A BOLD KISS

Tony framed Savina's face in his hands and took her lips, drawing them in as the kisses became more lingering, devouring, and he lost awareness of anything but their passion. Her arms were around his waist, and her lithe body pressed to his, points of fire igniting where they met.

"I'm sorry," he said, though for what he couldn't say. "I shouldn't have done that; it was unthinkably bold."

"Then I would have you be bold again," she whispered and moved back into his reach . . .

Books by Donna Simpson

Lord St. Claire's Angel

Lady Delafont's Dilemma

Lady May's Folly

Miss Truelove Beckons

Belle of the Ball

A Rake's Redemption

A Country Courtship

A Matchmaker's Christmas

Pamela's Second Season

Rachel's Change of Heart

Lord Pierson Reforms

The Duke and Mrs. Douglas

The Gilded Knight

Lady Savage

Published by Zebra Books

Lady Savage

Donna Simpson

ZEBRA BOOKS
Kensington Publishing Corp.
www.kensingtonbooks.com

ZEBRA BOOKS are published by

Kensington Publishing Corp.
850 Third Avenue
New York, NY 10022

ISBN 0-8217-7813-7

First Printing: June 2005
10 9 8 7 6 5 4 3 2 1

Printed in the United States of America

One

"I don't want to go! Why was I born a woman, and not a man?" Miss Savina Roxeter hammered her gloved fists on the polished railing of the ship *Prosperous,* docked in Jamaica's Kingston Harbor and being prepared for the long ocean voyage back to England. "Men can do as they please. Men can work and live anywhere they want. It's just not fair." She bit down on her lip to keep the tears from beading in her eyes. At least with only her maid, Zazu, to hear her she was safe from censure, but she would not cry, not now, not ever. Instead she stared down at the scene below; as the ship creaked and groaned in its moorings, a steady stream of workers loaded the last crates of freight into the hold, hoisting them up over the railing and then lowering them into the cargo hatch.

A breeze stirred and lifted the curls that escaped her bonnet, tangling them into elf-locks as she tugged impatiently at her gloves, wishing her hands would not perspire so in their confines. Panic welled up in her as she felt the confinement of everything: stays, bonnet, gloves, boots, ship . . . life.

"How will I do it? Will I even like England? I haven't been there for, oh, ten years now, almost. Why can Gaston-Reade and I not be married here and stay to manage his plantation?" When Zazu, her maid and companion, remained silent, she glanced sideways at the girl. Tears welled in Zazu's dark eyes and threatened to spill over; Savina followed her line of vision to a dark-skinned young man who stood on the dock and stared up at her.

"Who is that?" Savina asked. The young fellow was foreshortened by their position, so far above, but he was a well-set-up young man, and dressed neatly in plain clothes.

"Nelson," Zazu said, her voice oddly choked.

"Nelson who?"

Zazu waved at the young man and he waved back, but with such a forlorn expression, evident even at such a distance, that Savina's heart twisted.

"Nelson Walker. He is one of Lord Gaston-Reade's serving staff at the plantation."

"He's . . . not a slave is he?" Savina's breath caught in her throat. Even after so many years living in Jamaica, she could not accept humans owning other humans, nor would she ever. When she had arrived on the island as a child of not quite twelve years she had tried to befriend the dark-skinned children, only to be told by her governess that it was not possible, for they were chattel, not children. The shock of it had never waned and in her heart, though she had stopped speaking her mind openly, she knew there could never be any justification for the abomination of slavery. Her conclusion was that owning anyone was an illusion; you could not own the human spirit.

"No, but his parents are slaves. He was born free by Lord Gaston-Reade's father's decree."

Savina watched her maid's face, wondering how she had been so stupidly blind as to not see the changes there. "And you like him?" she said, gently. "You like this young man, Nelson?" Though phrased as a question, she knew the answer.

Zazu nodded, and a tear finally trickled down her

soft brown cheek. She wiped it away with an impatient gesture and took in a deep, quavering breath.

"You never told me," Savina murmured, putting her arm around her maid's shoulders.

Shrugging, Zazu said, "What would have changed?" Her melodic voice was thick with tears, and the words saturated with the lilting inflection of her island birth. "I knew we were leaving, even as I . . . even as I grew to care for him."

"I asked you if you wanted to stay in Jamaica or go with me to England. Why didn't you say anything then?"

"Say what?" Zazu turned her tragic gaze on her employer. "Nelson and I cannot marry, and if you left me behind I would have no employment."

"But . . ."

"No," Zazu said, putting up one hand. "It is better this way. To continue as we were would have been unbearable."

"What do you mean?" Savina was still struggling to come to terms with this unexpected side of Zazu. How could she have been so consumed with her own life that she had missed this momentous change in Zazu? But it must be so, that she had been selfishly caught up in her own concerns and so had not seen that Zazu was falling in love. She squeezed the younger woman's shoulders and released her. "What would be unbearable? What do you mean?"

Zazu hung her head, and in a low voice replied, "We have been walking out for three months now. Two weeks ago Nelson asked the earl for permission to marry, and he was denied. His lordship does not like his serving staff to have dependents. To stay here and not be with Nelson . . ." She broke off, one tear trickling down her cheek and staining the soft blue material of her dress bodice.

"Why didn't you ask me to intercede?" Savina asked, hurt by her maid's lack of faith in her.

Zazu, her full lips pursed against a choking sob, just shook her head.

"Didn't you trust me enough to ask?"

The maid compressed her lips and her tears dried. She wiped away the last remnant and raised her head. "It was not a matter of trust," she said, in her perfect, inflected English, her narrow chin tilting up.

"Then it was foolish pride," Savina returned, exasperated. That pride had served Zazu well over the years, keeping her strong, pushing her to learn so she would need no one's help to decipher her mistress's native tongue. At twelve, walking out of the mountains, barefoot and ragged but with an ineffable air of grace and dignity, she had spoken only a few words of English, her language being the patois of her people, the independent Maroons of the Jamaican Blue Mountains. But swiftly, rejecting help, she had learned English, and as her fourteen-year-old mistress had learned French, so she had. Her thirst for understanding of the wide world had led her to learn geography and mathematics and history, too, just by sitting in on Savina's lessons and reading in every spare moment from her duties as maid. She had been an inspiration to Savina, who felt she never would have learned so much if not for the constant example of Zazu's insatiable hunger for knowledge.

Zazu shook her head at Savina's exasperation but remained silent, gazing down at her young man. She waved again, put her dark, slim fingers to her lips, kissed them, then blew the kiss down to him. She then turned away from the railing and did not look back. "It was not a matter of trust," she repeated, her stiff shoulders indicating her awareness that Nelson Walker still stared up at her beseechingly.

Savina, her heart aching for the fellow, gazed at him for a moment, then back at Zazu. She waited. The ship groaned with impatience; the pace of the workers accelerated around them.

"And it was not a matter of pride," Zazu finally said. She met Savina's gaze. "I know you would have done your best to convince Lord Gaston-Reade to allow Nelson and me to marry. But why would you think his lordship would do anything for you?"

"We . . . we're to be married. He cares for me." Savina searched her heart and then told the truth. "I would have asked it as a great favor."

"And that he might grant you, but it would have a cost and I would not subject you to any cost for me."

Savina gazed into Zazu's chocolate eyes. Though she and her maid were close, she was aware in that moment that there was much the young woman thought and felt that they did not share. There was a chasm between them, and she felt the pain of it. After seven years together she thought they knew everything about each other, but she had been proved wrong. She nodded. "I understand." And she did. One might be willing to beg favors for oneself, but if the cost of that favor was to be borne by someone else, one might be reluctant. Zazu was proud and independent, the legacy of her freedom-loving people thick in her veins. She took favors from no one, nor would she complain about the loss she would suffer.

"It is too hot."

The new voice, clear and filled with irritation, was that of Lady Venture Mills, who strolled the deck toward them with her fiancé, Mr. William Barker, and her brother, Lord Gaston-Reade, Savina's fiancé. Savina's father Mr. Peter Roxeter, formerly a top governing official of Jamaica but now returning to England to retire, stepped up from the hatch in the middle of the deck and wiped his hand across his brow.

"It's too hot and this place smells. The whole island smells of decay." Lady Venture's haughty, plain face, her nose patrician in length and shape and her eyes prominent, was pulled down in a scowl that marred the straight line of her lips.

Savina steadied herself against the railing and awaited the others while Zazu murmured that she was going to retire below deck to see to Savina's things. Without a single look over her shoulder she did just that, and when Savina looked over the railing once, it was to see young Nelson Walker retreat, his shoulders slumped, his head down. She didn't even know him, but she felt his pain. Zazu was a rare treasure; to love her and lose her would be devastating.

"You have been saying that since we arrived in Jamaica, Vennie," Lord Gaston-Reade said to his sister of her complaints about the heat and smell. He approached Savina and nodded to her. "You didn't have to come," he said, still talking to his sister, "and you are returning to England now, so it would be a most pleasant change if you would cease your endless stream of complaints."

Mr. William Barker, a pleasant, round-faced young man, supported his fiancée with one hand to her back and one under her arm. He had been a minor government official in Savina's father's office, and he had first expressed an interest in her, but when Lady Venture had latched onto him, he had flopped once or twice and then allowed himself to be reeled in. She was a very good match for the young man, much wealthier than Savina, and it was acclaimed as a piece of luck on his part. Savina felt sorry for him, but supposed he would be happy, or at least wealthy, which for some people was the same thing.

Lady Venture and Lord Gaston-Reade bickered

back and forth for a few more minutes, and Savina let their voices become background as she leaned on the railing and looked her last at Jamaica, away from the bustling port of Kingston toward the misty Blue Mountains. If she closed her eyes she could see the cool green of the palms and ferns and feel the breeze that swept down from the mountains. She and her father had lived in an airy and spacious manse between the capital city of Spanish Town and the most prosperous seaport, Kingston. Though he had spent much time in Spanish Town, a beautiful old city, she had preferred to stay on their estate and oversee the household and attached farm.

She closed out the smells of the port, the sea, the cargo, the dirt and filth inevitable in any port city, and instead let her senses remember jasmine-scented breezes in the morning, and the forest after rain, earthy and rich as if the mother goddess of creation had perfumed her limbs with loam and dew. Home for her was a large stone house set atop a hill, with open windows, white muslin curtains fluttering in the breeze, teak furniture gracing the flagged terrace, and the mountains as her view. Her days were taken up with study, managing the farm, and entertaining for her father when he had company back from Spanish Town. It was there that she had first met Lord Gaston-Reade, and there, in her own lovely home, that he had courted her with the express approval and encouragement of her father.

And now they were sailing to England to be married. What would London hold? Her memories from childhood were of mist and rain, cups of bitter chocolate and toast in front of the fire, and long winters when the ice and snow made the streets filthy and kept everyone indoors. It would be a difficult adjustment after the lazy drift from day to day of warm sun, warm rain, warm breezes.

"Savina. Savina!"

Her fiancé's voice brought her back to the present and she looked up into Gaston-Reade's gray eyes. The tide was turning, and the ship creaked and grunted with the shifting waters.

"Your expression was most peculiar. What were you thinking about just now?" he asked.

"Jamaica," she answered, straightening with a sigh.

"But we're still here."

"Not this Jamaica," she said, waving her hand to indicate the port below them as the pace on the deck accelerated. With the turn of the tide they were about a half hour away from casting off, she supposed, and her stomach rumbled with anxiety. "This Jamaica," she continued, tapping her head. Then she covered her heart with one hand. "And this Jamaica. I'll miss it." She hesitated and gazed up into his gray eyes. There was still time, if she hurried. "Albert," she said, trying out his Christian name. He frowned but she surged ahead, undaunted. "Why don't we stay here? If you hurry, you could tell the captain and they could unload our things. Why don't we stay here, get married and look after your family plantations? Papa can stay too, then, and live on Tanager with us."

His secretary, Mr. Anthony Heywood, approached with Savina's father and stood, watching the interchange. He shaded his eyes in the midday sun and steadily stared.

Gaston-Reade, his handsome, bony face a mask of incomprehension, said, "Don't be ridiculous."

"Yes, don't be silly, Savina," her father said, irritably. His mouth pursed and he looked a little gray as the ship lurched.

"I'm not," she insisted, steadying herself against the railing. She knew port life, even though she had not lived in Kingston, nor even Spanish Town, and she knew there still was time to unload their belongings if she was able to convince her fiancé she was serious. She should have gathered her courage and done this earlier, but not one to be put off by what she should have done and hadn't, she pushed ahead. She put one hand on Lord Gaston-Reade's wool-clad arm. She felt the others' gaze on her, Lady Venture's horror-stricken likely, and Mr. Barker's sympathetic. Her father's stare was anxious. Mr. Heywood was watching her most intently. It would affect him if Lord Gaston-Reade decided to honor her request, but it was too important to think of anyone else in that moment, but what she truly wanted deep inside. And Zazu . . . how this would change her life! "I'm not being ridiculous. There is so much to do here!" she said, squeezing her fiancé's arm. "We could manage Tanager together," she continued, naming his plantation and estate. "I may not have experience with managing a plantation, but I know the country, and I know the people. I do understand plantation life."

"Savina . . ."

"And we could . . ." She gathered her courage like armor. "We could work on making Tanager run without the need for slave labor. You could free your slaves . . . pay them a wage, instead!"

Somebody gasped and even the ship seemed to quiver with outrage.

"Savina!" Gaston-Reade shook off her hand. Perspiration beaded on his forehead and ran in a trickle down the side of his face. "Enough! That was an extremely unladylike speech! We are going back to England, and we'll be married there in my family's chapel."

She bowed her head, but then lifted it again. One more try. "Then . . . please, can we not . . ." She hesitated and threw a look at the mountains.

The beautiful Blue Mountains. Once, she had gone

with Zazu to her family's village in the mountains. The journey was more than a physical trip to the interior of the island; they traveled back in time, it seemed to Savina. As they sat around a smoky fire the first evening, Zazu's mother told her, translated by Zazu, about the Maroon people and their revolt many years before from the bondage of Spanish slavery, and their eventual treaty with the British, keeping them free and independent. That memory had stayed with her and it urged her to push harder, to make that freedom grace the entire island population. She was not so conceited as to think she could affect the issue of slavery as an English institution, but if in some small way she could make a start for some people it would be the proudest moment of her life. She summoned her courage, despite the look of horror on her fiancé's face. "Perhaps it can't be done overnight, but let's work toward making Tanager a free plantation."

"Free?" His expression was one of bafflement, as if he had never heard the word before.

"Yes . . . free. No slave labor," she said, impatiently. "You know how I feel about slavery." She had tried to raise the subject before and he hadn't been receptive, but she thought it was just a matter of time before she prevailed. Now a niggling doubt wormed into her heart; she had thought that her fiancé, as a reasonable man, would agree that slavery must end, and soon. Had she been blinded by her own beliefs? Had she given Gaston-Reade too much credit? He had made vast changes on his own plantation that seemed to be heading in that direction, and that had led her to believe he was sympathetic, even if not quite ready to make the jump and free all of his workers. "But it's more than just my personal feeling, you know," she continued, launching an argument she had been preparing for some time but had never found the opportunity—nor the courage—to use. "I read a book—it's quite old but still important—called *The Wealth of Nations*, and in it the author stated that slave labor is really wasteful, because . . ." All eyes were on her. Lady Venture stared at her in disgust, and Mr. Barker in confusion, while her father still looked anxious. Her fiancé's reaction mirrored his sister's and added a kind of horror in his grimace. Only Mr. Anthony Heywood's gaze was unjudging.

"A book." Gaston-Reade's heavy brow was furrowed.

"Yes, a book," she said, becoming impatient. "I do read." This was not going how she would have wanted; she had waited too long and then spoken too precipitately. She must have been mad to leave such an important discussion to this moment. Why had she not spoken earlier?

"I know the book Miss Roxeter is referring to, by an economist, Mr. Adam Smith," the earl's secretary said. "Very well thought of."

Mr. Heywood's support was unexpected but appreciated. She smiled over to him but he only frowned. His employer, though, gazed at him thoughtfully.

"That's quite enough, Tony. Miss Roxeter can do without your valuable support." He looked back to Savina and a smile lightened his features, which had a tendency toward the beetling if one looked forward into his later years. "Now Savina, my dear girl," he said, tweaking her chin, "you must leave such matters to me. You only show your ignorance when you speak of weighty topics, and I will not have you getting fretful with too much learning." He patted her cheek.

Anger filled her, but she was speechless in the face of his condescension. Savina's father sighed in relief and began a conversation with Mr. Barker about London fashion and the likelihood of getting a new suit before the fall season.

"I hardly think it is ignorance that would lead Miss

Roxeter to a book like *The Wealth of Nations*, my lord," Heywood said, diffidence in his tone but not his eyes.

"She may have read it," Gaston-Reade said, his voice hard with suppressed anger, "but I'm sure she has misinterpreted the thrust of the fellow's arguments. How can slavery be economically unsound? Everyone knows you cannot run a sugar plantation without it."

"Actually, my lord, Mr. Smith was not alone in thinking that a paid workforce . . ."

"Enough, Tony!"

Anthony Heywood knew by his employer's tone it was time to shut his mouth or suffer a difficult couple of days. It would do no good to protest further, but he did regret his inability to shake Lord Gaston-Reade until his teeth rattled. Especially did he feel so when he saw the mortified look on Miss Roxeter's pretty face. He had admired, before, her feminine beauty—as a constant adjunct to his employer he had been witness to some of the courtship and betrothal of the two—but now he wondered if he had been hasty in condemning her as insipid. The assumption of insipidity had been based on his reflection that no woman of spirit and intelligence could voluntarily marry such a prig as his employer. Perhaps, though, he reflected, his lack of experience with the fair sex left him unqualified to judge the persuasion a young woman could be subjected to by family and friends. Lord Gaston-Reade was, in a worldly sense, an exceptionally good match for the daughter of a government official. A young lady of only moderate wealth would consider herself fortunate indeed to marry such a man as the earl, even if she had to endure his sanctimonious twaddle.

Miss Roxeter had turned back to the railing as the work of loading slowed and stopped. The ship heaved under them like a great lumbering beast of burden preparing for a journey. Anthony watched her, admiring again the dusky curls that fluttered from out of the confines of her bonnet and the pink of her cheek against her pale, lightly freckled skin. Her father had joined her at the railing and taken her arm. Mr. Roxeter was respectable and solid, but not forward thinking, exactly right by British government standards for work as a colonial official.

Judging by the pensive expression on her face she had been hurt by her fiancé's dismissive attitude, but really, what did she expect? Lord Gaston-Reade, earl and peer of the realm, had been raised with the attitude of *noblesse oblige* and was considered relatively kind to his servants and to the slaves of the plantation, but it did not mean he considered them as other than chattel. He thought, and had said many times, that the slaves would not know what to do with freedom. He was not alone in that belief.

But Miss Roxeter had only known him a few months, and he would not have spoken on such subjects with her. She would not know his opinions, likely, on such serious matters. Anthony watched her face, and when she turned and gazed at him, was startled by the question in her eyes.

Why had he come to her support? It was what she wanted to know, but dared not ask, hemmed in as she was by her fiancé and her father. He tried a smile and she offered a tentative smile in return, before turning her face so her bonnet concealed her eyes.

But the expression had shuddered through him like an electric current. He would never again dismiss her as vacant or insipid. Beyond recognizing her intelligence—the fact that she had made it all the way through a dry book on economic theory and had apparently understood it certainly guaranteed that—he dared not venture, though. He thought perhaps he was more comfortable when he could dismiss her as lovely to look at but vapid.

The vessel groaned as around them the sailors bustled. Shuddering, the whole ship heaved and creaked, moaning about the voyage ahead just as much as a camel Tony had once ridden in the Persian desert complained ceaselessly as it made its way to the next oasis.

They were about to leave Jamaica forever, he thought with regret, turning his gaze, as Miss Roxeter did, to the far mountains, a misty blue-green in color. He had enjoyed his stay; of the many places he had been in his twenty-seven years, Jamaica had suited him most, but he would likely never have the opportunity to come back, unless Lord Gaston-Reade made the journey again to his plantation.

The crew cast off and the ship moved away from the port toward the ocean, attended by two smaller vessels, the navy ship *HRH Wessex* and a merchant vessel the *Linden,* and the island receded in mist. It was the fate of those who served, Tony thought with bitterness, that one was constantly leaving places of which one became fond. Jamaica had filled his heart, and the gallantry of its people, the lushness and vivacity of its climate, the rhythm of life, like a thrumming heartbeat, had entered his soul. Even if he never returned the memories would live within him forever.

He glanced over at Miss Savina Roxeter as the ship caught wind and picked up speed. She stood rigid at the railing, eschewing even the dubious comfort of her fiancé's supporting arm. Jamaica, now visible only as a misty blue outline in the distance, was almost gone from sight and one fat tear slid down her fair cheek.

Two

When Savina awoke the next morning it was to an empty cabin; Zazu was already out of the room. Arising, performing a brief morning wash and dressing in a simple day gown with a plain bonnet, Savina reflected that she had wondered if she would still be a good sailor after over nine years between voyages, and it appeared that she was, for she had slept soundly, even with the unfamiliar night noises of boards creaking and groaning and the strange smells and sensations of a lumpy bed, not her own feather mattress.

She would fight the depression she felt at leaving Jamaica, she thought, with determination. What could not be changed must be borne with courage, and there was no one who said she would never return. She was, in her marriage, allying herself with a family that had vast interest in Jamaica, and it was very possible that she would return. After how many years and what a different person she would be after perhaps decades of marriage, she did not want to contemplate.

Her self-congratulation on being a good sailor could not be applied to her father, she found when she stopped by his cabin, for he was still in his chamber, with one of the ship's staff bringing him tea. His pouchy face was pale and he begged her to go away, for he couldn't bear to see her cheery face when he felt so dreadful.

Seeing him well cared for, she obeyed, navigating the narrow halls to the steps that led above deck and climbing up to greet a day that had gray clouds scudding across the sky, racing them, it seemed, across the ocean. She steadied herself, stepped down onto deck and took a deep breath of salty air.

Zazu was at the railing, but when Savina approached it was to find her maid shivering and clamping down on her lip.

"Zazu, what's wrong?"

The young woman turned to her, an ashen pall over her smooth dark skin, and said, trembling, "It is nothing."

"Liar," Savina said affectionately, then more seriously, for she could see how her maid quivered, added, "What's wrong, truly?"

Zazu was silent for a long moment, but then said, in a low tone, her grip tight on the worn, polished wood of the railing, "It is so vast. The ocean . . . it stretches forever, and I've never seen anything like it. Mountains, fields, meadows, hills, rivers . . . all have an end. Nothing goes forever, but this does. From shore it was different, you know; I had my feet firmly planted in sand, and the horizon . . . it was just a dream beyond which there was nothing. But now . . . what if we don't find our way? I dreamt last night that we were lost and we wandered so far, and I was alone, then, and in a small boat in the middle of this vast blue. I kept calling and calling, but no one could hear me." She bowed her head. "My grandmother would be ashamed to hear me speak like this, for she did not raise me to fear. When she sent me down from our home to find work with you, she told me never to be afraid, for she would always be here," she said, putting one hand over her heart, "no matter what."

"Don't be afraid," Savina said. She put her arm over the younger girl's shoulders. "Zazu, I don't know how they do it, but they find their way across the ocean all the time by the stars and the sun, because those don't change no matter what." She gripped her maid's shoulder briefly and then released. "And your grandmother would be proud, for you are very brave to come out here and face what you fear. I don't know if I would have had the courage to face my fear so squarely as you have." She stared out at the heaving gray blue of the ocean, the color darkening to indigo near the horizon. They were out of sight of the other two ships, and it seemed to her that it was getting a little windier and that the waves were larger, but it was likely just her imagination. She would not alarm Zazu with her speculation.

Behind them and around them, sailing men in their tattered clothes scuttled about doing mysterious chores, each with a purpose. They were brown and weathered, men whose lives had been tied to the ocean and the ship *Prosperous*; they served her like scuttling ants serving the bloated queen ant. It had been nine years since Savina's trip to Jamaica, but she still remembered much of the crossing. The days had stretched and elongated, each one seeming weeks, each week seeming months. Perhaps with the wisdom of age it would not seem so long.

"We have each other to rely on," she said, with a smile at her maid. "I hope you don't regret coming? Even after leaving behind Nelson?"

The maid took a deep breath and stiffened her back, staring out boldly to the horizon as if daring it to daunt her. "No, I don't regret it. When I went home just before we left, my grandmother told me that life is very short; I will honor my family by seeing more of the world and carrying my name to faraway lands."

"And you will," Savina said, gently. "You'll meet

many people in London, and Gaston-Reade and I may travel after our wedding, you know, to Rome, or Florence, or even Venice. You and I can explore the galleries and see the paintings, perhaps, that we have only seen color plates of in my books. You can write to your grandmama and your mother and tell them all about those places. They'll be so proud."

There were tears in Zazu's eyes, but Savina knew that they were not tears of fear. She well remembered what it was like to leave her homeland and all that was familiar for unknown destinations. But she . . . she always had her father with her. Zazu was alone but for Savina, alone and missing her mother, grandmother and Nelson.

"You know I'll never desert you, Zazu," she said.

Zazu nodded, wiped her tears and took in a deep breath.

From the hatch came Mr. Heywood, and Savina was reminded of the day before and the gallant way he had come to her support in the matter of slavery. Perhaps he was a like-minded soul, and she had met few enough of those in the nine years she had lived in Jamaica that finding one was a novelty. Of the many English she had come into contact with, few understood her revulsion for slavery, though there were societies aplenty dedicated to its eradication. But it seemed that economic necessity would be served despite the occasional protest over the immorality of slave-owning. It had been an unpleasant surprise, finding that Gaston-Reade didn't share her feelings, but she still had the hope of converting him. She had to believe it was possible.

Her fiancé's secretary, his aspect solemn, joined them at the railing.

"Good morning, ladies," he said, including Zazu in his greeting, as he always did.

Zazu murmured a hello and Savina covered her

hand on the railing and squeezed it as she greeted the gentleman. "Good morning, Mr. Heywood."

"We appear to be in for a rather fierce storm," he said, eyeing the sky.

Zazu moaned, and wide-eyed, glanced to Savina for confirmation. "I'm sure it won't be a big one," Savina said.

"I hope not, for my employer is not the best of sailors."

"Really?" Savina asked. It was something she would not have suspected of her fiancé. "I cannot imagine Gaston-Reade as other than stalwart."

"He would be pleased to hear you say that, Miss Roxeter," Heywood said, with a slight bow to her.

"But really, is he frightened? Or just incapacitated, as my father is? For you know, it isn't the same thing. Father is not fearful, but something about the motion of rocking on the waves seems to upset his stomach awfully." A gust of wind blew her bonnet back off her head and her knot came loose, her dark hair flying in tangled curls around her face. She swept them back impatiently as Mr. Heywood watched her. She had always had the feeling that he watched her to criticize, and he was no doubt thinking what a featherbrain she was that moment.

His answer was lost on the wind as another sudden gust came up.

The crew's pace accelerated and changed, it seemed to Savina, as she turned to watch them at their mysterious tasks. Some were taking down sails, while others worked at fastening the cargo hatches and stowing coils of rope. The captain, a bluff, weathered man who wasted few words, ordered them below deck; Savina took Zazu's arm and bustled to comply. "What do you think will happen, Mr. Heywood?" she asked the secretary, above the sound of the wind. "Will the storm blow for a while, or settle quickly?"

He took her free arm and guided her around a coil of rope, the boat's sway on the heaving swells more pronounced than they had been even minutes before. "I think the crew will handle the ship and we will ride out the weather," he said, his voice loud enough to carry but his tone calm. "How long it will last is a matter known to God and sailors only. But I trust the crew to do their duty."

Zazu, her expression stoic, sighed with some relief as they reached the hatch. Mr. Heywood helped the two belowdecks to the relative serenity of the hall.

"Would you ladies like to take breakfast?" he asked, steadying himself against the paneled wall.

When Savina indicated they would, he guided them down to the dining cabin. Insulated as it was from the external weather, one could still sense the heave and dash of the giant waves in the tilt of the cabinetry. Railings and pegs kept all of the dishes secure from sliding onto the floor.

Lady Venture Mills and her fiancé were in the dining cabin already, and as Savina took a seat, Lord Gaston-Reade entered, his clothing immaculate, his expression dour and his temper clearly uncertain.

As Zazu took a seat away from the others, Lady Venture said, "Miss Roxeter, surely you are not going to allow your maid to dine with us?"

Savina frowned across the table at the lady. "I certainly am."

"My maid is taking her meal in my cabin."

"That is *your* maid. It will be far easier on the serving crew if all who wish to eat, eat together, rather than making more work for them."

"Really, Savina, it would be better if your maid took her breakfast in your cabin. She is a servant, after all," Gaston-Reade said.

"She is *my* servant, though, not anyone else's," Savina said, disturbed by her fiancé's penchant for taking his sister's side over his fiancée's.

"Nevertheless," Gaston-Reade said. "Serving staff do not eat with their superiors."

Zazu had already risen and was on her way out of the cabin. Savina stopped her with a hand on her arm as she passed behind her chair. "No, Zazu, sit and eat."

The young woman pulled her arm out of her employer's grasp. "I go because I want to," she said, "not because they command it." In an undertone she added, "I . . . I do not feel very well. May I just return to the cabin?"

"Of course," Savina whispered and began to rise. "Let me go back with you."

"No," Zazu murmured back. "Stay, and fight the battle."

Savina grinned. They had spoken many times of Lady Venture's uncertain temper, and how Savina would deal with such a sister-in-law. Together they had decided the voyage would be the battleground of wills, with Savina sure to win. "All right. Go. I'll have a crew member bring you some seltzer, if it is available."

When Zazu had exited, Lady Venture, her mouth twisted in a sour expression, said, "She is impertinent. I would have slapped her if my maid had spoken in that insolent manner to anyone."

"What did she say but the truth?"

"Perhaps that's the problem," Lord Gaston-Reade said. "I have noticed before a penchant on your maid's part to impudence; I blame that on her heritage. I would never have hired as a servant anyone from those mutinous Maroons!" He shuddered, as many Jamaican plantation owners did, at the mere mention of the independent mountain dwellers. The Maroons were a constant concern, for runaway slaves were welcome in Maroon townships, though the plantation landowners constantly petitioned for help from the government to keep their chattel from slipping away in the night. "You must curb her behavior," he said, grimly. "What is tolerated in what passes for society in Jamaica will not be allowed in England. As your maid, Zazu will accompany you everywhere, and she must know her limits. Servants are like animals; a tight collar and short leash are advisable."

"That is a disgusting thing to say, Gaston-Reade," Savina said, accepting a dish of eggs from a young cabin boy. She gave the lad a warm smile and he ducked his head in embarrassment. "You cannot treat a human being like a pet."

"Why not?" Lady Venture said. "She's named like a pet!" She laughed, but when no one joined in, she fell silent with a petulant look.

"Though Vennie was being humorous, it is something I have been meaning to speak to you about," Gaston-Reade said, shooting his sister a warning look. "You must find another name for Zazu. Perhaps Mary. That's a good Christian name."

"I can't rename her as if she is a doll!" Savina said, staring at her fiancé, trying to tell if he truly meant what he said. It didn't seem possible, but he was serious. "I wouldn't even try! She's a person, and Zazu is her name. It came to her grandmother in a dream before she was born, and it's a part of her. You may as well say you will rename me after we marry."

"You must give her another name. And you must not let her speak out of turn." Gaston-Reade stared at her steadily. His tone mild, he said, "I will not have you flouting my wishes. Really Savina, you have a most unattractive streak of independence. You must learn to curb it. Your behavior must conform to society expectations or you will find yourself an outcast."

Though his voice was gentle, the words he spoke cut Savina to the soul. He made England sound so bleak and friendless, and marriage to him a prison. "I must do this and I must do that? I refuse to believe that English society is so devoid of humanity as you suggest that anyone who is not exactly the same as everyone else is shunned."

"I think, Miss Roxeter, that you should believe his lordship," Anthony Heywood said. As little as he liked seeing anyone's spirit crushed, it was perhaps better that she arrived in England knowing what to expect.

He watched her eyes widen, and her questioning gaze swung from his face, to her intended husband's, to Lady Venture's and finally to Mr. William Barker, Lady Venture's silent fiancé. Tony knew some of Miss Roxeter's history, and that she had come to Jamaica nine years before; that meant she was, at most, just a child of eleven or twelve when she left England and would not have mixed in society at that age. Raised in independence on the island by an indulgent father and with only occasional contact with other English inhabitants, she perhaps had no idea what returning to England would mean, nor how her behavior would be curtailed by marrying Lord Gaston-Reade.

His employer was a pompous ass, and Anthony had gotten into the habit of thinking that if Miss Roxeter could not see that, or saw it and accepted his proposal anyway, then she was a featherbrain who deserved her fate. It had not changed the fact that he admired her looks more than any lady he had ever seen. She was lovely, and the teasing wind, which had pulled her dark hair from its confines, had only made her more so. She had pink in her cheeks from the confrontation with her fiancé and his sister, and dark curls floated around her face, which was a pale oval dotted with a dusting of freckles.

However he now wondered if she had just accepted her fiancé as he was—and he could be charming at times—without thinking how she would be expected to modify her own behavior. If that was the case this might be the first time she realized what marriage would mean for her.

"Do you believe, Mr. Heywood," she said, staring at him and following up on his last comment, "that I will be out of place in English society, then?"

He considered his reply, aware that the others' gaze was on him. Working as Lord Gaston-Reade's secretary was a wonderful opportunity, even though he despised the man. The circles he traveled in allowed Tony access to people he would never have met in his normal life, and he had plans for his future, plans he had made advancements on, though not enough to strike out on his own yet. He still needed his employer's goodwill, but he could not remain silent, not with Miss Roxeter's eyes searching his, even if it meant offending his employer with his frankness.

"I do think you will be out of place, miss. Most ladies have no idea what they think, and you clearly do."

A gasp from Lady Venture told him he was treading on dangerous ground.

"And ladies in society never speak their mind, nor do they care about those in their employ. You will most certainly be an anomaly."

Mr. William Barker, whom he had never suspected of having a sense of humor before, suppressed a snort of laughter, turning it into a cough.

Gaston-Reade stared at him. "Have you lost your mind, Tony?"

"Perhaps, sir."

Lady Venture peered at him through the gloom of the dining cabin and said, "I think he was being rude to me, William. Was he being rude to me?"

"Why would you suspect it, my love?" Barker smirked over at Tony behind his fiancee's back, but Tony knew he was treading on dangerous ground and did not return the smile.

But when he met Miss Roxeter's lovely blue eyes, it was worth it.

She smiled at him and said, "You make me feel it may not be such a terrible thing to stand out in English society, Mr. Heywood." She settled down to her breakfast, turning away from her fiancé and his sister.

Tony was silent. It was, perhaps, better for him when he could dismiss her as a featherbrain. At this moment it was too abundantly clear to him that she had a brain to think with and a heart to feel, that in fact she was chock-full of important and valuable organs superior to those contained in most people's bodies. The discovery dismayed him, for as long as he could maintain his comfortable sense of superiority, he need not admit how perfectly lovely, amiable and sweet-tempered he had always found Miss Roxeter, and how beautiful he thought her. And now, to believe her intelligent and with a compassionate heart . . . her perfection was dangerous to him.

The meal was soon over with no more discussion; Savina had nothing more to say to Gaston-Reade, nor to his sister, though she had much to think about. As the day wore on, it became clear the storm was rising. Savina's father stayed in his cabin, as did Zazu, but the others gathered in the cabin assigned to them as a parlor.

The *Prosperous* was a merchant vessel carrying sugar to England, but the captain was not averse to mingling with his few passengers. He entered the parlor near dinner to reassure them that though it was clear to all that the storm had worsened, they would ride it out in safety.

Unfortunately, his speech was interrupted by a particularly bad heave, and a shout from somewhere among the crew.

"Now see here, Captain," Lord Gaston-Reade said, his face white and his breathing quickening. "I demand that you steady the ship this instant and calm your crew!"

Savina stared at him in dismay. Had she heard him correctly? Had he even thought about what he said?

Captain Gallagher glared at him. "I have a measure of power, my lord, but sorry I be that it don't extend to the heavens and the Almighty. But the ship, I assure you, is a sound one, an' we'll do. As for my crew, they be perfectly in control. Now, if you will all excuse me, I have a ship to command and a storm to ride out."

"What would that shout have been, Captain Gallagher?" Savina asked, politely, just before the captain exited.

"Could have been anything, Miss Roxeter," he said, turning back and speaking with a kind tone. "I'll let you know, if I find out, but don't worry yerself about it. Now, excuse me miss, ladies and gents," he finished, turning and bowing to the others. He disappeared out the door.

"Impertinence," Lord Gaston-Reade spluttered.

Savina held her tongue, for her comment would have been pithy. Though the company chatted, at times having to steady themselves against the heaving of the ship, most felt the tension. Anthony Heywood, Savina noticed, was tight-lipped and wordless, but that was often his demeanor. He occupied the difficult position between servant and gentlefolk, for as Gaston-Reade's secretary he mingled with the other passengers, and yet could not become overly familiar.

Though she retreated to her cabin at about ten in the evening, she didn't sleep. She stayed awake with Zazu, both of them unnerved by the howling wind and pitching and tossing of the ship, and both determined to comfort the other.

Toward morning the seas seemed to calm, and as daylight broke, Savina felt the urgent need to see for herself that they had come to no harm through the long night. She made her way to the deck to find that though they had indeed ridden out the night in safety, all was far from well.

Three

Another ship was lashed to their own, but it was not the *HRH Wessex*, nor was it the *Linden*, the two ships they had been accompanied by when they left Kingston Harbor. The flag the new ship flew was that of the United States of America, with whom her native country was locked in a war declared by that fledgling country, and the name she could make out through the rigging of her own ship was the *Gryphon*.

Savina scrambled onto the deck, shivering in the freshening wind of a gusty, gray day, but when she rounded a coil of heavy rope it was to find a confrontation taking place.

Anthony Heywood was already on deck watching the confrontation between Captain Gallagher and a uniformed officer of the United States Navy. The American captain was surrounded by many of his well-armed men, who held at bay the English merchant captain's crew.

Savina murmured her alarm and Mr. Heywood turned to her.

"Miss Roxeter!" he whispered. "You should not be up here. Go back immediately!"

"No. What has happened, Mr. Heywood?"

A couple of the American officers looked her way, and one smiled and winked at her, but she kept her expression grim, not willing to bring any more attention to herself than inevitably she would get.

"What's going on?" she repeated to her reluctant companion, tugging his sleeve.

"I'm not sure, but it doesn't look good," Mr. Heywood said, not letting his attention stray from the scene before them.

Savina thought that was a vast understatement, since Captain Gallagher had just been caught by the arms by one of the American commander's men. "Oh! Is he going to be all right?"

But Anthony Heywood had already started forward; Savina followed at a safe distance, not to interfere but to watch. She couldn't possibly retreat now, and besides, if things started to look dangerous she wanted enough warning so she could go below deck and muster Zazu and her father and the others to resistance, as futile as that seemed, confined as they were.

Hostilities between the two nations, in this late summer of 1814, were as unresolved as they had been in the two years the nations had been locked in enmity, and she had no desire to be taken by Americans. Savina had heard much from the officials who visited her father all summer; they had spoken about the coming raid on New Orleans, which they hoped would procure them some help from the local Creole population, chafing under American rule imposed upon them so recently as a mere fifteen years earlier. She didn't want to be forced to share the knowledge she had with these Americans, though from the indiscretion of the British officials, who were so sure of their own superiority they spoke openly of the coming raid, she had always felt certain the Americans would have much advance warning of the coming attack.

Mr. Heywood, his plain buff trousers and navy jacket a dull contrast to the smart uniform of the American commander, approached the group.

"Say now," Heywood said, his tone even. "Sir, please release Captain Gallagher. I assure you, his primary concern is the welfare of his passengers and crew; if he made any threatening gesture, it was merely in the aid of that goal."

The American cocked an eyebrow at him and looked him over. "And you are?"

"Mr. Anthony Heywood, passenger on this ship."

"I would think, sir, that you should shut your damned mouth."

Savina watched Mr. Heywood's hands clench into fists, but his voice, when he spoke again, was calm and unruffled.

"I think, sir, that rudeness is unbecoming your uniform."

The American captain stilled, then gave a signal, and the officer holding Captain Gallagher tight loosened his hold.

"You are correct, Mr. Heywood. I forgot myself in the urgency of the moment, but it is not politic to be goaded into returning rudeness for rudeness, is it?" He strolled closer to Heywood. "You, sir, must be a diplomat?"

"Nothing so grand, just a humble secretary. But with an interest in maintaining my hide, and that of the other passengers."

"But not the crew?"

"The crew is the captain's realm, sir."

"True."

Savina let out a breath of relief at the pacific nature of the exchange. The red-faced American captain, though he looked to be a hard man, seemed willing to be composed if met with calmness. But her relief was short-lived as Lord Gaston-Reade blustered above deck and charged toward the odd grouping.

"What is going on?" he bellowed. "Why is that ship there? Who are you?"

The American looked over the new arrival with an interested air. "Captain Charles Verdun. And you?"

"I am Lord Albert Gaston-Reade. What is the meaning of this . . . this outrage?"

Savina rolled her eyes, for there could not have been an utterance more trite, like a phrase out of the poorest species of adventure novel.

"Are there other passengers?" the American captain asked, turning to Captain Gallagher.

"Yes, of course," the English captain growled. "Damned rebel buffoon, let us go!"

The American captain refused to be insulted by his English counterpart. He strolled to the railing and looked at his own ship. For the first time Savina let her gaze travel it, and saw that it listed badly. Crew members lined the railings and watched avidly the proceedings.

When Verdun returned, he was about to pass by her but stopped, and bowed. "Miss, may I ask . . ."

"Step away from her, you damned jackanapes."

Savina sighed. Again Gaston-Reade insisted on sounding like the worst kind of novel character, one provided by a writer with no imagination beyond the trite and hackneyed.

The American stiffened and turned slowly. "Sir . . . pardon, *my lord*," he said, with exaggerated and insulting politeness, "I was merely going to ask the young lady a question."

"You will address me, not my fiancée."

"Glory to God," Verdun said, turning his gaze to her, his brown eyes wide with wonder. "This man is your intended, miss?"

Savina could not ignore him and nodded, restraining her quivering with hands clenched before her.

Gently, the American said, the expression in his eyes softening, "Miss, please be assured I mean you no harm. I don't know what you have heard of us *Yankees*, but as in any war, you have likely heard that we are monsters, which is the same nonsense spread about English commanders, who I have found to a man to be a valiant, brave, if hard species when crossed. I expect nothing less. But I was merely wishful to ask, are there other ladies on board?"

"Yes, there are, sir," she answered, her voice a squeak at first. She cleared her throat. "There is another lady, and our maidservants."

"Ah."

"And . . . and my father . . . he's older . . ."

The man looked pained. "Don't be afraid, miss. I have a daughter; I would no more hurt a lady than I would hurt my own golden child." The American walked to the railing. He shouted an order and the sailors began to scuttle about.

Gaston-Reade, a vein throbbing in his neck, trailed Verdun, shouting incoherent questions at him. Heywood dashed after him and Savina watched as he tried to speak to his employer, but was repeatedly brushed away. Finally Verdun rounded on Gaston-Reade and shouted an incomprehensible order, and two of his men seized the earl.

"Tie him up and place him in the hold," Verdun said.

Heywood stepped forward. "What are your intentions, Captain?"

Verdun glared at him, a nerve jumping on his cheek. "You said you're a secretary. Is that . . . that bumblehead your employer?"

"Yes."

Gaston-Reade grunted wildly and struggled at the insulting appellation.

"More the pity, sir, for you seem a reasonable enough gent, for all you're on the wrong side. But I will not have him blustering around causing trouble. We are taking this ship. Our own is foundering badly, as you can see, injured by a damned British naval vessel just two days ago. Storm made it worse. We're taking on water and bound to sink. This sweet vessel is a blessing from the Lord."

Savina quivered inside. They were taking the ship? What were they going to do with them? Were they prisoners of war? Would they be tortured, or . . . she shivered. She had heard tales of women suffering a fate worse than death, of terrible humiliations at the hands of Americans, and she was frightened, but it was vital that she remain calm and listen, to gather all the information she could.

Mr. Heywood, his backbone stiff and hands still clenched at his sides, said, "What are you going to do with us?"

"I haven't decided," Verdun said. He glared at Gaston-Reade, who still struggled, grunting and puffing.

The American sailors were unloading the *Gryphon,* hauling sacks of gunpowder, foodstuffs, and barrels of rum by a ramp over the gunwale until Verdun interrupted and told them only the guns and gunpowder until they saw what the *Prosperous* had on board.

Gallagher, his ire once more under control, said, "Captain, you'll hafta let go of my passengers. Do what you must to me and my men, but the ladies . . ."

With a deep, exasperated sigh, Verdun glared at the men facing him: Gaston-Reade, his mien finally frozen in impotent fury; Heywood, his steady glare demanding answers; and Gallagher, his lined face red with suppressed fury. When the American captain turned to her, Savina quailed, but then rallied her courage and faced him. But she was not prepared for what he had to say.

"I shall leave your collective fate up to this brave young lady. Miss . . ."

"Savina Roxeter, sir," she said, proud of her steady voice.

"Miss Savina Roxeter, you have three choices." He paced toward her and stood, hands clasped behind his back, his stance swaying with the rolling of the vessel. "We intend to take this ship. We need a vessel to get back to the United States, since the wretched British Navy has so badly damaged ours. It is our luck last night's storm seems to have separated your rich little brig from your companion vessels. It's small, but it will do, and the sugar in your cargo hold will be welcome. Now . . ." He smiled and smirked over at the men. "As I said, Miss Savina Roxeter, you have three choices." He held up three fingers. "One," he said, pulling down one finger and folding it against his palm. "You and your gentlemen swear an oath of allegiance to the United States of America. You'll get all the benefits of citizenship in the greatest nation in the world." He smiled, but the smile changed to a harder look. "I would not recommend taking this line unless you mean to abide by it, for we don't cotton to deserters. Two," he continued, folding the next finger down. "You, the other ladies, the crew and all of your gentlemen companions come along with us as our prisoners. If we can find a safe harbor to drop you off we shall do so, but there are no guarantees, for we are at war and we have a duty to perform. You will spend all your time locked in a chamber in the hold together." He moved toward her and looked her over, his brown eyes challenging. "I *will* guarantee your safety from any predation by my crew, though, for I'm a civilized man, no matter what your countrymen would have you believe. However, if we are engaged by the enemy, I make no promises at all. Three," he continued, folding the next finger down. "We find you a nice cozy island and drop you off with enough supplies for a couple of weeks and a good knife or two and a pot to boil in. We'll also make certain someone knows where you are, though I can't warrant anyone of your addled countrymen will care enough to find you."

"You can't let her make that decision!" Gaston-Reade sputtered. "She's a . . . she is just a woman. What does she know?"

"Do shut your mouth, my lord," Tony Heywood said. He turned to the American captain. "It's really not fair to the young lady, sir, to put her in the position of choosing in this way. Surely . . ."

"See how your menfolk trust your intellectual powers, miss? Young Mr. Heywood here puts a smooth face to it, but he's saying the same thing as your intended, that they don't trust your powers of decision. But I . . . why in my estimation women are mightily constructed for making life-and-death decisions, otherwise we wouldn't let them take care of our future, our children, am I right?"

Savina stared down at the deck, examining the pattern of the boards. Was he truly going to leave it up to her? And if he did, what should she say? Should she decline? She looked up and met his eyes. "Why are you doing this, captain?"

Verdun stared back, his graying beard bristling along his hard jaw. He looked weary. "We need the crew of this ship, so they're staying. And if the gentlemen have valets, we will be recruiting them to bolster our numbers. But frankly miss, you all—yourself, your lady's maids and the aristocratic gentlemen—are a nuisance to us. We're at war with your country, but I'm no barbarian."

"But why me?"

He shrugged. "Why not you? P'raps I find it entertaining to see his lordship there ready to burst a blood vessel. And Mr. Heywood, while he seems a likable enough young fellow, also seems a mite pompous.

And Captain Gallagher? I don't trust that he'll do what's best for you. He might figure we'd be more careful with the lot of you on board, should we run into another British naval vessel. We wouldn't, but he might think so. Besides, it tickles me to see them so vexed."

"But that places me in an awkward position."

He nodded. "That it does, miss, but that's not my concern. Make your decision. You have until we empty our vessel of as much as we can carry. Then, depending on your decision, we'll take a few more things off our ship for you all to use on your island, if that's your decision, and we aim to scuttle the poor *Gryphon*." He turned and walked away, but then turned back. "Think well, Miss Roxeter. You have 'bout an hour, at most."

Four

The hour dragged on as Savina and the others gathered in the gloomy state parlor, watched closely by American crewmen, who unabashedly listened in on her discussion with the others.

What should they do? Her stomach churned and groaned as she alternately sat on her hands and fiddled with the ribbons on her dress bodice. If there had been a consensus, it would have been a much easier decision, she reflected, glancing around at the disparate group, her father sitting stiffly, fear in his glazed eyes, and the others in varying states of anger, watchfulness and trepidation. Given the diverse personalities involved, unanimity was never a danger. It would have been much more difficult, in a sense, she supposed, if all had understood her dilemma and been more kind in their attempts to influence her decision. As it was, they variously questioned what enticement she had used to get Captain Verdun to allow her to make the decision, what right she had to make a decision for the others, and why she would not listen to each one of them and do exactly as they recommended.

"I still think it very odd that that barbaric American should have placed our fates in *her* hands," Lady Venture said loudly to no one in particular, glaring at a point to the left of Savina.

No one responded, but one of the American crew

members posted by the door snickered and whispered something to his companion, another rough-looking fellow in stained trousers.

It *was* odd that the American captain had done things the way he had, Savina thought, but it was so, and she took her duty seriously. At first Lord Gaston-Reade had assumed she would defer her decision to him; when he found it was not so—she didn't think it would be right to abdicate responsibility—he had lapsed into confused and resentful silence for a time, and then had occasionally burst into obscure and incensed remarks. But rather than influence her to give up her difficult charge, the sometimes rancorous comments merely served to harden her resolve to make the decision herself. She thought she was, perhaps, better suited than any of them to make the judgment; being a woman she did feel somewhat alarmed at the thought of being marooned on a deserted island, and yet having lived in Jamaica for nine years and understanding the climate and habitat, she knew that they would likely survive, even if rescue was some time coming. Also, she understood completely, through her father's involvement in government, the dangers inherent in being held captive of an enemy nation. She prided herself, too, on being calm and reasonable, not something that could be said for some of her companions, nor even her own fiancé.

"Let us consider the possibilities once more," she said aloud, aware of the ticking clock on the sideboard.

"All right," Anthony Heywood said, from his position near the far door into the captain's dining room.

Savina glanced over at the two seamen and found that they had gotten bored and had begun a game of mumblety-peg in the hallway, over which they argued vociferously. "Come closer, all, and let us talk," she said. "We only have twenty more minutes and must come to a decision."

"You cannot order us about like this, Savina," Lord Gaston-Reade said. "It is not right and it is not womanly."

She sighed and ignored her fiancé. There was no time, and she had no response, anyway. "I think we can agree that one of the choices Captain Verdun offered us is out of the question," she said, looking around at the various expressions of her fellow captives. "It is unthinkable that we should pledge allegiance to their flag and join them."

Lady Venture, her eyes gleaming, leaned forward and whispered, "But we could *pretend* allegiance, you know, and then when we had lulled the captain and his crew into believing us, we could murder them all in their beds and take the ship back."

Savina gazed thoughtfully at her soon-to-be sister-in-law, wondering how such bloodthirsty notions could hide beneath the facade of a perfectly demure ladylike exterior. Mr. William Barker, gazing with horror at his blissfully unaware fiancée, seemed to be thinking the same thing. "There are far too many of them, and it is just as likely we should all be murdered in the attempt," Savina answered, as if she had considered the idea. "No, we have only two choices. We can go as prisoners to wherever Captain Verdun will take us, or we can be deposited on a nearby island, with his assurance that he will inform our people of our whereabouts."

"My dear," her father said, glancing back, seeing the seamen well entertained with their game and looking back at his daughter. "Our valets are to be left here, with those dreadful Americans. I really think . . . well, at least as prisoners we shall be cared for and fed. If we are abandoned on an island, who would look after our needs?"

"Why, we should, sir," Mr. Heywood, said. "Presuming the captain would give us supplies, we could take care of ourselves, and there would be fish in the ocean to catch for meat, and fruit in the trees. Better that than an uncertain fate at the hands of the Americans."

Lord Gaston-Reade cleared his throat. "I say, why should we only accept that American's choices?" He lowered his voice and leaned into the group huddled together now, as far as they could from the door. "We muster arms and attack! Take the ship back now!"

"What, against trained, armed, *aware* naval officers?" his secretary asked, incredulous, glancing at their armed guard, who had quit their game and were watching with alert expressions of distrust.

"But they're American," Gaston-Reade said, disdain in his voice. He didn't bother to lower his tone this time, displaying what some may have mistaken for brash courage, and others would condemn as dunderheaded idiocy. "What danger can they possibly be? We are three . . . nay *four* British gentlemen," he amended, looking at Savina's father, "and can beat the stuffing out of them with little trouble, I think."

"Ah, yes, just as we beat them in the rebellion and just as we are beating them in this conflict." Anthony Heywood turned away from his employer.

"But what of the ladies, my lord? Would you subject them to armed combat, with nowhere for them to go if things went badly except the bottom of the ocean?" That was Mr. William Barker speaking up for once.

Perhaps there was more to Mr. Barker than a slightly vacuous, but opportunistic, young man. "Thank you, sir," Savina said to him, "for thinking of us. In any of our plans we must remember that the crew of the *Prosperous* are not fighting men, but merchant vessel sailors. We could not rely on them for support. Keeping that in mind, I think even four British gentlemen are vastly outnumbered by such a crew of men as those." She indicated with a glance the two tough sailors who grinned over at them, having no doubt heard the earl's preposterous plan. She turned to her maid, who was listening on the periphery of the group, as was Lady Venture's maid, Annie. "Zazu, almost everyone else has given their opinion; what do *you* think we ought to do?"

"You cannot mean that you are asking the opinion of your servant?" Gaston-Reade said, mortification in his tone and outraged bearing.

"That is exactly what I have been pointing out," Lady Venture said to no one in particular, as she folded her hands in her lap. "Miss Roxeter has the most odd ideas, and consults her maid on everything. Very eccentric."

Lady Venture's maid, Annie, timidly said, "We are in danger, too, my lady."

"Exactly right," Savina said.

"I think," Zazu said, raising her voice above the ensuing hubbub, and Lady Venture's incensed reply to her maid's impertinence, "that I would rather take my chances on an island than on a ship manned for war and sailing into an enemy harbor."

Savina nodded. "Yes, that did occur to me. Annie?" she said, turning back to Lady Venture's maid. "What do you think?"

"Really!" Lady Venture said, sniffing with disdain. "Even *my* maid is to be consulted? When am I to be asked? After the servants?"

"I see Miss Roxeter's point, my dove," Mr. Barker cautiously offered. "You have given us your opinion already, my dearest one. The lady servants will be suffering the same fate as us. Should they not have at least their word considered?"

"I . . . I think we ought to stay with the American captain, Miss Roxeter," Annie said, her voice trembling and her glance slewing to the tough-looking sailors. "At least it is not abandonment on a horrible bare island with wild animals and savages, perhaps."

"Savina, listen to me," Gaston-Reade said, his tone suggesting great forbearance on his part. "I will not have you flout my wishes, now or after . . ."

"But the decision was left up to me," she said, feeling that she was doing an admirable job of keeping her voice controlled. "And I've come to a conclusion."

As the last rowboat receded in the distance, toward their ship, *Prosperous,* Anthony Heywood felt a momentary qualm, but supposed no matter what course of action they had taken he would feel the same. He glanced briefly at the pile of provisions the American captain had allowed them, and then turned away from the ocean and looked up at their new island home, temporary though he hoped it would be.

It appeared to be one of the many small islands that rimmed the Atlantic on the outer edge of the Caribbean Sea. They had been marooned on a quarter-moon-shaped beach bounded by two high jagged outcroppings of ancient coral rock. Above the sloping beach was a jungle of slanting palms, thick underbrush and sharp beach grass.

The others stood in the hot sun, a tight knot of humanity watching the rowboat disappear, becoming a tiny bobbing buoy by the ship *Prosperous,* which then raised sail, hoisted anchor and disappeared over the far horizon. Though the whole procedure took over half an hour, no one moved nor said a thing, stunned into silence by the turn of events. Even with a group of seven others, Tony had never felt so lonely as he did that moment, and judging by bewildered expressions he was sure some, at least, of the others shared his uneasiness.

They were abandoned, and who knew when next they would behold any sign of civilization?

And yet he couldn't help but believe that what Savina Roxeter had decided was for the best. Sitting in a locked room in the hold of the ship for days, weeks, perhaps even months, would soon become a living hell. At least this way they had some measure of hope to have a hand in their own survival.

He examined the people he was mired with for the uncertain future. First those he knew best: Lord Gaston-Reade and his harpy sister, Lady Venture Mills. Gaston-Reade was a pompous windbag who would complain every moment they were on the island, no doubt, while Lady Venture was an irritable, condescending, desperately managing young woman who was fortunate in finding for a fiancé a fellow who didn't have a mind to make up on his own, anyway. Her maid was a sad-eyed young woman whose one attempt at speaking up had been punished, no doubt, by the frosty silence and poisonous scorn of her mistress.

Mr. Peter Roxeter, Miss Savina's father, he had spoken to on occasion, and though he seemed a clever enough gentleman for his position as an official in the colonial government, his was not an original mind in any way.

That left Miss Savina Roxeter and her pretty maid, Zazu. Zazu, he had learned, was a Maroon, a proud descendent of the original Maroons, the former slaves on the first Spanish-built Jamaican plantations who many years before had escaped to the hills and then fought for their freedom so fiercely. When the British took over Jamaica, the Maroons had managed after a series of wars to negotiate a treaty with the British government that left them free to manage their own destiny up in their settlements in the Blue Mountains. Why Zazu, then, would voluntarily put herself in service and leave her island home was a mystery to Tony, and intriguing. What went on behind those intelligent, chocolate brown eyes?

But the most fascinating to him was Miss Savina Roxeter, and he suspected the American captain had seen the same something in her eyes that made him give her the power of their fate over her fellow English passengers. He had, perhaps, wanted to see what she would do when given such command, but he couldn't have been sure she would retain the authority to make the final decision. Most young ladies in her position would have deferred to her husband-to-be or her father, her future master or her past. But Miss Roxeter had accepted the responsibility, taken it seriously, listened to all of their opinions and then decided for herself.

Interesting. It would not make her life any easier for the time they were mired on the island. No doubt everyone who had been for another choice would remind her every miserable day that they were there by her decree.

As one by one the watchers on the white sand beach turned away from the horizon where the ship had disappeared, Tony roused himself. There would be much to be done, and they would need to sort things out before nightfall; it was already late afternoon. He joined the others, who were examining the pile of goods that constituted all of their supplies.

Lady Venture sat down on a barrel of water and said, "I am not going anywhere until we are rescued."

"Don't be ridiculous," her brother said with an angry scowl. "It may not be for weeks . . . years! We could live here until we rot and decay into piles of moldering bones."

Annie, Lady Venture's maid, began to cry, huge tears rolling down her pale cheeks and dripping on her clenched hands. She plunked down in the white sand and bawled, fisting her eyes like a child.

"Now see here, Gaston-Reade, you mustn't say such things with ladies about." William Barker leaned over and patted the maid's slim shoulder awkwardly.

"That's not a lady, you idiot, that is my maid," Lady Venture said, with a scathing glance at her fiancé.

"Still a young lady," Barker grumbled, but turned away and seemed very interested in a sack of sugar among the supplies.

"We won't starve," Zazu said, unexpectedly. "And we won't die. These islands," she said, spreading her arms out wide, "supply all that one could need. If there is fresh water . . . that is most important and what we need to find out immediately."

Lady Venture turned her back on them all and sat, rigid, staring off into the distance, where the cloud-strewn sky met the indigo ocean.

"Perhaps we ought to get these things up into the shelter of the wooded area," Tony suggested. "So it doesn't get wet if it should happen to whip up in the night."

Lord Gaston-Reade gave him a long, steady look and said, "Don't think, Tony, that this hideous situation in which we find ourselves means that the divisions of our various positions will be lowered. We are civilized British people, not natives and not savages."

Tony caught a veiled look of contempt from Zazu, aimed at the earl, and an expression of open astonishment from Miss Roxeter.

"All Mr. Heywood was saying was that we must gather our wits and begin to think of approaching nightfall," she said. "I hardly think he was challenging the very structure of the British aristocracy."

"Savina, you are poorly equipped to understand how important and how fragile is that very fabric of our British civilization," Gaston-Reade said.

"No, but then perhaps I don't have the same idea of

civilization that you do. Civilization, to me, means civility. We are desperately lacking in that at the moment."

"You really mustn't behave this way, Savina, dear," her father said, drawing off his gray gloves and passing one hand over his perspiration-coated brow. "I know the American captain's odd decision—putting our fate in your hands—may have filled your head with strange notions, but your moment of ascendancy is over."

Savina felt a spurt of anger mixed with exasperation. They were all acting as if their petty concerns of the moment were of import, when she was mostly concerned with the fact that the sun was descending, and they were sitting on an open beach with no shelter. She caught Mr. Heywood's eyes and bit her lip, trying not to laugh, for he was making a face behind her fiancé's back. She shouldn't laugh. She really shouldn't. Gaston-Reade had a right to her respect, at the very least. He had always been very kind to her, so this boorishness was a temporary blot on his character, nothing more. The secretary's strange behavior—she would never have thought the grave young man the type to make such a face—was no doubt a kind attempt on his part to lend the drama some levity.

"Zazu," she said. "Why don't we begin? Mr. Heywood, I concur with your suggestion. We need to get our provisions to some kind of shelter before nightfall." She took a deep breath and went to her fiancé. If they were going to be man and wife, they needed to find a way to work together in harmony, and this calamity had not proved an auspicious beginning. "Albert," she said, touching his jacket sleeve. "I don't mean to supersede your authority, you must know that. I just . . . we need to begin to take care of ourselves here."

Though she disliked doing it she wanted the group to work together, so she cajoled and courted him into a better mood, and he took command, choosing a temporary spot back in the forested edge above the long white beach. While he, Heywood, Zazu, Barker and Savina transported the supplies—the American captain had been reasonably generous, given that he had absolute command over the vessel and its crew—Lady Venture sat on the barrel and refused to take part, nor would she allow her maid to help, commanding her to attend to her solely. Savina's father dithered, horrified by his daughter's turn at manual labor, sure it did not do his own dignity any good to take part, but irresolute, dashing back and forth asking everyone's opinion whether he ought to help.

Finally they were done, and even Lady Venture's barrel seat had been moved.

Exhausted, Savina sat on the sandy ground above the beach with her back to a wood crate. Her lovely blue and white cotton dress was soiled, her shoes were pinching her feet and her hair was ratted on her sweaty neck. She felt utterly miserable, and in the normal course of things she would have asked Zazu to get her hip bath ready, with her lavender scented salts.

But Zazu was curled up asleep, having hauled and toted more than anyone else but Mr. Heywood. That gentleman had murmured something about private business—Savina had blushed, feeling sure she knew why he needed to go off into the bushes beyond their temporary camp, for it reminded her of her own soon-to-be urgent needs—but now she saw him striding back through the thick brush.

"I think I have found a source of clean water," he said as he approached the slumberous group. "There are two tiny connected lakes inland about a half mile. The water is not salty, at any rate; whether it is safe to drink I am not sure, but it will do, I think, for cooking and washing up."

His enthusiastic tidings were greeted with sullen silence, and he sat down on the ground a ways away from everyone else.

"I'm hungry," Lady Venture said.

That announcement, too, was greeted with silence. The sky was getting grayer by the minute and a wind began to whip up, blowing cyclones of sand into whirling tempests. From their minimal shelter in the fringe of palms and brush above the beach, Savina could see the gusting wind whipping the waves into frothy peaks.

The grand achievement of working together to get the supplies up off the beach seemed so little now as it occurred to Savina that they should have decided on a camping spot, started a fire, retrieved the boiling pot from among their supplies and begun a ragout of the salt pork the American had allowed them and perhaps some of the yams. And yet it had taken all of their energy just to do what they had done.

As if he had thought the same thoughts, Anthony Heywood set to work gathering wood, while Gaston-Reade, his notebook on his lap, began to make an inventory of their supplies. He repeatedly called his secretary away from his labor to help him, setting him to work opening crates, counting bottles, and repacking the cartons. Savina, trying to mend Gaston-Reade's damaged opinion of her, did her best to fold her hands together on her lap, as Lady Venture did, and behave in a ladylike manner, even as she longed to be doing something to help, and as much as she wanted to remonstrate with her fiancé that counting supplies was not really doing them a great deal of good at the moment.

But when Zazu awoke and saw what the secretary was trying to accomplish, she set to work to help him, gathering wood and smaller twigs and dried grass into organized piles. Savina couldn't stay still, not when so much needed to be done, and she finally leaped to her feet and silently began to help.

Perhaps if the entire group had worked together they would have succeeded, but with just the three of them making any effort at all, they ran out of time. The wind intensified, and their position at the edge of the wooded copse didn't offer them much protection; with no fire to warm them, nor any light, as the sun descended unseen behind a curtain of dark gray clouds, they got a taste of what the night was to be.

Zazu and Savina huddled together under a shawl as the wind howled around them, the giant palms swaying with ferocious joy at the blow. When she heard Annie, Lady Venture's maid, whimpering in the dark, Savina called out to her but realized it was too hard to be understood over the wind. She reached out and grabbed the girl's arm and hauled her down with the two of them in the shelter of the wooden crates and barrels, and for the next hours the three of them tried to offer each other what courage and comfort they could.

It was far from morning still when the rain began, blowing up from the beach and soaking all of them with needle-sharp precision.

Five

When the sun finally rose and cast off the gloomy shroud of clouds that had descended on them at twilight the night before, Tony stood at the edge of the thicket and looked around him. Of his fellow castaways, Mr. William Barker was wandering down along the beach, but at least he was doing something, which could not be said for Lord Gaston-Reade, who sat on a crate in majestic silence, brooding as he stared off into the tangle of undergrowth.

Zazu, Miss Roxeter's maid, had disappeared at daybreak; she had whispered something to her mistress, the two had gone off together, and then Miss Roxeter had come back alone.

Of them all Mr. Peter Roxeter looked the worst for their awful night. The oldest among them had refused to hunker down behind the barricade of supplies, and was therefore covered in filth, his day-old scrub of gray beard clogged with sand and his eyes circled by dark rings. His always tidy gray hair was a scruffy mat rising in tufts, and his daughter was near tears as she tried to get him to rouse himself to stand and let her get into the wood crate in which the American captain had packed for them a couple of knives, two cast-iron pots, a firkin or two of lard and some canvas bailing pails. He was foggy and abstracted, but eventually she got through to him and he stood, staggering off into the bushes presumably to relieve himself.

Lady Venture was in rare form. Her eyes glittered with fury, and her gaze slewed from person to person, looking, no doubt, for an object upon which to vent her fury. When her dark eyes settled on her future sister-in-law, Tony knew what was coming next.

"This is all your fault, Savina Roxeter," she exclaimed, dropping each word like a poison droplet into the silence. "If you hadn't thrust yourself forward in a most unbecoming manner, that American captain wouldn't have left our fate in your incapable hands and we would be . . . we would be . . ."

Savina whirled and stood over her, her grubby hands fisted at her sides. "We would be in the hold of the *Prosperous* suffering who knows what, prisoners of the United States government. Is that better than this?"

Lady Venture stood and the two women were face to face. "Yes, it would," she screeched, brushing away an insect from her cheek with an irritated swat. "Someone would be getting me some tea right now, and some breakfast, and I wouldn't be cold and wet and dirty."

"How do you know?"

"What?"

"How do you know?" Savina asked. She was silent for a moment, glaring at the other woman. A bird called to another and swooped low over the encampment. "Have you ever been a prisoner on a ship before? Do the Americans dispense tea and comfort like elderly aunts, or would they more likely forget about us, or abuse us, or even if they wanted to treat us well, simply need to keep us in chains because of your *idiotic* suggestion that we murder them all in their sleep!"

"Do not *ever* speak to me in that manner," Lady

Venture started, her whole body quivering with indignation.

But Miss Roxeter whirled away and stomped three paces, then turned and said, "Don't worry, I'll have nothing further to say to you until you speak to me in a sane and calm manner. And if you could get off your nether limbs and help, if you want tea so badly, that would go a very long way to ameliorating our miserable condition."

Tony suppressed a grin, then decided not to conceal it at all. He smirked openly, enchanted by the vision of Miss Savina Roxeter, hitherto the very model of ladylike behavior, screeching like a banshee.

Lady Venture turned to her brother but Lord Gaston-Reade, now hunched over his notebook, held up one hand. "Do not speak to me, Vennie. I am counting and must not be disturbed."

Annie timidly stepped forward, twisting her filthy hands around each other over and over. "Miss Roxeter, I could make something to eat, if you like. I'm rather a good cook."

"Don't offer help!" Lady Venture shrieked, plunking back down on her seat, one of the water barrels. "You are my maid, and I need you."

"But . . ."

"No. Not another word."

The atmosphere around the camp descended to a frosty silence, and Tony sighed. He had intended to try to let his employer set the pace for the day; survival demanded that they make camp further away from the shore, clearly, construct some kind of shelter, build a firepit, start a fire, and decide who had what skills and should take what tasks. Lord Gaston-Reade had always been capital at delegating duties on his plantation, but today he seemed mired in the need to ascertain exactly, to the last drop, how much water Captain Verdun had left them, how much food, how much tea, and if there was any wine. Perhaps that was his way of coping with the horrendous situation in which they found themselves, but it was an exercise in uselessness when there were far more important tasks to see to.

When William Barker came up from his walk on the beach, he looked around and said, "Everyone looks ghastly. Beastly night, eh?" For his efforts he got a timid smile from Annie, frosty silence from his fiancée, a shrug from Miss Roxeter and a grimace from Lord Gaston-Reade, who pointedly began a loud count again, making it plain he was not to be interrupted.

It was enough. Tony squared his shoulders. "Mr. Barker, would you go with me to scout a new spot to camp? Last night was an indication that we need better shelter if we are to be even moderately comfortable for however long we are here." Barker nodded, eager to do something, it seemed. Tony turned to Miss Roxeter, who was burrowing in a wood crate and hauling out a cast-iron pot and the flint and tinderbox the captain had given them. It was clearly her intention to help, and he was relieved that he didn't have to ask her to. "I propose, Miss Roxeter, a temporary firepit, just to put together some tea and food to give us strength for the day's efforts."

"I quite agree, Mr. Heywood," she said, straightening, with one hand to her back.

She was as grimy as the rest of them, but he couldn't help but think she looked adorable, with a smudge of dirt on her cheek.

"I was just contemplating something like that," she continued. "We are all exhausted, but there is much that needs to be done before tonight. Those of us who intend to work will need some strength." Her maid came back just then, laden with more wood and tinder. "Zazu and I can manage, I think. Though I don't know if I can build a fire . . ."

"I can do that," Zazu said as she tossed the wood to the ground and brushed her hands together. "I was not always a lady's maid."

Tony gazed at the two young women, both pretty, one dark and the other fair, and nodded. If he was Mr. Robinson Crusoe, he would name them Intrepid and Fearless. His respect for them both that moment was boundless. "Mr. Barker and I will scout a new camp, then," he said.

"I would suggest, Mr. Heywood," Zazu said, "that you go to the left beyond the camp. There is a spot just a little ways inland that would seem to be adequate."

He paused and gazed at her. "In what way?"

Her expression serious and thoughtful, she replied, "It is on high ground, but clear, and surrounded by sturdy palms suitable for framing some kind of shelter. The freshwater lakes you found last night are just a ways beyond it."

Tony smiled at her and nodded again. The young woman was going to be a valuable ally, as was her indomitable mistress. Miss Roxeter was gazing at her maid in astonishment, and as Tony led Barker away, he could hear Miss Roxeter say to her maid, "How do you know so much?"

It was no mystery to him, though, when one considered the maid's background. The Maroon settlements in the Blue Mountains were primitive by English standards, but the people had settled into the way of life and learned how to take advantage of the land. Instead of fighting nature, they embraced it, and the result was a coexistence with their surroundings that though harsh, was brave. The Maroon people were legendary for their ferocity and much feared by the English, who never ventured into the Maroon settlements. They had fought fiercely, and even against the superior power of the British army had refused to surrender. Proving indomitable, they had won their freedom by treaty. He didn't know much himself beyond that common knowledge, for they guarded their history zealously, but he had looked upon them with respect rather than fear. Zazu, raised in that atmosphere of fierce independence, couldn't help but revert given their present circumstances. Much of what came to her was a part of her innate knowledge from a childhood spent with nature.

Followed by the quiet Mr. Barker, he strode into the woods to find the site Zazu had spoken of.

Savina was surprised by a spurt of something close to jealousy at the admiring expression on Mr. Anthony Heywood's face when Zazu offered her advice. It did not bear examining, because she feared the emotion would not reflect well on her character. Instead she joined Zazu in building a fire—after many tries by both of them, and with no one else's help, they did manage to get one going with the flint and tinderbox—and constructing a rough tripod of heavy branches over the fire to suspend the pot to boil some water, not an easy task and taking the better part of an hour.

Dusting her hands off, she looked down at them ruefully, and then at her filthy dress and torn hem. "What a mess I am," she said. She sat down on the ground near their fire, and continued, "But I'm too tired to care, really. Last night was brutal and I'm exhausted."

Zazu sat down near her, then grimaced and moved a branch from under her legs. "How odd it is," she mused, "that we should be mired here, when we thought we were leaving the Caribbean forever."

"I wonder how long it will take before we're found," Savina said, pulling her knees up, surrounding them with her arms and resting her head on her forearms. "Do you think Captain Verdun will keep his promise and send word to the nearest British settlement of our position?"

"Why should he?" Lady Venture, sitting in stately

leisure and being fanned by Annie wielding a palm frond, spoke up finally, though she would not meet Savina's eye. The dry palm frond rattled as Annie's hands shook.

"He won't," Lord Gaston-Reade said, glancing up from his notebook. "Filthy Americans . . . they never keep their word."

"How do you know?" Savina said, genuinely curious. "Have you had dealings with Americans?"

"Of course not; wouldn't soil my hands with that. But everyone knows what they're like."

"Who is everyone?" Savina asked, gazing steadily at him.

"Everyone!" he retorted, irritation in his clipped response. "I can't name names. Just everyone. Didn't they break their agreements with us?"

"Bertie, no one wants to listen to politics here," Lady Venture said.

"And no one wishes to listen to you," he retorted.

Savina stood and stretched, trying to get the kinks out of her back. Zazu stood, too, and both young women bent their efforts to the practicality of tea and food without another word to the earl and his sister.

One of the other choices the American captain had forced Savina to make was that as he was being quite charitable enough in allowing them so many supplies, she had to make a choice in the number of trunks, crates and boxes they took ashore. Given the choice, she sacrificed their trunks of clothing for more food and supplies. She regretted it when she thought of changing into a dry, clean dress, but food, eating implements and a good-sized tarpaulin of oiled canvas had seemed more important.

Zazu scooped some of the boiling water out of the large pot into the smaller pot, threw some tea leaves in, and then said, "I saw some fruit trees; perhaps I should gather some fruit. The more we can extend our supplies, the better."

As she moved off, Savina's father came back and collapsed on the ground near the fire.

"Papa," Savina said, crouching down beside him.

He didn't respond, his lined face marred by an expression of defeat. Her stomach clenched and she thought of Lady Venture's words, that if they had stayed on board even if they were prisoners, they would have someone to care for them. Her father may have chafed at his role as a prisoner of war, but this was worse . . . much worse.

"Papa, please, you must rouse yourself." She reached over for the brush, one of the few luxury items she had been allowed to pack, and, kneeling beside him, brushed his hair. He gazed at her at first as if he didn't recognize her, but gradually he took in a deep breath and sighed.

He stayed her hand with his own. "Savina, don't trouble yourself, my dear. I shall . . . I shall rally. I will try harder to be more valiant. Like you." He gazed steadily at her, his pouchy eyes like those of a fond basset. "Your mother would be so proud. She was the strong one, you know, never me." He stood with great effort, given his bulk, turned to Lord Gaston-Reade, and said, "My lord, I wish to be of assistance. What may I do?"

Lord Gaston-Reade asked for his help counting and cataloguing supplies—Savina gritted her teeth and said nothing—and he set to work happily helping his future son-in-law. She supposed she should feel fortunate they got along so well, but in her opinion there was entirely too much deference on her father's side and too much presumption on the part of her fiancé.

When Zazu came back, they cut up some meat and yams and set them to boil. For Savina it was a novelty, something she had never done before, and she was clumsy at first. But Zazu seemed to have slipped back into her youth in the Maroon settlement, chopping some of the vegetables with quick, deft movements, and by the time the others came back, there was food to eat. Though it was rough, and in normal circumstances most would have rejected it as disgusting, even Lady Venture ate her share without comment.

"Where do you think we are?" Savina asked, as people's appetites became sated and conversation was once more possible.

Lady Venture sat still on her barrel, with Annie on the ground by her side. Mr. Heywood had kindly set a couple of crates near the fire and Savina's father had taken one, with Mr. Barker beside him. The younger man had tried to give his seat up to Savina, but she stayed on the ground close to the fire by Zazu. Lord Gaston-Reade stood, unwilling to do the work it would have required to make himself a crate seat. He shot his secretary, who sat on the ground near the fire, disagreeable looks, but Mr. Heywood appeared not to notice as he rapidly consumed the stew of pork and yams from a tin plate.

No one answered immediately, but once the secretary's mouthful of food was swallowed, he said, "It seems to me that we are on one of the islands known as the Bahamas, perhaps, or at least close by."

"Yes, I was thinking the same thing," Savina said. "We were clearly blown off course by the storm the night before the *Gryphon* accosted us, and so to that group of islands. I've heard that the smaller ones are coral cays."

Mr. Heywood shot her a look of some surprise. "What is a cay?" he said, giving it the pronunciation she had used, of "key."

She blushed. She was not accustomed to being asked about her fund of knowledge. She read widely and had a reasonable amount of knowledge, devouring every book on Jamaica and the Caribbean she could find, but her fiancé had never spoken to her of such things, or of any serious subject, she realized for the first time.

"A cay is an island composed of coral, from my understanding. Coral is a primitive life form," she said, fingering the small cross around her neck, made of a pale pink coral. "But as the coral becomes hard and builds up into enormous reefs it forms a base, and sand gathers, then plant seeds, blown on the winds, grow. Thus, islands are formed."

Heywood nodded. "The sand is particularly fine and white," he said, gazing down over the tranquil beach.

"Does it matter where we are?" Lady Venture interrupted, with an agitated huff. "What I want to know is, how are we going to get home?"

Savina's father spoke up for the first time, perhaps buoyed by the steaming cup of tea he held in his hands.

"My lady, I fear our first necessity is going to be survival in this terrible place. I can't imagine how we're to do it." He glanced around at the group. "What are we going to do?"

Savina glanced at Mr. Heywood, and saw that he was looking to his employer, who lounged indolently against the trunk of a palm tree. When Lord Gaston-Reade said nothing, Heywood brushed his hands together and stood.

"This is my proposal," he said. "Mr. Barker and I have found, with Miss Zazu's invaluable help, a capital spot for a safe camp. We have a good, heavy, large oilskin. With that as a roof, we could have a rudimentary shelter constructed by the end of the day. Is everyone in agreement?"

There was silence, but finally, Mr. Barker stood, and said, "I'm with you, Mr. Heywood."

Savina's father nodded. "I will do what I can to help."

"You will be a welcome addition, sir," Heywood said, giving him a warm smile.

Savina caught the secretary's eye and thanked him with a smile. He nodded, took a deep breath and said, "Well, gentlemen, shall we get started?"

Lord Gaston-Reade, piqued by the group's lack of deference—it was clear to Savina that he felt he ought to have been consulted about the placement of the camp—stomped off into the bushes after luncheon. Savina and Zazu set to work repacking the utensils, for they would need to be moved yet again, talking in low tones as they did so.

Savina occasionally glanced over at Lady Venture, who stood at the edge of the thicket and scowled off to the horizon in angry silence. The woman was a complete mystery to her, and since she had always found mysteries intriguing, she had whiled away some time in trying to figure out her character and temperament. They had often been in company together, in the social gatherings in Spanish Town feting government officials, or other celebrations. Lady Venture, older than Savina by some years, could be charming and had a sharp, incisive wit at times that had startled Savina the first time she was exposed to it.

But she was bad-tempered and shrewish often, too. Why she was so angry and rancorous was the mystery. She had what she had appeared to be after, a devoted fiancé, but still she was often sour, her remarks tinged with acerbic venom.

She would try one more time, Savina thought.

"Lady Venture," she said. "What do you make of our situation here? What would improve it, do you think?"

The woman's gaze slewed around to Savina. "Improve it? Our situation would be considerably improved if everyone would just stop pretending that this was some jolly camping adventure and face the facts. We are abandoned here, and will likely never leave this abominable island. And it is all your doing."

Annie, her maid, gazed up at her in horror, then dissolved in tears and ran away into the bushes.

"Whatever is wrong with her?" Lady Venture said, gazing off after her as she disappeared.

"You frightened her! She's a very sensitive girl and you scared her, with your talk of being here forever."

"Miss Roxeter, just because you treat your maid like some kind of pet do not think you can make a pet out of mine."

"That is enough," Zazu said, standing and stalking over to Lady Venture. "You shall not speak to me that way. I am descended from a Coromantee queen, so my lineage is not merely equal to yours, but better. *Never* speak to me that way again."

"I wasn't speaking *to* you at all," Lady Venture said, standing and staring directly into Zazu's dark eyes.

"Then do not speak *of* me in that manner."

Savina laughed out loud and clapped her hands as Zazu whirled and stalked away.

Lady Venture glared at Savina. "I have never been spoken to in that manner by a servant! You will tell her to behave herself."

"No. It's simply too much fun watching you two spar." Savina gazed at her steadily for a long minute. "My lady . . . Venture, I don't know how long we're going to be on this island, but you're going to have to become accustomed to the idea that for as long as that is the case, you will have to live with things the way they are. Zazu is working harder than any of us, and I, for one, will not tell her to behave any way at all. I consider her manners to be better than many others' I could name."

From then on, silence again reigned in the castaway camp.

After hours of exhausting labor a new camp was set up, the dinner was cooked and much had been accomplished. The atmosphere was tense, with Lord Gaston-Reade speaking only to Savina's father, and his sister, Lady Venture, speaking to no one but her brother, and everyone else too tired to talk at all, but Savina just didn't care.

After the camp had been tidied, she crept off to the beachfront and sat on a log, watching darkness veil the water as the moon replaced the sun. As tired as she was, it was still a beautiful, fearsome sight, the glowing trail across the lonely water, the waves lapping the shore.

"Oh, I beg your pardon," a voice behind her said.

Savina turned and saw Mr. Heywood approaching in the gloom. He bowed and turned to leave her alone, but she said, "No, come and sit, if that was your intention, Mr. Heywood."

He came around the log and sat down gingerly a few feet away from her. They were silent for a time.

"Mr. Heywood, I just want to say . . ."

"Miss Roxeter, I just wanted to th . . ."

Both of them had spoken at exactly the same moment.

"Ladies first," Heywood said, laughing at their folly.

Savina, very conscious of her ratted hair and unpleasant dress, turned on the log and gazed through the duskiness at Anthony Heywood. Though he was dirty and disheveled too, as they all were, he carried within him an innate dignity that could not be damaged by a dirty cravat or stubbly beard growing in. His sandy hair, at least, was neatly brushed to one side. "I just . . . I wanted to thank you, for all you've done today."

"I was about to say the same to you, Miss Roxeter. If not for you and Miss Zazu, we would have starved."

Savina shrugged. "I don't know how to cook. Zazu does."

"But you very bravely organized things," he said, his tone gentle and blending with the night sounds from the forest above and behind them. "And worked like a navvy all day long. I know that today has not been easy for you. Lord Gaston-Reade . . ." He didn't finish, just shaking his head and looking away, then back directly into her eyes. "You weren't raised to labor, and so it is all the more commendable that you took such initiative."

"Thank you. And thank you, too, for including my father. I'm afraid this has all been very difficult for him." She stood and brushed her skirt down. "I . . . I think I shall retire now."

Six

Though their sleeping arrangements were rough, by any accounting, Savina had been so weary the night before that the palm fronds and thick tropical leaves they had used to create pallets had been as comfortable as a feather mattress. Awakening in the morning, though, she felt dirty and disheveled and saw that Zazu, too, habitually very tidy, was also unkempt, her hair sticking out in tufts and her neat dress dirty.

"We'll have to find some way to clean up today. I don't think I can go another day like this," Savina said, quietly to Zazu, as they lay face to face on their shared pallet.

Dawn was just breaking, and a scraping sound nearby made Savina look up from her crude bed. She spotted a lizard scuttling through their encampment, and squeaked a surprised gasp, but then calmed and pointed it out to her maid. They watched it scurry away, and then Zazu moved up to rest on her elbow.

"I cannot stay so dirty," Zazu agreed, picking a twig out of her hair, grimacing, and tossing it aside. "But first, breakfast and tea, I think."

"One thing before that," Savina said with a sigh. "I need to find a quiet and secluded spot somewhere for some personal business. Ugh! This is one of the many things I am going to have trouble becoming accustomed to."

They arose together, did what was necessary, and then came back to begin the day, their third on the island. Their "camp" was situated in an opening in a grove of palms, with the large oilskin tarpaulin stretched taut and lashed to four trees. That was their shelter, as rudimentary as it was, but angled to exclude wind from the ocean, and with the crates and barrels lined up to one side, it was some protection. The others slept on, oblivious of the two young women and their cautious movements.

As quietly as possible they unpacked one of the wood crates they had not yet gotten to the bottom of, and Savina was overjoyed to find a few extra things she hadn't considered necessary until she thought they would have to get along without them. One was a straight razor and strop. Her father would be pleased, she thought, as she gazed over at him, still asleep on his pallet. Perpetually neat, even dandified, he was distressed by his gray beard and scruffy appearance, she knew. It was something the American captain had clearly thought of that she had not, and she silently blessed his kindness. She would never say it aloud, but she knew he could easily have mired them with nothing but the clothes on their back, so his few thoughtful gestures were greeted by her with gratitude.

"Molasses!" Zazu whispered, pulling a heavy tin pail out of the crate.

Savina made a face. "What can we do with that?"

"You will be glad of it soon enough. We shall have to make it last; who knows how long we shall be here."

The others gradually rose, stretching and yawning, and set off in different directions into the bush. She hadn't noticed before, but Savina soon realized that Anthony Heywood had been gone before she and Zazu arose. As they prepared the water to boil over the fire, he came back, the cuffs of his white shirt red, carrying a slab of something.

"What . . . what is that?" she asked, straightening from her task.

"Turtle meat," he said. He indicated the long knife he carried in a crude sheath on his hip. "It's very good. I had it once fried, though most often it's used as soup or stew."

"Of course," Savina said, trying to fight back her distaste. "I've had turtle soup before. And Captain Gallagher . . . he had live turtles on board for the crossing; I saw the crew loading them."

Mr. Heywood nodded as he deposited the meat in the other pot. "I intend to try to catch fish, too, but this fellow wandered by, and it was too opportune to ignore. A gift from the sea."

Savina felt faintly ill, but Zazu was enthusiastic. "We will make turtle stew for dinner," she said.

"And I'll have fish for you ladies tomorrow, I promise."

Lady Venture returned just then, sat down on one of the crates and said, "Is tea made?"

"No, not yet," Savina answered.

Annie returned, too, and without hesitation picked up the brush and began brushing her mistress's hair.

"Annie will need some of that hot water for my toilette, first," Lady Venture said, pointing at the pot of steaming water. "Get some, Annie. I wish to wash."

Zazu stepped in front of the pot. "My lady forgets there are other people. Tea first, then washing."

Lady Venture slowly turned to face Zazu. "I don't think I heard you correctly."

Savina stepped forward. "You know you did. Everyone wants some tea. There are eight of us, so you can just wait to wash up until after breakfast."

"I cannot eat in this state," she said, hands outstretched in distaste.

Savina shrugged. "Then don't eat. Or use cold water to wash. That's what I did."

Anthony Heywood stood back and watched with a secretive smile on his face as he scruffed his fingers against the three-day growth of beard on his chin. Lord Gaston-Reade and William Barker came up the rough path from the beach to the camp just then, and Lady Venture turned to them, related in highly colored expression and with enormous exaggeration what had just passed, and appealed to both for their support.

William Barker said nothing, watching Gaston-Reade's face, clearly uneasy at taking a position until he saw how the other man was going to decide.

The earl said, irritably, "Vennie, I want my breakfast. You can wash your face after, but if Zazu is going to make breakfast, I say let her."

Triumphant, Zazu and Savina went back to work, and tea and food were soon ready. Lady Venture merely picked at her food, trying to indicate her ire, no doubt, by her petulance. Savina just rolled her eyes at Zazu and shrugged.

"Tony," Lord Gaston-Reade said, as he finished his meal of fruit and fried pork. "I shall require you today. I wish to work out a map of where we may be, according to our position when we were taken off course by that storm."

Heywood glanced up at him. Savina watched, knowing the secretary had other plans that day for fishing, hunting, and securing their shelter.

"Uh, certainly, sir," he said. "But can it not wait until this evening? I have things . . ."

"No, it can't wait."

"I was thinking of getting some fish, sir, for dinner."

"Others can do that," Gaston-Reade said, waving one hand. "Let Barker do it. You've fished before, Barker, have you not?"

"Well, fly-fishing in Scotland, yes."

"Then you can fish. Go on . . . Tony and I have work to do."

Barker, mumbling under his breath, wandered off, with Lady Venture calling after him to bring back a lot of fish, as she was tired of pork.

"He's not very clever," Gaston-Reade said, ignoring a gasp and glare from his sister.

"I don't think he's unintelligent, sir," Heywood said.

Savina could hear the irritation in the secretary's voice as the two men settled down with a wood crate as a table. Her father hovered, and she realized that he would have been delighted to be the one consulted, and with his knowledge of the area would likely have been a better fit for figuring out where they were than Mr. Heywood, who had no prior knowledge of the place than their sojourn on Gaston-Reade's Jamaican sugar plantation for the last seven months.

She sighed and turned her back on the scene. It was her experience that any suggestions she had ever made to her fiancé had been received with indulgence, a smile and forgetfulness.

"Let's get some water, Zazu," she said, picking up the firkins.

"Be careful, Savina," her father said, glancing up from his position looking over the shoulders of the two younger men. "There may be wild animals, you know."

"Nothing but lizards, sir," Anthony Heywood said, glancing up. He smiled at Savina. "And I don't think Miss Roxeter would be frightened of a lizard."

"Attend to what I am explaining, Tony," Gaston-Reade said, drawing a line on the wood crate with a black stone.

"Yes, sir," Heywood said, and bent his head back over the crude map.

The forest was lush, with palms and other tropicals competing for space with thick underbrush, but Anthony Heywood, using one of the large knives the

American captain had allowed them, had already cut back some of the brush so there was a crude pathway to the freshwater source. The two young women picked their way through the brush, having to hold their skirts up with one hand and carrying the firkins in the other. Zazu led the way, as she knew where the lakes were.

Birds flew overhead, calling to each other as they swooped from tree to tree, disturbed by the intruders. Along the way some flowers grew and butterflies flitted among them. But as the path got more tangled, the two young women had to pay more attention to the walk and less to their surroundings.

"Long skirts are a nuisance," Savina said, disentangling the lace ruffle on the bottom of hers from a dead branch on the path and wincing at the ripping sound. "A sovereign's worth of lace torn, there. Ah, well. Zazu, what are we going to do?" She glanced ahead at her maid, also picking her way carefully through the tangled undergrowth.

"Do? What do you mean?"

"Do. Here. On this wretched island."

"Survive, of course," Zazu said, finally stopping and knotting her skirt so it would stay above her ankles and not interfere with the arduous hike through the scrub.

"Will we be all right?" Savina followed Zazu's lead in the way she knotted her skirt and then the two proceeded.

They topped a low rise and looked over to a clear area where the two small inland "lakes" were. "These must be fed by rainwater, I suppose. Do you think, Zazu? I can't imagine there would be a spring on such a tiny island."

"Perhaps," Zazu said.

"So," Savina repeated, as they followed the slope to

the edge of the tiny lake, a small flat pond fed from the larger pond. "Do you think we'll be all right?"

"I think we will," Zazu said. "There is water here, there is food in the sea and on the land."

"You're so certain," Savina said, watching the face of her maid. Zazu was small-boned and delicate, but stronger than she looked, and determined. From the ladies of society in Spanish Town, Savina had learned that she should keep a distance between herself and her maid, making sure Zazu knew her place, but she had never been able to. Raised in isolation as she had been in her Jamaican home, with little company but what her father brought home from Spanish Town, her maid had become her friend, she realized, and she didn't really want it any other way. They picked their way around the edge of the small pond to the rivulet that connected the two. "How can you be so sure we'll be all right?" She plunked down on a rocky outcropping and dipped one of the firkins in, setting it aside.

"Is there any other choice?"

"No, I suppose not."

"My people, when they escaped bondage and moved into the hills," Zazu said, crouching on the mossy edge of the pool and running her hand through the water, "knew nothing about how to survive in the strange land their forefathers had been brought to in chains, but without even these things—pails, knives, pots—they made their way. And so shall we."

"You're absolutely right." Savina looked down at the warm water. It trickled from the larger pool, over a shelf of mossy rocks and down to the lower pool. The rivulet, just a few feet long and sloped, was inviting. She glanced down at her shoes and the cool water, and pulled off her shoes and stockings. She set them aside.

"What are you doing?" Zazu asked.

"Perhaps Venture had the right idea," Savina said,

wading into the lower pool. "Come, we deserve this. The upper pool will be for drinking water, and the lower can be for bathing. You and I have worked as hard as anyone else. Harder than most." Zazu pulled off her own shoes and stockings and joined her, and the two of them waded in the warm water. "Oh, that's so much better!" Savina exclaimed, pulling her dirty skirts up and knotting them higher over her knees. She wiggled her poor pinched toes, then splashed some water at Zazu, who laughed and returned the favor.

Then Savina pulled her ratted hair out of its clumsy bun, and began yanking at the knots. For a while both girls were too consumed with the wonder of feeling clean, and how simple a pleasure that was, to even speak. They rinsed their dirty skirt hems and wrung them out and sat on the edge of the pond for a while, feet luxuriously clean. Finally Savina sighed and said, "I suppose we should go back."

"Do you think Lord Gaston-Reade has figured out where we are yet?"

Savina snickered, understanding the sarcasm that was veiled in Zazu's careful words, though she knew she shouldn't. She had to keep reminding herself she owed him respect, though that was getting increasingly hard to accord him when he offered her none in exchange. "He's . . . very tedious, isn't he?"

"But not as bad as his sister," Zazu said, splashing her feet in the water. "That woman thinks only of herself."

"Venture *is* poisonous, isn't she?" Savina said, frank for the first time in her life about what she thought.

"But . . . she doesn't mean to be."

The quiet voice made both young women whirl around to find Annie standing behind them, gazing longingly at the fresh water. Savina was grateful that it wasn't her future sister-in-law, and then realized it never would be, for Lady Venture was poorly named; she would never *venture* so far into the forest on her own.

"Your mistress is mean to you. How can you defend her?" Zazu asked, searching the expression of the young woman who stood above them.

"My last position was much worse," Annie said.

"Sit, take your boots off and wash your feet," Savina said, indicating a spot between them.

"I . . . shouldn't," Annie said with the hesitance that was so customary for her.

"Yes, you should," Zazu said, with great firmness.

"But my lady sent me to find you, to ask you why you hadn't boiled more water yet for her toilette."

"I'm not her handmaiden, nor is Zazu," Savina snapped. "Sit, Annie. You will better be able to serve your mistress if you're more comfortable yourself."

That argument proved efficacious, and Savina had the pleasure of seeing the girl take her shoes and stockings off and paddle in the water. Soon, she was wading in the pool below the rivulet, holding her skirts up and winding them around her waist. She was a very pretty girl, plump and pink, with light brown hair as fine as silk.

"What did you mean when you said Lady Venture was better than your last position?" Savina asked.

"I was a maid at Langley Hall," Annie said, naming one of the plantations near Jamaica's northern shore. She glanced at Zazu and then dropped her gaze again, but her gaze was drawn back as though she was mesmerized. She approached the dark-skinned girl and said, "I heard that your people—those Maroons—are cannibals."

Savina gasped. Zazu's dark eyes were wide with astonishment, but then her expression changed to a wide grin and she laughed out loud. "How my grandmother would laugh to hear that. She would say it is better for your people to think such things . . . then you do not roam into our mountains and bother us."

"I thought it wasn't true," Annie said, with a shy

smile. "You're much too kind. You . . . you gave me a ginger bun once, when Lady Venture was visiting Mr. and Miss Roxeter. I was very hungry, for I hadn't had time to eat that morning, and you noticed how pale I was and made me eat."

"You remember that?" Zazu asked. "I don't remember at all."

The girl nodded. "It's true. You made me sit down, have a bun and a cup of milk."

Savina watched her, thinking how bad her former position must have been to make Lady Venture's treatment seem a relief. But as the girl continued her story, it came out that it was not her mistress at Langley Hall who was the trouble, but her master, who would not leave her alone, and who was always trying to get her alone. She had been afraid she wasn't going to be able to defend her virtue any longer, when Lady Venture, a guest at the house, found out and saved her by hiring her as her lady's maid.

"Venture did that?" Savina asked, amazed.

"She did, that very day. And she left with me so I wouldn't have to spend another night under that roof, and then she paid my former mistress a fee to take me away. I was so very grateful," Annie said, her voice breaking.

Perhaps Lady Venture was more complex than she had thought, Savina reflected. It had always seemed to her that her future sister-in-law was thoroughly spoiled and completely uncaring about anyone's comfort but her own. But if the story was accurate—and surely it must be—then it revealed depths to Venture that she had yet to plumb. She shrugged and relegated the information to her list of things she thought about when she was bored. It was a conundrum, and she liked puzzles.

Finally they all felt clean and refreshed, and clambered

back up the short rise, filled both firkins, and stood, overlooking the lovely spot.

"I'm not putting these wretched shoes and stockings back on," Savina declared, waving them with her free hand. "Even if it is rough walking back, it's better than the torture of those leather caskets!"

"Thank goodness," Zazu sighed. "I won't either, then."

Annie stared at them wide-eyed, but sat down on the ground and slipped her own back on her damp, clean feet. "I wouldn't dare do such a thing," she said. "It wouldn't be proper."

Savina glanced over at her suspiciously, but the maid seemed unaware that she was casting aspersions on the propriety of Savina and Zazu's decision. The three made their way back to the camp, Savina relishing the unusual feeling of bare feet. There were a few tough moments on broken branches and slippery moss, but it was worth it for the unaccustomed feeling of freedom. She vowed to herself that she would go down to the beach later. She had always wondered what sand would feel like under her feet, and soon she would know.

But their return was halted at the edge of the camp by the shouting they heard.

Savina handed her pail of water to Annie and raced ahead to find Lord Gaston-Reade and his secretary facing each other, with Mr. William Barker standing off to the side, holding his hand away from him. Blood dripped from it.

"What's going on here?" she said, tossing her shoes and stockings aside and striding into the clearing near their tarpaulin.

"Savina, you should not be here," her fiancé said, pointing back the way she came. "I sent Venture away. It is not seemly for a lady to hear men arguing. Go, now!"

"Fustian! Mr. Heywood," she said, turning to the secretary. "What's going on here? And why is no one helping Mr. Barker?" That fellow held his hand out with a pitiable expression on his pale face. She bent down, ripped a strip from the bottom of her now-clean skirt, and bound the cut on his hand to try to stop the bleeding.

"Barker is fine," Heywood said, irritation in his voice. He passed one hand over his sandy hair, took a deep breath, and calmed himself. "Miss Roxeter, it is just a surface scrape."

"I . . . I cut it on a sharp shell," Mr. Barker said with a plaintive whine. "I was trying to grab a fish."

"Trying to grab a fish?" Savina shook her head. "But what was the shouting about?"

"Tony is just being difficult, Savina, and it is no business of yours," her fiancé said, his beaky face set in an obstinate expression. His scruffy beard, a black shadow over his jaw and chin, made him look like a perturbed pirate. "I told you that you should retreat, and I meant it. Your father quite agreed, and took Vennie off somewhere."

"I am not being difficult, sir," Mr. Heywood said through gritted teeth. He folded his arms over his chest. "I just said that I thought our tasks should be delegated to those who could best perform them. Mr. Barker clearly has no idea how to catch fish, and I do. He would be better here with you, figuring out your dratted map . . ." he said, with an impatient gesture at the wooden crate with the crude outline of their position worked out on it.

"Language, Tony! Do not curse in front of my fiancée!"

"Enough, both of you," Savina said, as Zazu and Annie entered the camp. Both women went about their business, leaving the confrontation to Savina.

"I'm going fishing," Heywood said, taking the long

knife and a length of rope and heading out of the camp, loping with long, furious strides.

Ire in every line of his body and in his face, the earl stomped off in the opposite direction. The conflict was far from over, Savina realized. Far from over. It would likely brew, breaking out again in some other way. But at least there was peace for the time being.

It was like the weather. Savina had lived for many years on Jamaica. They were entering hurricane season, that time of year when vast storms would cross the Atlantic and ravage the islands of the Caribbean. There was nothing on the horizon for now, but one could approach any time, and they would be wise, perhaps, to seek shelter deeper in the forest when one did cross their path. But she wouldn't look for trouble. They would handle that if it happened; so it was with trouble among the castaways. Perhaps everyone would surprise her and learn to get along.

The day was long, but quiet. Mr. Barker was happily employed with cutting up the turtle meat and roasting it over the fire, as Savina and Zazu tried to make their home a little more comfortable for the night by getting more leaves and fronds for their beds. Savina's father sat and talked with a cleaner and better-humored Lady Venture in the shade of the huge palms, as they canvassed what acquaintance they had in common, and how the summer was proceeding in London. It was September, so some people would be coming back to town for the little season, and there would be a few balls before people disappeared again to their estates for hunting and Christmas.

As they talked, Savina and Zazu whispered together, and then, both agreeing they deserved a walk, slipped off down toward the beach.

The sun was midway down to the horizon, and the water sparkled like a sheet of ice, pinpoints of light dancing on the crests of tiny wavelets. The beach itself was a crescent of white sand curving like the blade of a scythe between two rocky promontories. Savina marveled that she had never seen so many shades of blue: the pale aqua of the water, the celestial sky blue above them, the indigo as the two met at the horizon.

"Oh," she whispered, as her bare feet dug into the cool of the sand just below the surface heat. "Oh, this is heavenly." She stopped and wiggled her toes. A movement caught her eye, and she saw in the distance a figure clamber to the top of the rocky promontory on their left. She shaded her eyes and watched, in a moment identifying the figure. It was Anthony Heywood. "It's Mr. Heywood. We should see if he's been successful in catching any fish."

She and Zazu moved across the beach toward the rocky outcropping in time to see the man jump into the ocean, a soaring dive that halted Savina in her tracks and caught her breath in her throat as she stared. "That . . . that looked terribly dangerous."

Zazu gazed at her with curiosity in her dark eyes, but said nothing.

They climbed together up the rocky surface to where Mr. Heywood had been in time to meet him as he clambered up the rock surface again. He was shirtless, and as he strained to pull himself up, Savina stared at the unaccustomed sight of wet, sleek muscles cording thick fore- and upper arms and felt a slow flush robe her body from forehead to bare toes.

"Mr. Heywood," Zazu, with more presence of mind, said, and he looked up at them as he clambered to his feet.

"Uh, ladies," he said, hastily grabbing his shirt and pulling it on over his wet skin. It clung, and as it dampened gave a very clear outline of his upper torso.

Seven

The flush on her cheeks burned a lovely shade of pink, Tony thought, gazing at the incomparable Miss Savina Roxeter as he buttoned his damp shirt—he had rinsed it out earlier to cleanse it of the turtle blood from his morning hunting expedition—and swept his wet hair out of his eyes. He should feel embarrassed that she had seen him in his undress, and at first he had been, but discomfiture had been replaced by an intriguing thrill of excitement fueled by the ready thrum of his body's response to her awareness of him. No matter how much he told himself it was just that she had never seen a man's nearly naked body before, his body insisted the attraction he had long felt toward her was returned.

And his own had heightened. At least when he had thought her lovely but brainless he could quell his passion, explain it to himself as just physical attraction, the kind he had felt many times before. But now he knew her to be brave and intelligent and curious, and he was intrigued by the depths the young lady had so successfully kept concealed. It all fueled an uncomfortable physical response he must quell if he was to stay decent in the ladies' presence.

When he glanced at her maid he saw amusement in her dark eyes. Miss Zazu was intelligent, too, and observant . . . disconcertingly so. Her gaze flicked down over his body and then she smiled and winked at him.

"My deepest apologies, ladies, I . . . well, I was swimming." And how idiotic that sounded, even to himself. He summoned his usual aplomb, and, dripping with seawater, crossed the rocky surface to the small tidal pool shadowed by the rocks. "Actually I was celebrating a successful day with one last dive." He reached down and pulled up part of the rope he had left with that morning.

"Fish!" Miss Roxeter exclaimed, clapping her hands together.

He examined his string of seven fish with pride. There were blue and black fish, the rope strung through their mouths and out their gills. "It was like being a boy again, but instead of a fishing pole and hook, I used this." He picked up a long stick from the rock by the tidal pool and showed them his makeshift spear, the long knife lashed on with another section of the invaluable rope.

"How ingenious," Miss Roxeter exclaimed, reaching out and caressing the long shaft with naïve interest.

Tony swallowed and hastily let go of the spear, releasing it into her hand.

The maid, with a sly sideglance, asked Miss Roxeter, "Do you like Mr. Heywood's spear?"

The young woman had caught hold of it and hefted it in her hand, closing her fingers tightly around the haft. "It's very nicely designed but a little too thick for me to grasp properly." She looked up at her maid's choked laughter. "What is it, Zazu? Did I say something?"

"Nothing at all," the maid said, with another saucy wink at Tony.

"We should make our way back to our encampment, ladies," Tony said, trying not to smile at the maid's wicked grin. Her earthy imagination left him shocked but entertained. He thought she might be younger than her mistress but of course, as a maid and previously in her Maroon village, she had not lived the sheltered life Miss Roxeter had.

"I suppose," Miss Roxeter murmured.

"I'm willing to go on ahead with the fish, if you wish," he said, noting hesitation in her tone. He slung the string of fish over his back and picked up his boots from the rocky promontory before beginning his descent.

"No," she sighed. "I know we have to go back and start dinner. This has been so delightful, this walk and . . ." She looked down at her bare feet, pink toes wiggling against the dark rock.

Tony glanced down at them and stared, mesmerized. Her feet were not especially small, but they were perfectly formed with smooth pink skin and delicate ankles just visible beneath the hem of her dress. "And?" He looked up into her eyes.

"Nothing. It's nothing."

But as they climbed down the stone projection and started across the beach, Miss Roxeter still carrying the spear, the maid ran ahead and began to pick up scattered shells in her skirt, and his companion lagged. Finally she stopped and planted the haft of the spear in the sand. The breeze had picked up and her dark, tangled curls fluttered in the wind. She looked like some ancient sea deity, Tony thought, watching her, memorizing every freckle on her sun-kissed cheeks.

She gazed up to the entrance into the forest above the beach. "Why do some people feel it is all right to do nothing while others serve them? And they don't really care who does the serving, as long as it isn't them."

"Do you mean . . . who *do* you mean?" Tony said, afraid to mention her fiancé and break the spell of amity they found themselves in. They had never exchanged more than a handful of words before being marooned together, but he felt at ease with her now that they were together alone. Everything had changed the moment they were cast upon the golden shore of their secluded little island.

"I'm speaking of Gaston-Reade's dreadful sister, of course." She looked up at him, searching his eyes, her own shadowed against the deeply slanting sun with her free hand. "Who else could I have meant?"

"Oh, Lady Venture. Yes, of course." He dug his bare feet in the cooling sand and waited, for she clearly had more to say; he could see it in the pensive expression in her celestial eyes.

"I think that even though Zazu and Annie are maids, and perhaps the work would in the normal course of things be left up to them, this is an extraordinary circumstance, and we should throw our lot in together and all work." She clasped the spear with both hands and leaned on it, gazing, still, up at the edge of the forest. "We could be so much more comfortable, Mr. Heywood. If we worked together we would have more food, more bedding, a better shelter . . . but instead, even though she sees me working alongside Zazu, Venture will not raise a finger, nor will she let her maid help, even though the poor girl would like to, I think."

Tony reached out and allowed his bare fingers to touch her hand. "Such is the world," he said. "If we all worked together, how much better a world could we build?"

She gazed into his eyes and her own widened. "I . . . hadn't thought of it like that, but it's true. And yet each of us behaves as though the world was constructed for ourselves, to give us what we desire."

Zazu glanced back at them, and Tony took Miss Roxeter's free arm. "We should walk while we talk, or Miss Zazu will get very far in front of us."

She began to stroll again, dragging her feet in the fine sand.

"Lady Venture does seem to feel that she is owed something for simply being who she is," Tony said, moving their conversation back to their peculiar situation. "It is her lot in life to be among the helpless, as I have often thought of all who need servants even for the most everyday tasks."

Miss Roxeter was silent, so Tony went on.

"But it seems to me—and I have known her three years—she is unhappy most of the time, no matter where she is. Jamaica was too hot, London, when she is there, is too dirty and damp and the countryside is boring. This is too primitive and uncomfortable, Brighton too busy and crowded. She is always looking ahead to that which will make her happy."

"But she has a fiancé. That's what she came to Jamaica to obtain, isn't it?" She looked sideways at him and searched his eyes.

Tony laughed out loud, thinking how refreshing Miss Roxeter was, and how outspoken. And he was glad that his employer's habit of correcting her constantly and belittling her often hadn't silenced her. "Well, yes, it is what she came to Jamaica for, since no one in London would have her. But we are not supposed to acknowledge that, you know."

"I know," she said with a sigh. "I never would in front of her."

They began up the sloping sand to the fringe of palms that topped the crescent-shaped beach.

"You should just make your case to Lady Venture," Tony said, glancing sideways at his companion as they entered the shadowed palm forest behind Zazu.

"Perhaps." She picked her way carefully over dead palm fronds and twigs.

"You sound reluctant."

She shook her head. They caught up with Zazu and walked in silence the rest of the way.

Mr. Roxeter glanced up as they entered the little

clearing that was their temporary home. "Savina! Where have you been?"

"Zazu and I were out walking, father. We met Mr. Heywood and he has fish for our dinner!"

"Fish?" Lady Venture, patting at her brow with a delicate handkerchief, showed interest. "Finally something different to eat from that dreadful pork. I was beginning to feel quite ill. I have a delicate stomach, you know, and too much pork is bad for one's digestion."

"Good, then as you are so looking forward to fish for dinner, you may help me gut them, my lady," Tony said. "I could use someone's help."

"Tony, you are quite out of order," Lord Gaston-Reade said, looking up from his crude map.

Staring at his employer, Tony reflected on the many times he had had to bite his tongue quite literally to keep from retorting to the earl's sometimes inane remarks. "I thought, sir, that your sister, since she is so hungry, might want to speed the process of making dinner by helping out in some way."

"Vennie? Never!" Gaston-Reade said with a snort. "She couldn't help. She would be quite useless and you would be sorry you asked. She's never done anything in her whole life."

Lady Venture, who had been looking smug at her brother's support, glared at him, but seemed unable to offer any retort.

"I was merely being humorous, my lady. I shall, of course, do the honors myself," Tony said, bowing and taking his catch a ways away from the encampment.

Dinner was a change, at least, everyone said, but Savina knew the fish was burned due entirely to her own inattention—she hadn't been able to keep her mind on the meal—and she was sorry after all the work Mr. Heywood had gone to. But he had kindly said he didn't mind it overcooked at all, and that it was far preferable to undercooked. The turtle, too, was overcooked and tough, but all were ravenous, and even Lady Venture ate her meal in silence, a lovely change.

As she and Zazu tidied after dinner, she could not stop thinking about the day, and Mr. Heywood, and the unexpected sight of his half-naked torso and bare arms. In her mind's eye she could see little details: the lashing of golden hair across his taut stomach, the blue veins wrapping over his thick forearms, the way the water droplets had trickled down his bare chest. Why such things were so fascinating she could not imagine, and wondered if she was quite normal. About men she supposed she knew little or nothing but that they were different from women and that the marital bed was where one explored those differences. She had always supposed that men's bodies must be roughly analogous to male animals', and so the act of intercourse must feature some details already familiar to her; she had some vague idea of what to expect. It was not something she anticipated greatly with Lord Gaston-Reade, but she wasn't afraid. All married couples did such things, and if one wanted children, it was how one got them. And she did want children. She thought it would be great fun to have lots of rollicking babies.

But she had heard whispered among the married ladies of Jamaica that men liked such things that married couples did much better than women, and that they were filled with animal lusts, unpleasantly so at times, especially when they had too much wine. She had never seen any evidence of uncontrolled lust, even from the young men who had occasionally courted her, and certainly never from her fiancé, who had always been most circumspect and careful of her reputation and delicate feelings.

She had never felt anything in return but mild interest. When Lord Gaston-Reade proposed, her father had counseled her that it was by far the best proposal of marriage she would ever get, and since they had to return to London, anyway—his time in Jamaica was done and his replacement already installed in the governmental office—she may as well return to England an engaged woman. It was by far preferable, he said, than to have to endure the marriage market and find another young man she could marry.

Marriage was her goal, of course, as it was for every young lady of her acquaintance, so it had sounded like sensible advice, and her fiancé had been polite and pleasant to her. Life promised to be interesting and enjoyable. An earl, the ladies of Jamaica assured her, was far above what she would have been expected to marry, as she was just a plain "Miss" with no interesting family connections. Lord Gaston-Reade had pressed her hand most earnestly and said he begged the "honor" of her hand in marriage. He had then taken her in his arms and kissed her forehead, releasing her immediately after.

And she had not felt so much as a thrill of anticipation. That had been delayed until she had seen Mr. Heywood's wet skin and muscled arms. Then she had wondered how it would feel to be held close and kissed. By him. It had left her shocked at herself and nervous. It was so seldom she experienced any feeling she was not in control of, that she felt as she had on occasion when as a child when ill, feverish and unlike herself.

His great kindness had relieved her nerves somewhat, but now all she could do was steal glances at him while he worked, remembering that beneath the layers of clothes—he had put his jacket back on over his shirt—there was a very interesting male physique. Gaston-Reade would look much the same, perhaps, unclothed, so why did she not wonder about that? Was it merest chance, simply because she had seen Mr. Heywood partially unclothed first?

The group was scattered, with Zazu and Savina

working still, as had become the routine, at tidying the dishes and piling them back in one of the crates. Lady Venture was lying down on her pallet, turned away from the rest of them with Annie fanning her; Savina's father had gone walking on the beach, having discovered an interest in shells sparked by Zazu's collection; and William Barker and the earl were talking about politics.

Mr. Heywood had been working at something for some time, and he carried his creation over to Zazu and Savina. He set down his rough contrivance in front of them. "I was thinking, ladies," he said, as he took the pot Zazu had been scrubbing and set it down on his invention, "that it would be easier for you if there were some benches to put things on, rather than the dirty ground or back in the crates. You should not have to pack and unpack each day, just to keep things clean."

It was a crude bench of sticks lashed together with vines, and it kept the pot well up off the ground. Savina set a stack of tin plates next to the pot and clapped her hands.

"Thank you so much, Mr. Heywood; what an ingenious thing!"

"It will save us time, to be sure," Zazu said.

He sat back, elbows on the ground, and said, "I was thinking that if I could find enough straight, long sticks, I could replace these pallets of palm leaves with cots, at least for you ladies and Mr. Roxeter. It will help if you ladies can sleep up off the ground, for it is so very damp, at times."

"Heavens, you don't think we're going to be here long enough for that, do you?" Lady Venture said, turning over and sitting up.

Lord Gaston-Reade looked up and said, "Tony, you are enjoying this camping adventure far too much. I was just thinking that we ought to be doing something to be getting off this dreadful island, instead of sitting day after day and doing nothing."

Savina had to hold back the retort that some of them may be sitting around doing nothing, but a few of them were very busy. She and Zazu exchanged looks.

"Perhaps that is so, sir, but we must be comfortable while here . . . or at least as comfortable as possible."

Behind the mild words, Savina sensed a tension, and she watched the two men, waiting for another explosion. Anthony Heywood was now sitting erect and alert, and Lord Gaston-Reade stared at his secretary with an inscrutable gaze.

"I think it would be a mistake to get too comfortable," the earl said. "A level of discomfort will make us strive to get off this wretched island."

"I would agree to any level of discomfort for myself and the other gentlemen, but I think the ladies . . ." He paused and threw a glance at Zazu and Savina. "Especially the ladies who have been doing such an excellent job providing food for us all, deserve some amenities."

"I must say, sir, that I do think the ladies should be provided for," William Barker said timidly.

"I doubt if it is worth all the fuss for the short time we will be on this awful island," the earl said.

Anthony Heywood sighed. "I, too, hope to be rescued in short order. However, my lord, this is deadly serious, not some game I am playing. Survival requires us all to do our best together, something we have not been doing at all. Some are doing too much, and some nothing at all. We all need to exert our abilities to keep us alive and comfortable. I have been thinking, too, that perhaps I ought to show you other gentlemen how I managed to get the fish we had at dinner. If something should happen to me . . ."

"Now that is just enough Tony," Gaston-Reade said,

standing. "You are taking too much on yourself, thinking you are the only one capable of doing anything."

"I have proven so far to be the only one capable of getting us dinner!" Heywood said, standing too.

Savina watched the two men confronting each other. It felt to her that there was something else beneath what they were saying. She had many times seen ladies speaking around a subject in the same way, if more slyly, but men usually came right out and said what they were thinking. Perhaps there was something they did not want to admit, even to each other. She exchanged a glance with Zazu, who was watching with intent interest.

"Now you are overstepping it, Tony."

"But he's only telling the truth, sir," Barker said. He shrugged and added, "You sent me out and I had no more notion of how to get a fish than an infant would. I would welcome some instruction. I think Mr. Heywood is just saying . . ."

"I don't need you to defend him, nor explain his notions to me," the earl said, pacing forward, his stance rigid and defensive.

"Yes, don't be an idiot, William," Lady Venture said, sitting up straighter, her eyes gleaming as she sensed the coming battle. "As usual you don't know what you are talking about. Bertie is right. Mr. Heywood is being intolerable."

Savina jumped to her feet. "But he's only saying we ought to be prepared! Doesn't that make sense? He has proven to be the *only* one catching any fish. He's only saying, what would happen if he became incapacitated?"

"Savina, please do not speak," her fiancé said, holding up one hand. "You are only exposing your ignorance . . . uh, innocence, rather."

She glared at him. At that moment her father came wandering back into the camp, emptying his pockets and mumbling about the marvelous shells he had discovered. When silence greeted him, he looked up and seemed to catch wind of the confrontation.

But his arrival had dispelled the angry mood and the different factions went back to their pastimes, though with a tension, still, that was unresolved. In the treacherous surroundings of a deserted island perhaps amity was too important even when the tension between the two men seemed ready to flame out in open hostility. But Savina burned in anger, the first time she had truly felt that desperate emotion. "He will never see me as other than a helpless ninny," she muttered, clashing pots together and rattling tin dishes.

"Who are you talking about?" Zazu asked.

With a darted glance, Savina indicated Gaston-Reade, who had already returned to conversation, this time with Savina's father. He appeared to be recounting the argument, making his own case quite successfully, as the older man shook his head, tut-tutted, and cast worried glances over at Mr. Heywood and his daughter.

"Did you truly expect anything else from him? Has he not always treated you thus?"

Savina put aside the rag she had picked up to rub sand over the bottom of the stewing pot; she had discovered that damp sand removed the black charring from it rather effectively. She wound her arms around her knees and stared across the encampment at her fiancé. "I suppose I thought that in time he would see me as his intellectual equal."

Zazu laughed.

"What's so funny?" She stared at her maid, shocked at her levity.

The maid shook her head. "From my observation, his lordship is incapable of admitting that anyone is his equal in any way," she murmured. "Nor even of giving credit where it is due."

"Why do you say that?"

At first Zazu just shook her head, but then she scuttled closer to Savina and said, "Lord Gaston-Reade seems a very shrewd gentleman, does he not?"

"I have always thought him so. And the ladies of Spanish Town spoke of him so very highly, of his charm, ambition, intelligence. Everyone approved so of the many changes he made to Tanager, and the many more he has planned for the future."

"Yes, well . . . Nelson told me that Mr. Heywood was the one who truly planned all of those changes for Tanager."

Savina experienced a sick sensation of disappointment mingled with horror. One of the reasons she had accepted Lord Gaston-Reade's proposal was that she felt his reform of the formerly corrupt and cruel plantation practices on Tanager spoke well of his heart, his mind, and his possible plans for the future. Though she had never been able to bring him to discuss such things with her, she thought marriage would change all of that, as their relationship would inevitably be closer, more intimate, and he would listen to her. She had been sure she could convince him to give up slave-owning, since the reforms on Tanager had already been heading toward making the sugar growing and harvesting more efficient, safe, and sustainable with hired labor.

But now, to learn that her fiancé had no part in those reforms?

"But . . . Gaston-Reade at least agreed to the reforms," she said, with a wistful hope, staring at the earl and her father through the dusk, so involved in conversation, two English gentlemen absurdly untouched by their tropical forest surroundings.

Zazu shook her head. "Only when Mr. Heywood proved that it would bring him higher profit. But Nelson said that Mr. Heywood pushed past his employer a few reforms that improved conditions for the slaves, but did nothing to really increase sugar production. And when Mr. Heywood found that Nelson knew how to read and write, he took him into his confidence, hoping to be able to sustain changes after the earl and Mr. Heywood left Jamaica."

"Why did I know nothing of this?" Savina whispered. She covered her eyes and bowed her head for a moment, contemplating a lifetime tied to a man whom she feared she could not respect. When she looked up again, she said, "If I had known it may have changed . . . I might not have . . ."

Zazu, her dark eyes filled with concern, slumped down in the sand. A solitary tear welled in the corner of one eye. "I didn't know it would make a difference. You never said that your acceptance of Lord Gaston-Reade's proposal was predicated on his reform at Tanager."

"Zazu! I thought it was understood between us. How could it not have a part in my decision? Above everyone else, you know how I feel about the . . . the situation in Jamaica, and how I abhor slavery."

"But everyone was telling you to marry him," Zazu said, a pleading tone in her voice and worry in her dark, tear-filled eyes. "I just thought . . . I thought you were doing as you were advised by your father, by the other ladies . . . by everyone."

"I was, in part, I suppose. But you know me." She reached out, and in the dim and fading light grabbed for Zazu's hand. "I could never agree to marry a man unless I believed him to feel as I feel, to want what I want, and to have plans for the future that would coincide with what I believe is right and just. There would be no comfort for me in such an unequal marriage."

"I'm so sorry," her maid whispered, squeezing Savina's hand. "I should have said something, but I didn't know . . . didn't think . . ."

"What have I done, Zazu?" Savina whispered, the

sound echoing up off the canopy. "Who is this man I've agreed to marry?" She pulled her hand away and turned her gaze from her maid's worried expression. She watched Mr. Heywood for a long minute; when he looked up, their eyes met, his dark and unfathomable in the failing light. He smiled. It was a simple expression, warm, sincere, and it frightened her beyond belief not for what it said about him, but for the emotion it summoned within her.

She looked away without returning the smile.

Eight

The others had long since laid down on their humble pallets to submit as the deep slumber of the exhausted overwhelmed them. Zazu was curled up sound asleep, Annie near her. The other maid, though older than both Zazu and Savina, looked to Zazu as to one more experienced, stronger, and wiser, and clung to her whenever she was not at her mistress's side. Though she had been frightened of Zazu at first—the legends of her Maroon forebears were fearsome indeed—that fear had turned to hero worship and gratitude.

Lord Gaston-Reade had secluded himself away from the others as much as possible, but Mr. William Barker and Savina's father were the opposite, keeping their sleep pallets close to the camp, hoping, to no avail, that that would keep away the tiny reptiles and insects that clambered in mysterious processions over their recumbent forms. The irritation of the insects that feasted on them nightly was one of the unsavory facts of their new life that all were dealing with, with varying degrees of success.

Even Lady Venture had claimed to experience great weariness and fallen asleep early, though Savina was of the opinion in her case it was boredom, since the lady did nothing for herself but complain. *That* she would not delegate, since no one could do it so well as she did.

But Savina still sat by the fire, staring into the embers that glowed and sparked against the backdrop of the dusky palm jungle. At a noise nearby she looked up, to find Mr. Heywood watching her from the edge of the palm forest. Seeing her glance up he swiftly made his way to the fire and sat down by her.

Her pulse raced. She had not been able to erase or explain the disturbing attraction she felt for him, but she thought given time to reflect, it would soon assume its proper importance as a fleeting sensation, nothing more. Regardless of her current feelings, she was affianced to a worthy man and it was not an agreement she took lightly. Once she gave her word on anything, it was firm and unshakable.

But it would be so much simpler if she could learn that there was some great good within him, some worthy ambition. And if Lord Gaston-Reade could make her tremble and sigh with his merest touch it would be enough, united with that thread of goodness, to give her hope for their marriage.

"I want to thank you," he whispered, leaning close to her, "for supporting me in what I was saying earlier."

"It seems merely common sense to me that more of us should know how to catch fish," she said with a shrug. "On my little farm in Jamaica, Nancy, the old hen mistress, said it was foolish to place all of one's eggs into one basket. If you should drop it, all are gone." Keeping her voice matter-of-fact and even in tone was an effort. She could feel a warmth emanating from Mr. Heywood that enveloped her, and it was tempting to lean into it, to bathe in it and absorb it.

"Regardless, thank you. You went against Lord Gaston-Reade, and I appreciate your daring."

"Should I not be able to disagree with him from time to time?" She shook back her curls, free from any restraint now she had discarded her bonnet except when the sun was at its zenith and she needed protection. She wore her hair up as much as possible, but tendrils would still escape and drift down over the course of the long day, the heat and dampness coiling them into long ringlets. "Does marriage mean subjugation of my free will and even my ability to think?"

He stared at her. "How could I have been so wrong about you?"

Taken aback, she stared into his dark eyes and said, "I beg your pardon?" Her father, in the encampment just a few yards away, stirred in his sleep. "I beg your pardon?" she whispered, reminded to keep her tone hushed.

Mr. Heywood sighed, and the sound whispered up to the trees and disappeared. "You were so quiet, I thought you dull and uninformed. I was very, *very* wrong. I apologize."

Savina ruefully thought that if she had just opened her mouth and spoke to Anthony Heywood months ago, she might have learned for herself what Zazu had told her that very day. But she had only seen Lord Gaston-Reade formally and with others around, except for the occasional walk in the garden. When Mr. Heywood was there, he was a silent presence looming in the background. She could say much the same about him, that she thought him dull and uninformed. "Tell me, Mr. Heywood," she said, quietly. "I have been talking with Zazu about the reforms on Tanager."

He raised his thick eyebrows. "Oh?"

"She told me that every one that came down on the side of humanity and decency and . . . and fairness emanated from you."

"And how does Miss Zazu know anything about Tanager?"

"She and Nelson Walker have an understanding . . . or did until we left Jamaica."

"Ah," Mr. Heywood said, nodding. "Young Nelson. A bright lad with a good heart. I knew he had a lady friend, but I did not know who she was." He didn't go on.

"Well?" Savina stared at him, watching him in the flickering light of the embers, challenging him with her eyes to tell her the truth. When he didn't answer her challenge, she spoke. "I want to know the truth, Mr. Heywood. I agreed to marry Lord Gaston-Reade, and I will not jilt him easily. It is not in my nature to break an agreement once I have made it. But I went into that agreement, that engagement, thinking one way about him; I believed that beneath his occasionally harsh nature, under the cool facade, there must be a warmth and compassion and general benevolence. I based my surmise on the changes he made at Tanager, changes I foresaw would eventually lead to him abandoning slave labor on the plantation. I would know the truth now, so I may enter marriage with a clear vision."

Tony stared at the lovely Savina Roxeter in horror. That she had affianced herself to Lord Gaston-Reade on such a premise had never occurred to him, and now, though he would not take back the reforms and could not wish that more people knew they came from him, not his employer, he regretted the bitterness of her future if she remained affianced to a man she would, ultimately, come to disrespect.

"Miss Roxeter, I'm so sorry . . ."

She held up one hand. "Mr. Heywood," she said, quietly, "I'm not asking for an apology. The consequences of my actions are my own responsibility, and no one else's. I could as easily bemoan that I allowed my father's wishes to influence me unduly, or that I failed to examine the earl's behavior in the right light.

I thought him imperious, but kindly." She stared into the fire. "If what I have heard is true, then I just must find in him something I can respect and come to appreciate. I fear, too, that the earl will find himself affianced to a woman with ideas and beliefs he will abhor. For now he thinks that eventually I will bend my will to his, but how will he accept it when he finally understands that I have my own heart and mind, and will subjugate my beliefs to no one?"

Tony couldn't think of a thing to say. He was numb with regret, and filled with a powerful yearning to hold her and comfort her. She was calm, but distress underlaid her composure; he could feel it in his gut, and it twisted and roiled with bitterness. If he could just reach out, if he could only touch her, hold her . . . but what he wanted was impossible and what he wanted to do unthinkable. He put one hand over hers, where it clutched the sand between them.

"Miss Roxeter . . . Savina . . . I am sorry. I did institute the changes on Tanager."

She took in a deep breath and released it slowly. "Did Gaston-Reade at least agree to them with open eyes?"

Tony thought about evasion, but it wasn't in his nature except when absolutely necessary, and it would serve her poorly. "I presented every idea I could to him in the light of a measure that would improve production or lower costs. Those that did neither, those measures designed to improve the living conditions in such an abysmal, destructive, despicable practice as slavery, I slipped past him by enlisting the help of certain sympathetic people at Tanager." He sighed. "Lord Gaston-Reade will never voluntarily agree to free his slaves on the plantation. Like the other owners, he sees no viable alternative. It would mean, he feels, the end of any profit for his Caribbean holdings, and he could be right. But the price being paid for his profit is too high; the cost is human suffering so acute it is unbearable to see at close quarters."

When he glanced over, it was to see her head down. He thought she was looking at something on the ground, but her shoulders were heaving. "Miss Roxeter . . . Savina, are you all right?"

When she didn't answer, he put his hand under her chin and raised her face to be visible in the flickering firelight, trails of tears tracking wetly down her cheeks and glittering. She pulled away. Compulsion ripped through him and he took her in his arms and held her against his shoulder, rocking her gently, feeling her slim form heave with muffled sobs. Tenderness trickling through him, he pressed his lips to her forehead, his heart thumping so loud with the anguish he felt for her that he was sure she would hear it.

But she pulled away and dried her eyes on her sleeve. Taking a deep, quivering breath, she shuddered and calmed. "How awful," she said. "How awful to be so completely wrong about everything one based one's future on." She tried to smile, but it was a trembling, tentative expression, her cheeks still wet and her nose dripping.

His handkerchief was stained after so many days in such rough condition, but it was relatively clean. He took it from his pocket and wiped her cheeks. "Here," he said. "Please use it."

She dried her eyes and blew her nose. "Do . . . do ladies in England ever change their minds and . . . and disengage themselves?"

As much as he hated it, he had to be honest with her. "Yes. But when the gentleman is a man of such standing as Lord Gaston-Reade, the young lady is sometimes called a jilt, and especially for a young lady as yourself, with no friends in society at all. You might find your reputation in tatters before you can even establish one."

"I don't care about that."

"But your father might." And she might after learning how vital was a good reputation for a young lady in London, he thought, but did not say.

She was silent. After a long pause, she said, "Tell me, Mr. Heywood, why do you work for Lord Gaston-Reade?"

He struggled with his response as he took up a stick and poked the fire, watching the shower of sparks pop and crackle up into the darkness like the fireflies he had once seen while encamped in the Canadian wilderness. He had pledged to honesty, but how much honesty? And did honesty require him to shatter every fond hope she could have? With emotions awoken within his breast of such depth and fervor that he still did not quite know how he felt, he was apt to say too much, and he could not be sure he would be fair to his employer with his new awareness of Miss Savina Roxeter's infinite worth.

She perhaps mistook his long pause for unwillingness, for she amended her question, her tone low and her face hidden in shadow. "Rather, tell me something good you know of his lordship. That is really more to my purpose."

Tony nodded. This was reality. She was his employer's fiancée and must now find peace in her future life. "Lord Gaston-Reade," he said, "is not an unkind man. When we first arrived in Jamaica there was a perfectly foul man named Jarvis as the overseer on the plantation. Jarvis was like a mad dog: cruel, vicious, impossible to reason with. His lordship soon took the measure of the man and wasted no time in getting rid of him. The outside workers celebrated long into the night, and his lordship gave them an extra measure of rum and a pig to roast for their jubilation. That was all his own idea, and he spoke quite vehemently about the cruelty of the man he had discharged."

The young lady nodded and heaved a deep sigh. "I think I will be going to sleep now, Mr. Heywood." She rose, went to Annie and Zazu, and laid down near them, leaving Tony to stare at the fire long into the night.

The new day brought new determination to Tony. What he had said the previous day about the band's ability to survive should he be incapacitated had not changed. Someone needed to know what he had discovered so far about the best places for fishing, and he needed to share the knowledge he had long had about survival in the open. Lord Gaston-Reade was clearly out of the question, and Mr. Peter Roxeter was as well, simply by his inability to think of their situation in any realistic light. He seemed to think that some miracle would bring them a ship. William Barker was a jolly fellow, but clumsy and awkward and not too brilliant, though worthy and good-natured. Lady Venture, he knew from long association, was inveterately superior and aware of her position. She would never condescend to do anything to contribute to her own subsistence, and she was adamant that her maid tend only to her own needs.

His best choices were, unfortunately, the ladies who were already doing far too much for the sustenance of the group. Miss Zazu, from her childhood in the Blue Mountains, knew all of the fruits and edible plants of the forest, but seemed unaware of what good food came from the ocean. Miss Roxeter was learning from her maid and combined her native intelligence with a willingness to do things no lady in her position could have been expected to.

But could they learn to dive, swim and fish? Would

they even be willing to, when so much of their time was already taken up with work?

The day would tell.

Savina, coming back after breakfast from a solitary foray into the forest, saw some of the men gathered down on the beach and wondered what was going on. She wandered down the path onto the golden sand and to the group which comprised her father, her fiancé and Mr. William Barker.

"What's going on, Papa?" she said, tugging his sleeve just as she had as a young girl when she was trying to see something at the fair and was too small.

Affectionate, as he always had been, he put his arm around her shoulders. "It is the most exciting thing, Savina! Lord Gaston-Reade is the most brilliant young man. He is devising a way to get us off this island."

"Ah, Savina," Lord Gaston-Reade said, clearly in a good humor, for he only allowed himself to use her Christian name in such a mood. He clapped his hands together, his gray eyes alight with reflected sun. "I have decided, as your father has probably been telling you, that rather than wait for the dastardly American to send word—I'm sure he has no intention or desire to procure aid for us—I shall find a way that we can leave this dreadful island ourselves and get to civilization."

Savina felt a trill of fear. "How . . . how will you do that?"

"We are going to build a boat!" he said, gathering all of their admiring glances to him, looking around the group and rocking from his heels up to his toes and then down again, his dark boots digging into the sand.

"How marvelous, my lord," William Barker said, applauding. He blinked and nodded, his weak eyes watering in the tropical sun.

"Stupendous," Savina's father added. "What a mind you have, Lord Gaston-Reade, and how proud I will be to call you my son!"

"But . . ." Savina stopped.

"Yes?" her fiancé said, with a kindly look in his cool eyes.

"But if the American captain *is* sending help, it will be to this position, where he last left us. If we leave . . ."

"I'm afraid you don't know the way of the world very well, Savina," Gaston-Reade said, shaking his head. "But it does your feminine heart credit that you would think that riffraff capable of decent behavior. He has no more intention of sending help than I would, in his position."

Taken aback, Savina fell silent. It was a new and unwelcome vision of her fiancé's behavior that he could even say that. She could only think that he had not seriously thought through that statement, and that, presented with the same situation, he would be more humane than his words suggested.

As the men went back to their plans, she slipped away, back to the encampment and the work that waited.

The day was long and the work hard, but she had occasions throughout the day to see what progress the gentlemen were making, with Lady Venture deigning to sit in the shade nearby and offer her invaluable suggestions. They had drawn in the sand a gigantic map of the island and where they thought they were in relation to Jamaica and the Windward Passage. With the war against the Americans a couple of years old already, there had been much talk of the strategic importance of the Caribbean, and the British plans to take the United States from a southern vantage point with naval power. It was a topic of much conversation among the gentlemen plantation owners of Jamaica, and so all three of the men were somewhat familiar with the territory. However, in Savina's estimation that did not equate with being able to navigate the waters in hurricane season on a boat made from, as far as she understood their plans, lashed-together palm logs.

By the end of the day they had made no progress at all on the actual boat-building, not being able to agree even in principle on the construction. It was clear to Savina that once Gaston-Reade decided on one model, the others would fall into line, but as yet he had not made his final decision.

As twilight dimmed the view, and the gentlemen, weary from all their laborious efforts, straggled back to the encampment to eat their evening meal, Savina watched carefully the interaction between Lord Gaston-Reade and his secretary. The rift from the previous day had not healed, and neither man was ready to cry friends. She wished she had persisted in her question to the secretary of why he worked for the earl, but supposed the answer would merely have been that it was a good position, and lucrative. And she wondered how she could have not even really seen the secretary for all those months, and yet now be so very aware of his presence every second he was near.

For that sensation of extreme awareness had not subsided. They had spoken often through the day, and he had tentatively approached her and Zazu about teaching them to fish, which they had both agreed to try the next morning after breakfast, but she had held back, not getting too close, not looking into his eyes too often.

He had taken her into his arms briefly the night before as she sobbed out her fears of what she had committed herself to, and the memory haunted her; she still felt raw and exposed in his presence. Every second he held her had brought a new sensation, his fingers stroking her back, his rough beard chafing her cheek, his tender voice whispering consolation in her ear. Drawing away had been difficult but necessary because what she had really wanted to do was raise her face and kiss him on the lips, and that impulse frightened her. Clearly she was becoming far too fond of him and the attraction she had felt as a frisson of desire was deepening hour by hour, in a startlingly quick time, into friendship, dependence and tenderness, all of the things she had hoped for with her husband-to-be. With the weariness of her daily work her spirit was wearing down, but just speaking with him buoyed her and gave her courage to go on. It was what she had always imagined marriage would be, that mutual giving and taking of comfort and support, though she couldn't think where she had gotten that notion but from her own fading memories of the tender love between her father and mother.

It was not too late to crush those developing emotions toward Anthony Heywood though, and she would be ruthless where she knew she was right. She had given her word to wed Lord Gaston-Reade, and though she was still deciding if that decision must be held to, in light of what she now knew, she would make no hasty moves.

As tired as she was from a day of work, she had fallen deep asleep the moment her body came to rest on her rough pallet. But sometime in the wee hours of morning she had awoken with the urgent need to relieve herself, had gone as far into the forest as she dared, and then hastened back to sit down by the banked fire for a moment.

She heard someone else stirring, and of course it was the one person she would have avoided if she could have, Anthony Heywood, who joined her at the fireside on the log he had dragged there for them to sit on. Were they the only two people in camp who ever had a sleepless moment? They seemed cursed to be perpetually awake at the same moments.

"Miss Savina," he whispered without preamble, "I'm so glad to catch you alone like this. I have been worrying all day that you would fear the effects of our conversation last night."

What did he mean? Had he sensed her divided emotions and inappropriate attraction to him? If so he must be ruthlessly disabused of that notion. She stayed silent and stared at the fire, stirring it to a flame and tossing a piece of wood on it.

"I would never reveal to your fiancé that you went into your engagement with a misunderstanding of any kind. It is your secret, and not mine."

"Thank you, Mr. Heywood," she said, when she could find her voice.

There was silence for a few more moments and then the secretary, clearly sensing that no further conversation on that topic would be welcome, asked her what she thought of the men's determination to build a boat and go for help.

"I don't know," she admitted. "It really depends, doesn't it, on whether one believes the American captain's vow to send help for us. If he does send help, then it would be foolish beyond belief to risk anyone's life on the open sea in a boat of such crude construction. But if his veracity is not to be trusted, then going for help may be our only chance at rescue for some time, perhaps years. This cay is not populated, nor does it hold anything of interest except as a provider of tropical fruits."

"Your summation is admirably succinct, Miss Savina."

"So," she said, directly, and looked him in the eyes for the first time that day. "Do you believe that Captain Verdun will be as good as his word, or do you side with my fiancé and think he was lying?" She examined his face. The gentlemen had taken turns using the razor and strop to good effect, but Mr. Heywood's beard came in quickly, if rather straggly and patchy. He had assumed the habit of scruffing his chin when thinking. He did so then and gazed into the fire.

"I think he was telling the truth. American naval men are as honorable as our own, from my understanding, and as tender toward the fair sex, but my fear is that as good as his intentions are, he can only do what he can. He may not be able to get a message to the British, his enemy. If he does, he may not be believed. Our naval force may think it is a trick or a hoax, at least until our own ship doesn't arrive when and where it is supposed to. We have no idea what happened to the *Linden* and the *Wessex,* but they may have sailed on for England, or they may have gone down in the storm." He sighed deeply. "Even then, even if he does manage to send a message to the British Navy and they believe it and send help, his directions may not be exact and the navy may find it hard to locate us."

Savina nodded. She had come to some of the same conclusions herself. "I know it is very much dependent upon chance, to some extent, but I do believe that he will get word out of our position, and it's possible that even this moment a party is being put together to come find us. To that end," she said, "I think that we should be setting up a system for making our presence known. I was thinking a signal fire on the rock promontory . . . smoky during the day, and flaming brightly at night. It is vital, in my estimation, that we make our presence known."

Mr. Heywood gazed at her with open admiration. "You, Miss Savina, are the cleverest person among us. I should have thought of that."

"Not only that," she said, with a grim set to her mouth, "but I think that it is time for Lady Venture to do something other than sit on a log and complain. I think the signal fire shall be her and Annie's chore."

Heywood chuckled. "If you manage to make Lady Venture do that work, I will forever think you a magician, Miss Savina Roxeter."

Nine

Instead of merely surviving, Savina thought, back on her pallet to try to sleep until sunrise, she had to begin to think of their sojourn on the island differently. If it had never happened, she would be halfway to England by then, serene and unruffled, still thinking that Lord Gaston-Reade was a progressive, kindly, forward-thinking man who, if a bit stiff in his manner, was a man of the future. She would be able to eventually work with her husband, she would still be thinking, to end slavery on his plantation, and free the poor people who labored so hard in the Jamaican heat for his profit and toward their own death.

She lay on her back, just out beyond the edge of the tarpaulin that protected their encampment, and gazed up at the radiant blanket of stars that arched above her. Around her she could hear the various sounds of the night, from those close by—the snuffling and deep breathing of her sleeping companions—to those distant, the call of some night bird in the forest beyond their camp and the unidentifiable scuttling of reptiles in the underbrush. Though there was unceasing work in this beautiful, dangerous, exotic place, so was there peace for reflection and time to contemplate.

Reality was a bitter potion to take, but sometimes the bitter medicines were those most efficacious. This time out of civilization was given to her as a lesson.

What had she done when faced with a difficult reality? She had seized control, asked no permission, and found a way to survive. She was under no illusion; without Zazu and the others she didn't know if she would have been successful, but she would have died in the attempt.

The lesson for her was that she was far more resolute than she had ever realized, and stronger. Her fear was that those attributes were guaranteed to make her marriage to Lord Gaston-Reade turbulent. The lady-wives of the diplomats she had entertained as her father's hostess had practiced a kind of gentle submission, for the most part, to their husbands' will, preferring to find ways to subvert spousal decrees with devious stratagems Savina had always thought underhanded. Perhaps it was the only way to express their own determination and do as they wished some of the time, but it seemed a poor exchange for an open understanding between marital partners. If she married Gaston-Reade, would she in time become one of those wily wives, devising schemes for getting around his commands? She'd rather die. And yet her father's one wish was to see her well married, settled in the kind of affluence beyond what he could have ever provided for her. Marriage to the earl was a surety against poverty or want for her and any children she might bear.

"What are you thinking?"

Savina looked over toward Zazu, who was awake and had rolled over to face her. Moving to her side to face her maid, Savina whispered, "Zazu, what made you leave Jamaica with me? I know you said you couldn't marry Nelson, but you could have gone back to your village in the Blue Mountains to your family, or found other work. You could have hoped for something to change."

Zazu, her dark face indistinct in the thin moonlight that peeked from clouds overhead, said, "When I first came down from the mountains to find work, I was afraid. But my mother and grandmother . . . they are descended from a long line of queens. If our people had not been tricked into coming to Jamaica, I would be perhaps a chieftess, or warrior princess."

"You mentioned that in your confrontation with Venture the other day, but I wasn't sure if you were serious, or merely putting her in her place," Savina whispered, fascinated by the glimpse into a hidden history. The Maroons did not tell the ancient stories to many people, preferring to keep their history a secret, but Zazu did occasionally tell bits of their history, as she had heard it from her grandmother. Propping herself up on one elbow, Savina said, "I can't believe I have a princess for a maid. It seems backward."

"Why?" Zazu murmured. "Even being a princess is a kind of servitude."

"I never thought of it that way. But that doesn't answer my question."

"I know. You interrupted me."

"Excuse me, Princess Zazu," Savina whispered, ending on a soft giggle.

Zazu pinched her elbow. "Listen; I came down from the mountain because my grandmother thought I should learn about the great world. She wanted to know why your people do what you do, why you keep slaves. She thought I could learn. It is said that our people kept slaves once in the old land; if a man or woman was indebted to you for something, they could pledge their service to you, and be your slave. Or, if two nations went to war, those people who were conquered would become slaves, sometimes. My grandmother wanted to know how your people thought, whether all of your people felt they had a right to own us, to enslave us. After the peace, it was thought that the English would leave us alone, but still your government wished to make trouble for us. We didn't understand."

Zazu referred to the peace accord many, many years before that allowed her ancestors to live free in the Blue Mountains in their townships in return for a cessation of hostilities between the plantation owners and the bothersome Maroons, who would raid supplies and stores from them, and offered a place for runaway slaves to live freely.

"But my grandmother thought that I should learn all I could. She told me that there was something within me, a restlessness, that would never be content with guarding the pigs and chickens, that only the wide world could satisfy my needs. My mother agreed, and so I walked down out of the mountains and came to you, of whom I had heard even among my people, as a child of great promise."

"I didn't know you knew of me before we met. How had you heard that?" Savina asked, eyes wide in the darkness that enveloped them.

"One of your serving staff was friendly with our people. He was courting my aunt, and he would bring her things from time to time, a loaf of bread, an iron pot. He was the one who told my mother about the girl-child of the house where he was employed. He said this unusual girl would look him in the eye and ask him things, and would listen when he spoke."

"Just that?"

"Among your people you must know how rare a thing that is. Even children are taught from infancy, I know now, that servants are not to be acknowledged directly except to give orders. Why were you so different?"

Savina stared into the darkness and thought about it. "I don't know. I didn't realize then that I *was* different, only that I wanted to learn about people. Jamaica was new to me; I had never seen such dark skin before, and I thought it was beautiful. No one else would tell me why other people's skin was dark, so I asked the servants. One in particular—perhaps the one who was courting your aunt—told me it was like hair color or eye color, just a part of who he was. That made sense to me. Given that, how could slavery be right, then? I've never really understood it."

"You *are* rare," Zazu said with a low, dry chuckle. "Most of your people see the differences; you see the similarities. I knew that the moment I met you, and you asked me if I would like a sweet cake. I barely understood your language, but cake . . . I knew that word! After I had been working for you for a year or so I took you back to meet my mother and grandmother. Do you remember?"

"Of course I do; it was my one wish for my fifteenth birthday. It was thrilling!" Savina clutched her only covering, a thin blanket, to her chest. "How worried my father was, and how he was warned not to let me go, but I would not be denied. Though he was too nervous to go himself, he sent that young guardsman with us and felt somewhat better. Papa had been told so many stories of your people . . . when I think about it now, I still think it was a miracle he let me go at all. I wore him down with my whining. I'm sure he thought I would be frightened and turn back."

"He took me aside and told me to take care of you," Zazu said, "for you were precious to him. I asked him if he wished to come, but he said he felt that his presence would only be a hindrance, and that a British official would cause some trouble for my people, if it was known he had visited them. I didn't think he was nervous; I thought him a wise man."

"I didn't know he had spoken to you, and I'm amazed he thought so profoundly. I think I've underestimated him in some respects." Savina was silent for a long minute. "I still remember so vividly the trek up through the forest and into the Blue Mountains. Your grandmother and mother were very gracious, though, very hospitable."

"When grandmother met you she thought you were a tolerable 'backra,' not so ugly as most." Zazu laughed, a low husky sound in the night.

"What is 'backra'?" That was Annie, Lady Venture's maid, joining in. It was clear that she was wide awake and had likely been listening in for some time in silence.

"It is just what my people call your people."

From the sound of Zazu's voice Savina could tell she had turned over on her back, to share her stories with the young women on both sides of her.

"Are you really a princess, Miss Zazu?"

The maid's breathless tone made Savina smile in the dark. So she was right; Annie had heard the whole conversation.

"It is an old title and doesn't mean anything among my people now. It is from the old country when we were Coromantee, not Maroon."

"Where was that? The old country?" Savina asked, surprised she had never thought to ask before. She knew some of the old history, that Zazu's people were African, and used to trade gold for copper with the Spanish but were tricked or conquered—it was not clear which—into traveling as slaves to the new world.

"I sometimes looked at the maps in your father's library," Zazu admitted to Savina. "I think, from the stories, it is perhaps along the coast of the African continent, the large curve that juts into the ocean."

"I don't know where Africa is. Is it across the ocean?" Annie said.

"Very far," Zazu said. "My mother," she continued to Savina, "said you were good 'backra.' The old woman in our village thought you had magic, and I should follow you to capture it. But I stayed at first not for that, but because I learned so much. So many books!

After I learned to speak your language and to read, I thought I would stay until I had read all of the books in the library, and then I learned there were more books all the time, and I couldn't think to go until I had learned more."

"And then you met Nelson," Savina said, hastening the story back to her original question. "But still, you decided to go with me to England, knowing it might mean you would never see Nelson again."

"Men are only one part of our lives, my grandmother said. They think women do nothing but think of babies and cooking and men—even Nelson thought so of women until I taught him my truth—but we know there is more. It was my turn, she said, to go out in the wide world and let them know there were people such as us in it."

Savina thought about Zazu's words as Annie questioned her about the Maroons and her life as a child in the mountains. There was more to a woman's life than babies and marriage. Among the ladies—the wives and daughters—of the governing officials of Jamaica it didn't seem that there *was* more. From the time she was fifteen they were constantly talking to her about who she could marry, and how pretty she was, and how that would surely attract the gentlemen. When the earl had shown an interest in her soon after his arrival to manage his plantation, Tanager, they had done everything in their power to put the two together in suitable social situations and had counseled her as to her hair style, clothing and jewelry. And it had done what they hoped. She had felt the weight of all of their hopes and dreams on her shoulders when the earl had offered his hand in marriage, and had said yes, unwilling to disappoint such kindness as they had shown. It had pleased her father so, too, and she loved her father with all her heart. All he wanted out of what was left of his life, he said, was to see her well married and have grandchildren. He had been on the verge of marriage himself a couple of times in Jamaica, but always he had drawn back, and it was due to his concern for her, she thought, and his fear that a stepmother would not be acceptable for her. And so she had said yes to the earl's proposal. To be part of the freeing of a hundred people would have been a noble thing, too, and something worth her life, she had thought, when she believed that Gaston-Reade had as his aim freedom for his workers.

But now, on this island, it all seemed a sham. The deeds she had valued, the worth she had admired, were all Anthony Heywood's. She would be married to a slave-owner, and every guiding principle of her life compromised.

She drifted to sleep as the other two whispered, and when she awoke as golden sunlight filtered through the canopy of palms and other trees, it was with a new determination. This awful, dangerous, arduous time was a gift. At the end of it, if they were rescued and safe, she would know if she could marry Lord Gaston-Reade, or if it was worth damaging her reputation and risking her father's deep unhappiness to break the engagement.

Until that time her task was to help them survive.

Her morning routine was, with Zazu, to prepare the papaya, coconut, plantains and other fruits that would be their simple breakfast. Zazu, thankfully, had an amazing recollection of the fruits, roots and nuts her mother and grandmother used to collect when she was a child, and so they wouldn't starve, not with guava, hog plum, taro root, custard apple and star apples to eat on their little island. With rice, molasses and flour the American captain had given them and the fish and turtle meat from the sea, they would survive however long it took to either be rescued or find a way off the island. As much as some of the others complained—and that was mostly Lady Venture—she knew they were fortunate.

It occurred to her, as she peeled a ripe custard apple, to wonder why, when she had been raised in luxury and with servants, she didn't act as Lady Venture, who resolutely refused to do anything for herself. But even as a child she had been fascinated by the rhythm of the kitchen in their London house. Her mother—gone for twelve years now—was often busy in the stillroom, or managing the making of preserves, or discussing with their cook the week's menu. Standing by the cook's apron and stealing a piece of dough or a shred of carrot or a handful of raisins was her constant preoccupation. So when it was necessary, stepping in and taking over seemed natural.

This was life: preparing food, collecting food, managing food. In Zazu's village, she had witnessed firsthand a communal life with all of the women gathered and singing old songs as they prepared meals. Using the large knife that served so many capacities, she peeled the fruit and cut it into chunks as the others rose, stretched, and disappeared to perform their morning ablutions, such as they were in such crude surroundings.

Lord Gaston-Reade was the first back, and he glanced at her, then looked again. "Savina," he said, his tone severe. "Your feet are bare."

"They have been for two days," she said, not looking up from her task.

"That is unseemly. Really, Savina," he admonished, "just because we are living on this island, does not mean we stray so far from our civilized mores. It is what separates us from the savages."

Zazu, returning from fetching some water, looked askance at him, then just shook her head, poured the water in a pot, and began peeling plantains. Savina watched Gaston-Reade for a long minute, so correct in his jacket, even if the cuffs were filthy and the neckcloth stained. "And the savages are . . . ?"

He frowned. "Don't be deliberately obtuse, Savina, and mind your tone; you sounded very challenging just then."

She set the knife aside, stood, unbound her hair, shook it out and let it ripple down her back. She pushed up the sleeves of her dress and straightened her backbone, staring directly at him. Challenging? Perhaps. But she was a woman, not a child, and would never placate him again. She had pretended demureness for too long, and had played what the lady-wives of the Jamaican officials had taught her was her role, but it had never been hers. Now she would be herself. He stared at her, but then turned away without comment.

She was not deluded; they must discuss their future some time, and if it wasn't that moment, it would merely wait until another day.

The others gathered and ate breakfast, picking at the fruit, some complaining and others, in particular Mr. Barker and her own father, talking longingly about rashers of bacon, fresh eggs, ham and toast . . . piles of golden toast dripping with butter. Savina ate papaya as her stomach growled in unladylike complaint. She was dirty, exhausted and constantly hungry for food she could not have, but she was alive, and would never forget that simple fact and would be grateful for it.

Soon the fruit was all gone, but the group still sat variously on crates, barrels or the ground. Savina stood and cleared her throat. When the others looked up at her, expectantly, she said, "I think we are all agreed that we don't wish to stay here forever."

"Of course, Savina, dear," her father said, irritably.

"But we are disagreed, some of us, as to our best chance for escape. Some of us believe that the American captain will keep his word and send help." She heard Gaston-Reade snort, but charged on. "Some of us think we must take escape into our own hands. But regardless, I think we would all agree that we must cover every possibility if we want to get away from here."

"What is the meaning of this drivel, or is there a meaning?"

Savina turned to Lady Venture, the speaker. "Do you agree that escaping this island is vital?"

"Of course!"

"And would you do anything to see that accomplished?"

"Of course," Lady Venture repeated, but more slowly, and with a distrusting eye on Savina.

"It occurred to me last night that if the American captain did keep his word—and it must be admitted by everyone that that is a possibility—that a rescue ship may be on its way already. But how are they to know we're here? I think we need a signal fire, day and night."

There was silence, but Savina could see that everyone was digesting the idea, and then several nodded, William Barker, for one, and her father for another. She noticed Anthony Heywood checking the others' reactions as well, and then he met her eyes and nodded.

"So, I think we all agree that it is important . . . vital, in fact. Flame at night and smoke during the day. Now we need to decide who is going to . . ."

"Wait just a moment, Savina," her fiancé said, standing. "Rather good thought of yours. Now we need to figure out where best to put this signal fire, and I propose . . ."

"You interrupted me," Savina said, calmly, though her heart was pounding and her hands shaking.

"I beg your pardon?" he said, staring at her across the shadowed enclosure their tarpaulin afforded.

"How impertinent," Lady Venture said, clasping her

hands together on her lap and squeezing them until her knuckles whitened. "Tell her, Bertie. She is getting entirely above herself."

"Shut up, Vennie," he said.

"Stop!" Savina felt a welcome spurt of anger bubble up within her. Anger was good. Anger always helped her be more bold. She glanced around at the others, Annie wide-eyed, Mr. William Barker the same, Zazu with a secret smile on her narrow face. Her father stared at her with alarm, and she faltered for a moment, but then took a deep breath. "We must work together. My proposal," she said, "is that whoever is not busy should man the fire. Isn't that fair?"

Anthony Heywood, her secret confederate, murmured, "Couldn't be more fair, I think. Mr. Roxeter? Do you not agree?"

Looking befuddled, but willing to go along with the group, Savina's father nodded. "Sounds right, though Savina dear, I didn't like how you interrupted Lord Gaston-Reade just now."

"Who is not busy?" Savina said, unwilling to be diverted from her goal.

Mr. William Barker finally spoke up. "His lordship, Mr. Roxeter and I are busy with the boat we are building. Going to take some time, since we haven't even begun yet, really, you know."

"Hmm, and Mr. Heywood is busy procuring the fish and turtle and building our shelter stronger. Zazu and I, well . . . we have been doing just about everything else," Savina said, with a long look at Lady Venture.

"That just leaves you," William Barker said, looking at his fiancee. "You and Annie. Shall you have a go at it, my dearest dove?"

"Of course not. I've never heard anything so absurd . . ."

"Stop whining, Vennie," Lord Gaston-Reade said, tossing his tin plate aside.

"And I say," Savina said, raising her voice to cover the murmuring that had broken out. "That the rock promontory is the best place. If the gentlemen can haul wood for her, Lady Venture and Annie will be well able to do the chore, at least for part of the time. Perhaps we can take turns at night," she said, glancing from face to face, "for it wouldn't be fair to expect Lady Venture and Annie to do it all the hours of the day and night."

Lady Venture narrowed her eyes and glared at her future sister-in-law, but Savina, unwilling to be engaged in a feud said, "Just think, my lady, you could be the one responsible for getting us rescued. What a marvelous thing that would be!"

A glorious rout, Tony reflected, as he secured the knife on his spear once more and checked that his knots would hold. It was vital they not lose their best knife, and so he checked and tightened the lashings constantly. Savina Roxeter's final statement had served to cement the position as an important one and Lady Venture as its holder.

He looked up from his task, and saw, on the opposite end of the beach on the other rocky promontory, the gentlemen piling wood and helping Lady Venture set up her bonfire. As he watched, Miss Savina and Miss Zazu strolled down the crescent-shaped beach between the two rocky projections, picking their way around scuttling crabs and rocky outcroppings.

When they came to a silvery clean stretch of sand the maid stretched her dark, slim arms above her and quickly bent over, turning a sideways flip using her hands to catapult herself. Her mistress stood to one side and clapped, jumping up and down, her long, dark, silky hair dancing and fluttering on the ocean breeze and her skirt belling around her bare ankles and feet. Tony sat down on the rock and watched, enjoying the pantomime, as the young maid clearly tried to talk her mistress into trying the same action.

Miss Roxeter glanced over her shoulder, up to where her fiancé was helping his sister set up the signal fire. Would she refuse, since he was watching her that moment?

But no, with Lord Gaston-Reade's attention clearly on her, she stretched her nearly bare arms over her head and attempted the same sideways flip, tumbling onto the beach and laying back on the wet sand, laughing as Miss Zazu stood over her and urged her to try again. She stood, flipped her hair out of her way, and executed a perfect turn, her dark hair tangling, her slim white legs exposed by the motion.

Lord Gaston-Reade was gesticulating and shouting from his rocky viewpoint, but Miss Roxeter gave one long, cool gaze in that direction, then turned and walked toward Tony's rocky ledge.

He hastened to hide his laughter, but when the two young ladies achieved his vantage point, he saw concealment wasn't necessary. Miss Savina, her cheeks pink and her dark hair clogged with wet sand, was laughing, her eyes sparkling in the tropical sunlight. Out of breath, she took his offered hand and let him pull her up to the rocky point, as Miss Zazu followed, clambering independently up.

"That was a display worthy of some acrobats I saw in Persia many years ago," he said.

"Are you not shocked?" she asked, with a mocking frown, pursing her lips and pushing them out in a good imitation of her fiancé's most outraged expression. "Are you not appalled that I behaved so, and in front of an audience?"

"If you had done so in the middle of Hyde Park at the promenade hour, I suppose I would have been.

But we find ourselves in such different circumstances that I am not at all shocked."

"I am," she confessed, sitting down on the rocky surface beside Zazu, who watched her mistress with a secretive smile on her face. "I am shocked at myself, a little. But . . . it looked like such fun." She glanced at Zazu. "And she dared me to try it, you know."

"I am a bad influence, certainly," Miss Zazu said, gravely.

Tony examined Miss Savina's face; her skin was becoming lightly tanned, the freckles darkening, and he reflected that but for this awful circumstance he would never have come to know her as he now did. She would have remained, to him, a lovely but dull enigma. Instead, he now knew her to hold the same defiant beliefs as he had. Gaston-Reade had no idea, clearly, and when he found out, would be appalled at the viper he had clasped to his bosom. Freedom for slaves? Reform of the plantation system? One or the other of them would have to give up their values, and with all of the power in their society held in the husband's hands, how could it help but be Miss Savina who would be vanquished?

He cast aside his gloomy thoughts. It was out of his power to correct mistakes already made. For now she was his friend, and they would be friends until rescue parted them and thrust them back into their well-defined roles. He stood and offered her his hand.

"Miss Savina, Miss Zazu, shall we begin the fishing lessons?"

"Better to start with swimming lessons," Miss Savina said, wryly. "I have never swum before, and would drown if I flung myself off this promontory as you do."

Ten

Down on the beach, Anthony Heywood led them into the water; Savina found her cursed skirts a nuisance, so she knotted them up between her legs as best she could. The morning sun rose above the jungle behind them, but dark clouds lingered on the horizon. As she waded in, she stared down through water so clear she could see her own feet and she wiggled her toes in the sand, giggling with Zazu, who was doing the same.

"As far as swimming goes," their tutor said, leading the way, "Salt water makes one more buoyant, so it will aid you in staying afloat. Swimming is really just an extension of our natural instinct when in the water to tread and thrust our arms, keeping ourselves afloat. Come farther . . . the water is calm today and safe."

Savina grasped Zazu's hand and they both waded out farther to where Mr. Heywood awaited them. Zazu's hand trembled as much as her own, she was happy to note, so the nervousness she felt of the engulfing waters that swirled around her waist was not her own alone.

"Are you sure," Zazu asked, her teeth chattering, "that this truly is safe?"

"Would I bring harm to you two ladies?" Heywood said, a grin on his tanned face. "Who else would make the meals?"

Savina splashed him using her free hand, and he returned the favor. "Drat these heavy skirts," she exclaimed, as the sodden material tugged at her. "Even knotted up they are such a nuisance. I wish I could take them off." When she caught the expression of merriment in his eyes, she blushed furiously. "I didn't mean I would! Merely that . . . that . . ."

"Never mind," he said. "When you ladies practice on your own perhaps you can strip down to something less confining. For now, we will just get the rudiments. Miss Zazu, come to me. You can try first." He put his hands on her waist and lifted her in the water and, her eyes wide, she began to flail her legs. "No, calm! Just relax yourself. Move your legs, but don't flail, just easy."

He helped her float in the water and she was soon moving her legs and arms, and when he let her go, she clumsily moved a few yards before stopping.

"That's a beginning," he said. "Practice, and I'll show Miss Savina."

Zazu paddled away toward shore, and Mr. Heywood moved toward Savina. She felt shy, all of a sudden, but could think of no excuse to stop the lesson.

"Here," he said, putting his arm around her waist. He lifted her and she leaned forward, feeling the strength of his arm as he held her close to his body and encouraged her to move her legs and arms, just gently. But she was breathless and gasping for air, partly panic at the unaccustomed feel of weightlessness in the water, and partly a surge of yearning as he held her close.

He let her go and she stood, head down, aware of his body close to hers.

"Are you all right, Miss Roxeter?"

"Yes," she said, feeling foolish. "I'm just fine. Let me try that again."

He took her waist in his hands and lifted her, and

she looked down at him, the rising sun reflecting on the sharp planes of his angular face. He stopped, gazed steadily at her and wrapped his arms around her for a moment, gazing directly into her eyes. She stared back. He swallowed and pushed her away, holding her lightly by the waist.

"Uh, just relax in the water, let it carry your weight, Miss . . . Miss Savina. Just relax; I won't let anything happen to you. Trust me."

Zazu was rapidly perfecting her swimming, and she stroked efficiently back to them. "I think I have it! It's so much fun. I used to paddle in the river at home, but it was shallow and I didn't go in over my knees. This is much better!"

"Yes," Savina said. "Much better."

Zazu splashed to a halt by them, and looked from one to the other. She muttered something in her people's patois, a language she only rarely used around anyone but her own family, and shouted out a laugh, then splashed away, leaving Savina and Anthony Heywood staring at each other.

Anthony put his hands on her shoulders. "Miss Roxeter, may I just say that I think you are . . . are wonderful. You will try anything, you work hard, you are so good to your father . . ."

"Stop! Mr. Heywood," she said, drawing away, "I think the swimming lesson is done for now. I have the rudiments, and I'll practice for a while with Zazu."

His expression dimmed and he stepped back. "Yes. And I should begin to fish. Learning to fish we will leave for another day, for you still must learn how to dive." He turned and dove into the water, swimming with quick, efficient strokes until he came to the rocky promontory, where he clambered up, stripped off his shirt and commenced his hunt for fish.

* * *

"Savina, my dear."

Savina turned at her father's voice behind her. She had come down to the beach at sunset to watch the horizon and wonder if their signal fire would be visible. Were they even on the right side of the island? Perhaps the east side of the island, toward the Atlantic, would be more sensible. Or should they be on the higher ground in the center of the small island?

"Yes, Papa?"

Her father approached and put his arm over her shoulders. She glanced over at him, thinking how weary and troubled he appeared. He had even fallen from his usual immaculate appearance, and the stubble of gray beard on his chin was unfamiliar and oddly alarming.

"His lordship came to me after dinner tonight."

"Yes?"

Her father stared out at the horizon and pulled at his stained neckcloth with his free hand. "Uh, he is, uh, concerned . . . that your . . . hmm, your friendship with Mr. Heywood is . . . is influencing you to behave immodestly." He sighed, as at a burden shrugged off.

"Behave immodestly?"

Still staring out at the horizon, he replied, "Yes, uh, your performance on the beach this morning, and your behavior while learning to swim."

Points on her treacherous body pulsed with remembered sensitivity, and Savina reflected on the day, and her own mixed feelings during the swimming lesson. The unaccustomed feel of the water, warmed by the sun, had been unsettling at first; it felt like bathwater, but to be sharing it with Mr. Heywood felt shockingly intimate, especially when Zazu had splashed away from them for her own private practice. The sensation became agreeable and she soon grew to relish it. But then came her lesson, and the agitating sensations that had coursed through her as Mr. Heywood talked her into surrendering to the buoyancy of the water and reclining in it, and she had felt his strong hands at her waist, holding her up, and then pressing her to his chest. The longing in his warm brown eyes had been unmistakable and mirrored her own craving for his touch; everything was etched in her memory and left her confused and shaken. Supported by his hands, thrust against his torso, the gentle motion of the water rocking their bodies together; it had all given her much to ponder of the physical relations between women and men, and as she went mechanically about her business for the rest of the day she had thought how wise, perhaps, were those matrons who limited interaction until a firm commitment was made by the gentleman to wed the young lady. Temptation to prolong those moments of contact was strong.

And yet Zazu, later, when questioned, had claimed not to feel those same feelings. Was it because she was already committed to Nelson in her mind and heart, if not in fact? Her own engagement to Lord Gaston-Reade, then, ought to have protected Savina from any mere physical response. Unless there was something between Mr. Heywood and herself that needed to be expressed . . . or quashed. She already knew she liked and admired him, but was it more?

She glanced over at her father, who was casting her worried glances. Having said what he had to, he was silent now. She doubted if he would even have noticed her swimming lessons, much less her burgeoning friendship with Mr. Heywood, if not for Gaston-Reade's interference. Even if he had noticed, he would never have said anything to her, but his dread of his future son-in-law's disapprobation was more powerful than his reluctance to broach the subject with his daughter. "So, Lord Gaston-Reade sent you to admonish me to behave myself?"

"It was not quite like that, Savina, dear." Her father

was looking at her with alarm, and she understood in that moment that even in his eyes, she had changed. He didn't know what to make of those changes.

"What is your feeling in this, Papa?" she asked, kicking at the sand with her bare toe. "Am I behaving immodestly?"

He looked askance at her. "Savina, you must know you are. I understand that we are among friends, but really . . ."

When she was silent, he bolted back into speech. "I beg you, Savina, not to risk your engagement to such a wealthy, well-thought-of, prosperous, dignified, powerful fellow as his lordship just for the friendship of his secretary. Is it worth it? Truly."

Savina caught sight of her fiancé depositing a load of wood on the rock promontory where the signal fire was. Mr. William Barker had volunteered to take the first night's tending of it so his fiancée could get some rest, as he solicitously put it. The earl said something to the other man, then began back towards the camp. Excusing herself from her father, she raced across the beach to meet Lord Gaston-Reade as he clambered down from the rocky outcropping.

He stopped and waited as she approached him. Once she stood before him, she gazed up at him. Somehow, even in the primitive circumstances of their tropical marooning, he managed to stay relatively impeccable, waistcoat on, cuffs exposed just the right amount, cravat tied, even though it was wilted and stained. She felt grimy in comparison, her dress salt-rimed from the morning swim, her hair gritty and her skin chapped from wind and sand. It made her feel even more irritable, but as angry as she was, she wasn't sure her fury was justified. Perhaps he had every right to expect more circumspect behavior in his fiancée. It was a dilemma, to be sure, between her true feelings and her uncertainty about those feelings. But it was not his anger over her behavior that infuriated her.

"Albert," she said, trying to calm herself enough to hide the trembling of her voice.

"Savina."

"I was just speaking to my father. He tells me that you find in my behavior today much to disapprove of."

"I would not say I disapprove, merely that I expressed my concern."

Staring into his cool gray eyes, Savina searched for something, anything, to show what he was feeling. Was it jealousy at her easy friendship with Mr. Heywood? That she could understand, and in that it would indicate some emotional attachment toward her, would alter her behavior to appease him.

"If you had a concern," she said, carefully, broaching the real source of her anger with him, "why did you not raise it with me? Why did you approach my father, as if he is in control of my conduct?"

"He *is* in control of your conduct."

"He is not! Nor has he ever been."

"Then he should be."

She was taken aback by his emotionless tone. His expression was unreadable, his eyes cold and dark, the gray like lead. "He is my father, not my . . . my jailer. He cannot command me in matters of my personal deportment."

"Then that is a failure of his that I did not notice before. You are under your father's protection and control until the moment you marry—I should not need to remind you of this, Savina—and then it becomes my burden to assume."

"Burden? I am my father's burden, and then I am to be yours. Do you mean that I am never in my own control?"

"Really, Savina, you must know this is so; by law as

well as by obligation I will be your keeper . . . or rather, your protector, and it will be up to me to correct and admonish you when you stray from the path of virtue and moral probity."

Said with such finality and acceptance it sounded like the voice of doom rather than the tones of a loving fiancé. She would be his burden, his chattel. Though she had always known it was so, she supposed, spoken aloud it had the air of death about it. Surely if he cared for her, he would not have said such a thing. But then, if she had offended his moral sensitivity perhaps he felt he had to say it aloud.

Her anger had changed to a cold dread of her future. She turned on her heel and walked away, toward the ocean, facing the horizon as the signal fire blazed and lit up the sky with new orange flames.

Eleven

Days passed, blending into each other, and yet each unique for Savina in that she learned something new either about the island, or about her fellow castaways. Lady Venture had, after an initial time of silent fury over being expected to perform the same task every day, become quite managing and particular about whomever took over her task for the night. She was, as Zazu called her, the mistress of the flame, and took her duty seriously.

From intense dislike, Savina had come to at least respect aspects of the other woman's character and understand her a little better. Manipulating William Barker into an engagement had, Savina believed when she considered it, been Lady Venture's attempt to grasp control over her own life by choosing as a suitor one who would never dare deny her, restrain her or attempt to assert his mastery in the marriage. She could sympathize with that goal, seeing, as she now did, what her own life would be with a man who would not allow her any personal freedom.

Though she had long thought Mr. Barker weak-willed and insignificant, she had come to appreciate his self-deprecating humor, his kindness, and his chivalry . . . true chivalry, the kind that had as its source a profound respect and genuine affection for femininity. He was invariably respectful and good-natured. But it seemed to Savina that Lady Venture was turning him into her lackey; soon, there would be nothing left of him but what Lady Venture allowed. Savina couldn't respect his lack of firmness, but she could still appreciate his kindness.

Zazu she had come to cherish as a sister. Their differences were many, but their similarities more numerous. Without speaking the words, they each knew, Savina felt, that she could depend on the other for anything, even life. It changed everything. How could Zazu be her maid, when she was her friend and sister?

But that was a conundrum she needn't solve while they were on the island, for they were no longer maid and mistress, but just survivors.

Of the others, the surprises were more subtle. Her father she worried about. He was at his best when Lord Gaston-Reade and he bent their heads over a problem concerning the raft they were building down on the beach above the tide's reach. He was at his worst when faced with the food, which he despised, the insects which feasted on him and the lizards, of which he had an unreasoning fear. The sleeping arrangements he considered scandalous and could not conceal his perturbation over.

Annie, Lady Venture's maid, troubled Savina, but it was in some way she couldn't fathom, and she feared she was being unfair to the girl, who appeared to do no more than become more comfortable with the men of the group than she may have in other circumstances. Annie's easier manner was no different, Savina told herself, than her own friendship with Tony Heywood, and since even Lady Venture didn't comment on her maid's demeanor, Savina could only keep her thoughts to herself and reflect on the secret wellsprings of jealousy in a woman's heart; she must be envious in some fashion, she decided at last, or the girl's artlessly beguiling manner wouldn't concern her.

Lord Gaston-Reade, still nominally her fiancé, she had come to feel an aversion toward that was distressing in such a small group. That he appeared oblivious of her feelings was even more irritating. She wanted him to ask her what was wrong. She wished he would just show some sign that he cared that there was a rift between them. It wouldn't resign her to the engagement, nor to her future husband, but it would at least show he had the tiniest bit of sensitivity to her emotions.

But the most profound alteration was in her feeling toward Tony Heywood. She couldn't even look at him without feeling a spurt of attraction and affection. That it was doomed to dwindle, if she was fortunate, given their respective positions, into a sisterly affection did not ease her agitation in his company at the present.

She would conquer the feeling, she determined. And that could only be accomplished by either becoming used to his company, or finding some part of his personality that irritated her as much as her fiancé's smug superiority did. Either goal could only be accomplished by spending time with him, and so she steeled her will and threw herself into his company as often as she could, disregarding her fiancé's perturbation and her father's worried glances.

For his part, Tony found every notion of his carefully planned existence changed, and it had little to do with being marooned on a tiny cay in the outer reaches of the Caribbean with a disparate group of grumbling complainers. It was Miss Savina Roxeter, and how he felt whenever she was near that had made a muddle of his thoughts and emotions. In all his controlled, organized life he had never felt the terror of being on the edge of something greater than all his careful plans. But it was there, the knowledge that in her he had found the one other soul in the world that felt like he did, thought like he did, wanted what he wanted, even if she didn't know it. As a well-raised young lady she was limited, perhaps, in what she could imagine for herself and her life, but he could see in her the magnificence of her mind and heart, and given free range, the endless possibilities of her life.

Was he misled by the utter enchantment of her face and form? There was no doubt, he thought, as he watched her graceful litheness after breakfast as she and Zazu rinsed the tin plates, that he was attracted to her physically. There was more than that between them, though, much more.

"Let me help," he said, drawn to her side by a force more powerful than magnetism.

Zazu, whom he often suspected of knowing his feelings, smiled and melted away to the path toward the beach, saying, "I have promised to help Lady Venture this morning with wood."

Savina smiled and waved to her, and then turned to Tony. "I'm almost done," she said, holding out a basket filled with hog plums and papayas. "But if you would conceal this, I would be grateful. I find that the birds and lizards are almost as voracious as we are, and all of our careful picking will come to naught if I don't do my best to hide the fruit."

He took the basket from her, his hand brushing hers as he did so, and set the basket in one of the empty wooden crates, covered it, then turned back to her and said, "I was thinking of going to a spot I found above the ridge beyond the north rock promontory to get a better view of the island. Would you, uh, like to accompany me? I don't suppose you've ever seen the island from there."

There was silence for a moment, other than the

sounds he had become so accustomed to, the chirring of insects and the trill of birds calling back and forth between the trees. She was studying his face.

"I suppose we could; I would like to see more of the interior. Are you asking anyone else?"

"We'll only be gone a couple of hours at most. No one will even miss us, I think."

She hesitated, looking up at him for a long moment, and, heart pounding, he pictured moving toward her, taking her in his arms and kissing her sun-chapped lips until she was breathless. If only . . . ah, but that was the problem. There were so many phrases to add after "if only": if only she wasn't already engaged, and to his employer of all men; if only she was not the daughter of a government official, retired but still well-respected; if only he had enough wealth and power to promise her everything he could ever want to promise her. If only.

"All right," she said.

He grabbed a canvas sack to bring back fruit and coconuts, if they found any—every person had been admonished by Zazu to collect food whenever they could—and they moved away from their encampment through the thick tangle of undergrowth. In one spot, over a damp rock, he reached back and took her hand in his briefly, trying to keep the quickness of his breathing from seeming like anything but the exertion of the journey. He had never behaved like this, never been so unnerved by a young lady's mere presence or touch. Flirting he had done in his past, and with ladies who spoke many different languages, but this one young English lady made him tremble with suppressed yearning. He had to conquer those feelings, he decided, and proximity was generally the best cure.

"There's a bit of a climb involved," he said, as they reached a slope in a clearing. He looked down at her bare feet and his own, and smiled over at her. "At least we are similarly shod."

"Scandalous," she said, returning his smile. "The earl cannot look at my naked feet without frowning."

"I don't know why. I find them very pretty."

She colored pink, and looked around. "I've never been to this part of the island before. Zazu and I walked around the other way by the beach, but we have never yet entered the interior of the island farther than the freshwater lakes."

He took her hand and helped her up over a rocky outcropping, and they started their ascent. "Miss Zazu is a fascinating young woman. I must say, I enjoy her childhood stories very much."

"She is telling us more now than I ever heard in all her time as my maid," his companion admitted. She stopped to catch her breath and gazed up at him. "Why don't you just call us Savina and Zazu, instead of adding 'Miss'?"

"If you like," he said, looking down at her, the blazing sun making her eyes sparkle and picking out golden threads in her dusky hair. "As long as you don't think it disrespectful."

"I would never think you disrespectful, Tony. And I have so long thought of you by your first name, it seems ludicrous not to admit the informality of our surroundings." She shook her head. "Unlike my father and the earl."

"Would you like to sit a minute and catch your breath?" he said, indicating the rocky ledge. He laid the canvas bag down for her to sit on.

She sat, and he sat beside her, feeling the warmth of her slim body radiating toward him in waves.

"Do you find his lordship a little stuffy?" He was treading dangerous ground, and he knew it. He longed to hear every manner of complaint about his employer from her lips. He wanted to belittle Lord Gaston-Reade, and it was a hideous sensation, the urge to verbally pummel a man he considered a rival. And yet her reticence, her refusal to disparage her fiancé, no matter how ridiculous he occasionally appeared to Tony, was something he respected about her.

"I think," she said, the words coming slowly, "that he is afraid to allow himself to waver from the behavior he considers necessary to call himself a gentleman. And that includes wearing a cravat, his boots . . . all of it."

Tony considered his next words carefully, given how little he still understood about her feelings toward Lord Gaston-Reade. "My feeling is, a gentleman is not his clothes, nor is he the polish on his boots. Neither is it his insistence on adhering to the formalities of address in a clearly informal setting. A gentleman is a man who, in difficult circumstances such as these, provides for the women in his care, protects them, and allows them to explore means of aiding in the survival of the group."

"*Allows* them?" She was staring over at him, trying to capture his gaze.

Her tone told him he had stepped wrong. "I didn't mean 'allows' in that sense, Savina. Please don't misunderstand me."

"Good, or I shall begin to think you as pompous and condescending as the American captain found you."

"I used entirely the wrong word." He gazed directly into her eyes, and saw her expression soften. "Let me say, unequivocally, that I believe in self-determination for every rational human creature, man or woman, of any country, of any color skin."

She took a deep breath. "So . . ." She paused and stared at him, then nodded. "I have long felt that you and I think alike on some subjects."

He covered her hand where it rested on the rock between them. "I've felt the same, ever since that first conversation on board the *Prosperous*, when you spoke to the earl about slavery." She turned her hand palm up and he clasped hers, thrilling at the touch, feeling the trembling connection between them strengthen. This was not right, he thought, and yet could not draw away. He had hoped time alone would reveal to him some fatal flaw, some awful insipidity or hideous defect. But of all the young ladies he had ever met, not a one combined her steady and serious intelligence with such a rich sense of the ridiculous, and united it with a lovely lightness of being, a freshness of expression, and an unutterably breathtaking sweetness.

She broke the connection and looked away, staring at the horizon and biting her lip. Her expression cleared, though, and she said, "What a lovely view from here."

"It is beautiful." He gazed down over the palm-dotted slope to the turquoise water of the ocean, deepening to a true indigo toward the horizon. Fluffy white clouds dotted the sky, lazily floating across as if in a slow-moving stream.

"I haven't been in England for almost ten years," she said. "What is it like? My memories are dim and clouded with uncertainty."

"Parts of it are beautiful. I was raised in Devon until I was fifteen and think it the loveliest spot on the island, but you know, every Englishman is fiercely particular to his own home county."

"What of London, though, for we—my . . . my fiancé and I—are to spend a good portion of our year there."

"And I will be there as his secretary," Tony said, fighting back his wretchedness at hearing her talk of her coming marriage to Lord Gaston-Reade. "Let's see . . . there are amusements in London one cannot find anywhere else, opera houses, theaters . . ."

"I don't care about that kind of thing. What of the people?"

Tony shrugged. "There is a mix of good and bad, as one finds . . ."

"Tony," she said, and put one slim hand on his tanned arm, where his sleeve was rolled up.

He looked down at her hand and felt his muscle flex involuntarily at the warmth of her touch.

"I'm not looking for platitudes about good and bad people. Tell me the truth, please. First, how much time have you spent in London?"

"Too much," he said. "Or, too much for someone who dislikes it as intensely as I do. I could hardly be fair about the city when I despise it so."

"Then don't be fair. Be biased. Be cruel. Tell your own truth about the city. I have a brain. I can sort out what is prejudiced by your own feelings. But be honest."

He stared into her eyes: the clear color, like the ocean at sunset, the untainted white, the long dark lashes. And then he stood, put out his hand, and said, "Let me talk while we climb. I want to get over the crest and to the interior. You haven't seen it yet, and it's truly magnificent. There is another freshwater lake beyond the hills."

Somehow, he never let go of her hand and Savina didn't mind; while they were alone they were just two children of nature, a part of the beauty that surrounded them. They scaled the hill, standing on the top for a long while just looking. The island, she found, was an irregular oval, only a few miles from one end to the other. Cradled in the basin of hills there was another larger freshwater lake. In the hazy distance, on the far horizon, she could see what looked like other islands. That they were uninhabited she thought was safe to assume.

Once they had canvassed Tony's mostly negative feelings about London—he called it a vast, dirty, smelly sewer where the people acted worse than the rats and Savina laughed at him, saying he was right that he could not be fair about the city—they spoke of things of more immediate importance.

"What do you think of Albert's raft?" Savina said, as they scaled down a long slope into a jungle interior alive with birdsong and the sound of iguanas scuttling away from them. Birds flitted from tree to tree above them as they picked their way carefully among the damp bushes. There were no paths, so they had to follow the contours of the vegetation.

Tony put his free arm around her shoulder as they negotiated a tricky outcropping of sharp coral rock. Distracted by the warmth of his hand and the feel of his flat, hard chest at her back, she tried to control her treacherous breathing, which would defiantly quicken with his proximity.

"I was at first concerned that his lordship would be precipitate and go off on the raft, losing his way and perhaps getting into trouble. But I should have realized, the earl never does anything precipitate."

She giggled. "No, if anything, he takes so long with every decision and every momentous pronouncement that we shall be old and gray before he has built the craft and charted his course."

The temptation to join her laughter was difficult to resist, but he was ever aware of his intense feelings of rivalry toward his employer, and he quashed his impulse. "I do hope the signal fire serves its purpose and finds us a rescuer."

Savina did not reply, and he wondered if rescue held as many varying connotations to her as it did to him. It meant comfort and safety for the first time in weeks, and a welcome change of clothes, good food, a warm bed. But it also meant going back to England and all of the stultifying conventions society demanded. It would end their easy association. It would mean she was engaged and expected to marry Lord Gaston-Reade.

They walked on, chatting desultorily about other things. One thing she confessed she was relieved about was that there were no dangerous animals on the island. Iguanas and snakes were all, along with a delightful array of birds and butterflies. She already missed the gardens of her Jamaica home, and asked him about having a garden in London, which he admitted was an unlikely thing, except for a garden such as Londoners would expect, a few potted conifers on a formal terrace or a conservatory full of orchids.

"Why did you say yes when the earl asked you to accept his hand in marriage?" As he spoke, he was very aware of her slim hand in his own, and how he was betraying his employer's best interest in his mind and heart, if not in fact, and how little he cared. Lord Gaston-Reade would be a fortunate man to marry a lady such as Savina Roxeter, more fortunate than Tony thought he deserved. The earl would ultimately make her unhappy, but he was helpless to do anything but watch and pray.

She was silent for a long few minutes, and he thought she was not going to answer. They walked on through the palm forest, swishing underbrush aside, heading for another elevation. When she stopped and turned to him, he threw down the canvas sack and took her other hand in his, so they stood linked, facing each other.

"I'd . . . rather not speak of that right now, Tony, please?"

He swallowed hard, looking down into her pleading eyes, shadowed by the palms that arched over their heads. His body urged him forward and he released her hands and took her in his arms, holding her close and gazing down into her lovely eyes. There was no retreat, not when he felt her relax in his embrace and her eyes fluttered closed.

The touch, when their lips met, was sweet and

tender, and warmth flooded his body. He surrendered to the sensation, unable to think clearly, incapable of abandoning the one perfect moment in his life.

He framed her face in his hands and took her lips, suckling and drawing them in as the kisses became more lingering, devouring, and he lost awareness of anything but their passion. Her arms were around his waist, and her lithe body pressed to his, points of fire igniting where they met. He jammed his fingers in her dusky hair and unaware of how far he was going, he thrust his tongue into her, tasting her, feeling her warm, wet mouth.

But she didn't draw back from the invasion. He did, though, finally releasing her and stepping away, staring at her, his breath coming in short gasps. She was trembling, her arms out, her eyes beseeching.

"I'm sorry," he said, though for what he couldn't say. "I shouldn't have done that; it was unthinkably bold."

"Then I would have you be bold again," she whispered and moved back into his reach.

Twelve

Lost in new sensation, when Tony kissed her again, Savina was prepared this time for the invasion of her mouth and gave back, finding a ferocious pleasure in the thrusting duel of their tongues. In seconds he had backed her against a slanting palm trunk, and she felt the heat from his body, and the press of his muscular legs and torso against her. Her hands found their quarry, and she pulled at his shirt until her hands were flat against the marvel that was his chest, and the intriguing musculature she had first seen when he was shirtless and swimming.

He paused and stared into her eyes, his look searching, questioning. She was acutely aware of everything about him as she ran her fingers over his smooth skin, feeling him shiver under her touch. A wave of dizzying delight swept through her as he slowly lowered his face to hers and gently kissed her once again, tracing the outline of her lips with the tip of his tongue. She closed her eyes, running her hands under his shirt, feeling the pounding of his heart as he murmured something against her mouth. He clasped her close to him, and then his hands snaked up from her waist to her breasts, sending a trill of thrilling disquietude down her backbone.

The cupping of his hands over her breasts awoke her to the impropriety . . . or no, more the danger of the game they were playing. But still, the temptation was to linger just a moment longer, to feel the fascinating flex and taut strength of his shoulders as his fingers— "Tony," she gasped, pushing him away. His brown eyes were clouded and his pupils large, as if a drug was coursing through his bloodstream. He shook himself, took a deep breath, and passed one hand over his unruly hair, turning away for a moment and bending over. He walked a few paces away, took another deep breath, and then paced back.

When he returned to her again, it was with a gaze more like one she had seen before. He shook his head and with a rueful grin said, "You are so very beautiful, Savina. And kissing you . . . I don't think I've ever felt quite like that in my life. I suppose I shouldn't say that, but it's the truth."

"It was a new sensation for me." She patted her dress down and straightened the fabric as she stared into his dark eyes, wondering why she felt so lost, so bereft. They could not have gone on with what they were doing, though the temptation had been strong just to follow urges and see where they led. Was that something the island was doing to them, or would the same forbidden desires be tugging at her in a London drawing room? "Why . . . why is it this way between us? Why do we both feel so . . ." She broke off and examined his face. Why did she not feel the same disquieting desires when facing Gaston-Reade, who was certainly more what people would call handsome? Tony was darker of mien and shorter of stature than her fiancé, and yet it was Tony who made her pulse quicken and her breath short. He entered her dreams and caressed her, and now she had so many new sensations to dream of, she would never be at peace in her sleeping hours again, she feared.

"I don't know how women feel," he said, simply. "I only know from a man's perspective."

"So tell me," she urged, pacing a ways away from him, feeling the need for distance. "I would like to understand it . . . how you feel."

Reluctantly, he acquiesced, watching her, still wanting her, she could tell. It was thrilling and frightening.

"The feeling is raw, primitive, an urge of the deepest, most animal part of me. I don't understand it, I just feel it, and it's a need to possess you, to . . . to conquer you." He shrugged, looking perplexed and mortified at his own words. He thrust his fingers through his increasingly shaggy hair, pulling it back from his eyes. "I shouldn't tell you such things," he said with a shake of his head. "I wouldn't have you alarmed or . . ."

"I'm not alarmed," she quickly said, feeling breathless, swept along by his vivid description, remembering the delicious abandonment of their kisses. "Tell me more."

"It is all those ferocious things, and yet . . ."

He stepped forward and threaded his fingers through her hair, pushing it back off her face. She stared up at him and saw the tenderness in his eyes, communicating itself to her on some level.

"And yet," he continued, his tone filled with wonder, "it is united with such overwhelming sensations of protectiveness toward you, tenderness, affection. I will be honest this once. I have never said anything like this before, nor will I likely again. You are the woman I never thought to meet, a woman of intelligence, sweetness of disposition, exquisite beauty. And more. You're so strong and combative and contrary and . . ." He broke off and just stared into her eyes as he stroked her cheek.

"Tony, no one has ever . . ." Savina paused as a stiff breeze swept up the hill and fluttered her skirts. She looked up as a sudden gust of wind thrashed through the palms overhead. The blue ceiling above had turned an alarming shade of gray, and the soft, fluffy white clouds had become towering thunderheads. "The weather has turned," she cried, pushing herself away from the palm she was leaned against. "A storm is brewing; we should go back. How far away are we from the camp?"

He looked up and his expression turned to one of grave concern. "As the crow flies, only a mile or two, but a couple of hours of climbing in this treacherous hilly terrain. I lost track of time. You're right. We have to go *now.*"

He grabbed the canvas sack he had thrown down, put his arm around her shoulders and they started back, but before they had gone far a cold pelting rain began, finding them even amongst the foliage of the underbrush, and as they scaled one hillside, the surface became muddy beneath their feet, greenery mashing into a slick, slippery trail. Savina slipped and slid back down a ways, and Tony had to half guide, half pull her up the hill.

They crested the rise to see a much different sight than they had just a while before. The ocean was an iron gray, and the wind lashed the palm forest in waves of shuddering violence. Savina felt a thrill of fear but refused to let Tony see her terror. It was hurricane season. Having only been in Jamaica for seven months, Tony had never before experienced that dangerous time of year when tropical storms could smash through the Caribbean at any time, with little warning. But she knew the danger. She only hoped Zazu and the others were making preparations and lashing things down as best they could. This could last hours or it could last days. It could be just the edge of the storm, or it could be the precursor of much worse to come.

They started down the other side, but Savina felt Tony's hand jerk out of her grasp as he tripped and slid, losing his balance and tumbling over a rocky outcropping that a half hour before had seemed so benign.

"Tony," she screamed, above the noise of the rising wind. She skidded down the side, trying not to lose her own footing, and found him a few yards below, holding his ankle and swearing richly, using language she had never thought to hear from a gentleman. She crouched at his side.

His face twisted in a grimace, he glanced up at her as she came to his aid. "I'm blasted sorry, Savina, but I've twisted my wretched ankle."

Pushing her rain-soaked hair out of her eyes, Savina stared down into his eyes. "You put it rather more forcefully just a few seconds ago!"

He laughed, a sharp bark of sound that ended with a yelp of pain as he tried to stand. "Damn, but it hurts!" He sat back down again on the muddy ground.

Savina took his foot in her hands and felt his bare ankle, disregarding the caking of mud she was getting on her hands and dress. "I can't tell; is it broken, do you think?"

"I don't think so. Look, we can't stay here." He pulled his foot from her grasp and tried again to stand. He sat back down abruptly in the muck. "Or more to the point, you can't stay here. This rain is getting worse, and the dirt and filth . . . Savina, I'm so sorry! What a wretched protector I am."

"Then I shall take a turn," she said, straightening and gazing around, wiping her hands on her dress skirt and impatiently swiping rain out of her eyes. "I saw, on my way up this slope, a cave opening. It will be shelter at least, even if it is cold." She helped him rise again, supporting him on her shoulder, and they descended the hill a ways further, then moved laterally to the cave opening Savina indicated.

Using her as a prop, Tony was able to limp into the opening of the cave. "It's very dark."

"It will get darker yet," Savina said, feeling a shiver of apprehension. But she must be strong; this was no time to allow her fears to overtake her. "Let me go ahead and see if there is some place to sit comfortably."

"I can . . ." Tony tried to step forward on his own but stumbled to his knees. "No, I guess I can't."

Savina shook her finger in his face. "Behave, and let me do this." She turned and advanced a little way into the cave, out of the wind and rain, as far as the weak light would let her walk. It was not an enormous cavern, but there was a cool breeze from the interior and Savina had the sensation that it went much deeper. The floor was descending toward the back. It would not be a good idea to go too far in, for if one of them slipped and slid into the cavern, the other might not be able to help. There was a spot to the side that had an outcropping that looked smooth enough to sit on at least for a while.

She returned to Tony and helped him in, guiding him to the spot she had scouted for them to sit. Outside the opening of the cavern the wind picked up and howled louder, rain driving at an angle and actually into the cave, though it didn't quite reach the two huddled together in the crude shelter. They didn't speak for a while, but finally, Tony's arms stole around her and he held her close to his body.

"I can feel you shivering," he said, his tone grim. "I even lost hold of the canvas sack, or we could have used it for a makeshift blanket. I'm so sorry about this, Savina."

"It's not your fault the weather turned. We've seen it happen before here, many a miserable night. And I've lived in Jamaica for nine years; I should have been the one to notice the turn of the weather."

"But we never should have left the encampment

without telling the others where we were going. What was I thinking? And I should have been watching the sky. I allowed myself to become distracted."

"Not your fault, either," Savina said. "Shall we say we both were distracted?" She turned to him and sought out his mouth and kissed him, feeling the warmth between them grow and banish her shivering.

Lost in a sweet haze, when Savina was again aware it was to note absently that she was almost on Tony's lap, her legs over his, his strong arms holding her close to his chest and her own wrapped around his neck. It seemed an efficient way to share their body heat.

It was not conducive to rational thought, though, she found. Her mind was muddled by a quivering deep inside of her that made her agitated and fretful. She wanted him to keep kissing her, but his face was turned away. She reached out and turned his face toward her. His expression, though, seen in the dim light from the rainy day outside the cave, sobered her instantly.

"What is it, Tony? You seem very . . . distressed."

"This is serious, Savina. I brought you to danger, ignored the weather, and now your father will be worried frantic about you. I should be hung by my thumbs for doing this."

"You only suggested we go for a walk," she said, "so stop taking all of the responsibility for this on yourself."

He shook his head, unconvinced. "I took you away from those who are your protectors, and that wasn't right."

She swung her legs off of his and moved away enough that their bodies weren't touching anymore. The rocky outcropping jutted and poked tender areas, and she was supremely uncomfortable. "I'm so weary of all this talk of protectors," she complained, taking a corner of her skirt and wiping dirt from her face. "Are women never to look after themselves? Are we so weak, so frail, so fragile that the merest breeze will knock us off our feet?"

"Obviously, that isn't so," Tony said. "After all, you're the one who found this cave and helped me to it." He stretched his legs out in front of him and grunted with the effort.

"How is your ankle?" she said, distracted from her ire by the memory of his injury.

"Damnably painful, but it clearly isn't broken, nor is it even truly sprained, I don't think. If this weather clears, we can go on."

"If." Savina gazed out of the mouth of the cave at the driving force of the rain and the greenery beyond, lashing wildly. "In my experience at home, once one of these deluges sets in, it is here for the day."

"All day? I hadn't considered that. We can't stay here overnight," he said, his dark eyes wide.

Savina thought about it. "We can if we have to. I'll not risk our safety just to calm my father's fears."

"But . . . what about Gaston-Reade? He'll be worried."

"Do you think so?"

"I do," Tony said, firmly. "It may not seem like it, but he does care for you."

"How do you know?"

"He asked you to marry him," Tony said, simply, his tone hollow.

Savina could no longer see his face in the dying light, and could not read his tone. "I suppose I never really examined what that meant."

"Trust me, Savina, in England the earl had ladies throwing their hats at him, and mothers desperate to arrange a marriage for their daughters with such a catch. I was surprised when he showed such interest in you, and then asked you to accept his hand."

"Why?"

He hesitated. The wind whipped up outside and

howled into the cavern. They huddled close together again, driven by necessity.

"Don't be afraid of hurting my feelings," she said, raising her voice over the wind. "I know that in every material sense he could have done better."

"I think you know by now that I think he could do no better if judging by your sweetness and intelligence."

"Ah, but Albert wasn't judging by my intelligence, was he?"

"No. But . . . he does seem to care for you."

Savina fell silent. After what they had experienced together it grated on her nerves for Tony to be defending his employer. Did he *want* her to marry the earl? Didn't he care for her himself? He had said as much when they spoke of their feelings; he had said he had never felt as he did now, toward her. Or perhaps that was just the heat of the moment.

Her feelings a jumble, she began to fret for her father's worries, and Zazu's. They didn't know where Savina and Tony were, didn't even have a clue as to the direction they had taken. Her papa would be so unhappy, for despite every evidence to the contrary he still considered her his little girl, a helpless, sweet and fragile child.

Hours passed. They spoke of the others, and wondered how they were faring through the storm, and admitted to each other how hungry and thirsty they were and how foolish they had been to set out on any trek so ill prepared.

"Do you have family in England, Tony?" Savina finally asked, disliking the echoing sound of the pounding rain and lashing palms.

"Not any more," he said. "My parents are both gone, my older brother is in Europe, and any relatives I have, I lost touch with over the years."

"Is there no one?"

He took her hand and squeezed it. "I have one old friend who will miss me if I never go back to England," he said, understanding what she was really asking. "I was apprenticed, when I was young, to a jeweler, and he has been my benefactor; he made sure I had schooling, and helped me find my first position as secretary. Do you have family? You must."

"Not really," she admitted. "Papa is everything to me. Oh, I do have some family on my mother's side . . . cousins, and a couple of maiden aunts, one of them very wealthy and very peculiar. It is she who gave my papa the money, when we were on our way to Jamaica, to buy me something to remember her by, she said. She gave him a gold sovereign and he bought, from a native craftsman, this little coral cross." She lifted the cross from her neck and Tony caressed, it, feeling the shape in the growing gloom of their cavern.

"It's very pretty," he said. "I have often admired it, thinking how well its delicacy suited you. She must have cared for you."

"I only remember meeting her once. I think she did the same for all of her nieces and great-nieces."

"You must have been special," Tony insisted. "I will have it no other way. The woman you have become can only have had her nascence in an extraordinary child."

She touched his cheek and brushed away the drying grit. With much left unsaid between them, conversation dwindled and night fell, the rain settling into a steady, heavy downpour. She could hear it coursing down in heavy streams past the cavern mouth, some trickling in past their seat. Savina thought about those back at the encampment, and worried that Zazu and her father were frantic. But just as she feared her thoughts would make her mad, she turned them to pondering again what had happened between her and Tony that day.

He told her he cared for her, and she had discovered a depth of feeling toward him that could not be denied. But she was still affianced to Lord Gaston-Reade, and it was clear from Tony's words that he still considered her his employer's intended bride; he had even found a way to state that the earl cared for her in some way. For some reason that irritated her more than anything else. She could accept that he considered her another man's possession, but then to have him defend that man—

She shifted her cramped body on the rock ledge and felt Tony slump heavily on her shoulder, clearly asleep. How typical. She was worried and fretting, and he was asleep.

Perhaps the kisses they had shared and the desire present between them was not enough for anything more than a few stolen moments, and Tony knew it. To her it felt like an awakening, but perhaps, having more experience in such matters, he knew it was fleeting and not the solid foundation a lifetime of togetherness required.

She shifted positions again and offered him her shoulder to lay his head on. He nuzzled her neck, and she felt the awkward flare of warmth his proximity always enflamed. Those minutes in his arms, drugged by kisses sweeter than mead, had been strange for the quality of forgetfulness; she had forgotten where they were, what their supposed purpose for walking out was, in short, she had forgotten anything but the sensations coursing through her. His hands on her body had taught her how much she would enjoy the more intimate aspects of love, and it had made her understand some of the actions she had thought ridiculous in the romances she had read and characterized as absurd. Yearning and powerful need, expressed in overblown expressions in those books, really did exist . . . unfortunately not with her fiancé.

She turned her face in the dark and felt Tony's lips

close. Kissing; such an odd custom, she thought, but then gave herself up to one more caress of his lips. Even slumbering, he kissed back, and soon they were reclining on the rocky shelf, all discomfort dissolving as his warm caresses generated again the lovely forgetfulness she craved.

His heavy body pressed against her and new sensation coursed through her as she felt his passion grow. Unnerved by feelings she could not explain and dared not act upon, she turned her back to him, and curled awkwardly in the protective curve of his body, shivering not from cold, but from inexplicable yearnings.

She closed her eyes and tried to settle herself to get some sleep with the distracting knowledge that Tony was pressed against her and held her close, sleepily curling his body around hers. Marriage. When she was married and felt such cravings, she would be able to satisfy them. There would be no stopping, no turning away from passion just as one wanted to go on. But would it be with a man who made her feel thus? Or had she never experienced such feelings with Gaston-Reade simply because they had never been in such a position, both literally and figuratively?

Despite such puzzling questions as her mind taunted her with, she finally grew weary and her eyes closed, and she lost all awareness.

Tony, cramped and cold, awoke to find weak light penetrating the cavern entrance. The rain had stopped and the wind had died overnight; he could surmise that much from the lack of sound other than morning birdsong. He had his arms around Savina and she was curled up to his body, which was responding in a natural way. He must conquer that treacherous passion before she awoke, and to aid that aim he gently disengaged himself and tested his damaged ankle by putting his foot down. Would it carry his weight? It was a little swollen and uncomfortable, but it wasn't broken, nor even sprained, just bruised, he thought.

He limped to the opening and gazed out. The sun had arisen and the forest was steaming, a mist rising from the vegetation and slick ground. He took a deep breath, thankful his body was responding appropriately, though he felt an overwhelming urge of a different sort. He exited, did what he had to do, and limped back into the cave, gazing down at Savina, still curled in a tight ball and asleep.

He couldn't conceal from himself what he felt for her. He was in love for the first time in his life, and it wasn't mere passion that spoke, though his body longed for her in the most indecent of ways. She inspired tenderness, too, and he was filled with the certainty that she was the perfection of all womankind, the most adorable, the sweetest, the most intelligent, and the kindest of all females. What he had laughed at in other men he now saw in himself, the urge to put his beloved on a pedestal so high she couldn't possibly earn her ascent to such a dizzying and lofty height. And yet he acknowledged her faults, if faults they truly were. She was hasty, at times, and argumentative. She could be stubborn and unruly, and he found those blemishes wholly endearing, providing the salt in a personality that would be cloyingly perfect without them.

But she was not only affianced to his employer, he didn't even have a right to try to take her away from the earl, not by any measurement he could fathom. He was not rich, nor did he have any expectations of wealth. His life's plan was not calculated in any way to make him wealthy. His birth was good, but without the cachet of nobility in his background.

He would impoverish her if he told her his feelings and asked her to share his life; though he was confident in his emotions, he had seen poverty before and what it could do to those who married for love despite a lack of income to support them comfortably. Love alone could not feed nor clothe two young people, but worse was the effect on the inevitable progeny that would come from such a passionate union. A large brood plus too little money for good food, proper schooling, or even an adequate house equaled squalor and misery; such were the mathematics of poverty. He loved her too much to see her become a threadbare and workworn woman, old before her time with care and strife.

But she had a sweet and passionate nature, and if he confessed his feelings to her and she felt the same, she might eagerly throw her lot in with his, daring society to condemn them.

No, as much as he longed to hear a confession of love from her sweet lips, he knew his duty now. He knelt by her side and stroked back her mud-encrusted hair. She murmured in her sleep and turned her face up to his, but he denied himself the right to kiss her awake, though he longed to; he wanted to kiss her muck-streaked cheek and take her in his arms. He had to ignore his own feelings and hope, against all of his inner desires, that her emotions were not engaged. He had to get her back to the encampment, exaggerate his injury, and make it seem like her night was spent nursing him, not kissing him. Whether she would go along with his charade was doubtful, but if he put it to her that it would soothe her poor father's understandable anxiety, she would likely acquiesce. He knew that what she would not do for herself she would do for those she loved.

"Savina," he said, shaking her shoulder. "Savina, it's morning. The weather has improved and we must get back to the others. Every second we delay is another second of torment for your poor father."

She sluggishly sat up, passed one hand over her eyes and gazed at him. "Tony, you're filthy! What a sight we both will be in the light of day." She arose and stretched, holding one hand to her back and grimacing at the ache. "All right. I suppose we must go. I am so hungry and thirsty I would even drink seawater right now."

The way back was awful and treacherous, taking more than an hour and a half. When they finally limped back into the encampment they were a wretched sight, he knew, clothes torn by rocks, mud caking their hair and clothes and limbs, misery on their filthy faces. It was good, he thought, good that they looked so wretched as to forestall any suspi-cion of their pastime while away. The memories would stay locked in his own heart forever.

Zazu was the first to see them, and she dropped the pot she was carrying and ran to them, crying out incoherently, and supporting them both. Savina's father went to his child the moment he spotted her and held her close, sobbing uncontrollably from his fear. The earl and Mr. William Barker were just about to set out to look for them, and were clearly relieved that they didn't have to do so with no idea of where to look. The explanations were tedious and lengthy, but finally they sat on crates and drank hot tea provided by Zazu, who was brushing Savina's hair, cleansing it as best she could of mud and tangles.

"I still don't understand what could possibly have prompted you to wander off in that singular way," the earl asked, his face a mask of incomprehension. "Where were you going?"

"Only up to the rise, to see if there was any better spot for the signal fire," Tony hastily offered. "We got lost, though, and then that wretched rain came and I sprained my ankle. It was all we could do to find a spot to shelter."

Savina glanced at him, and then looked away. Tony sighed with relief. She was not going to reveal anything more, he felt sure. For both of their sakes he was relieved.

Thirteen

Once they were alone, Savina and Zazu, repairing the damage the overnight storm had done to their encampment, were able to talk unguardedly. Savina would never think of keeping anything from her friend, and sorely needed someone to unburden her conscience to anyway.

"What really happened?" Zazu asked, while they brushed drying mud from the barrels and crates that made up their encampment's seating arrangements.

The tarpaulin had come down in the wind, Savina saw, and they must have had an exhausting, terrifying night, perhaps worse than she and Tony in their protected cave. Wearily, Savina slumped down on one of the crates and put her head in her hands. Then she looked up and met her friend's intelligent gaze. "I think I'm in love with Tony Heywood."

Zazu sat down opposite her and took Savina's hands in her own. "Are you sure?"

"No! I'm not sure at all. How can you tell, Zazu, if you're in love or not? You must know. You love Nelson."

"I don't know if it's the same for everyone. I only know how I felt . . . how I still feel."

"How? Tell me."

"I want for Nelson everything that is best. I hold him here," she said, releasing Savina's hands and covering her heart with one hand.

"But . . . but do you shiver when he touches you? Do you long to disappear with him and . . . just run away and never come back?"

Zazu's expression was grave. "Are you truly speaking of love, or something else? What happened up there overnight?"

"Nothing! We just . . . he kissed me. And I kissed him." Savina covered her face, scrubbed her eyes and then opened them again, staring over at her friend. "I wanted to do more, but we both knew we couldn't. Is that what love is?"

"There is a part of that," Zazu admitted, speaking slowly. "But Savina, it's so much more! Nelson and I trust each other. We believe in each other. I know in my heart that I will love Nelson always, and that he will always love me."

"Then how could you leave him behind?"

She shrugged. "It hurt more to be so close, but know we could never be together. And there were other things, other decisions . . ." She shook her head and looked away, her dark eyes welling with tears that threatened to spill over. She dashed one away impatiently. "We talked it over, and he said I needed to do what was best. He said he loved me, and that would never change, but that I had to make the decision for myself. I've told you the rest, and there is more in my heart . . ." She stopped and gazed meaningfully at Savina.

Savina sighed and nodded. "I think I do understand." She stood and looked around the encampment, the sandy muck piled up against things and the wet blankets strewn about. The tarpaulin had been folded and set aside for the men to put back up later, after the tropical sunshine had dried out the encampment. "It looks like you had as restful a night as I."

"It was awful," Zazu said, simply, rising too. "But worse for your father and myself was wondering where you were, and if you would be all right. I thought you would be. I know you; you're a resolute woman. Lot of good spirit, my grandmother would say. But your poor father—he doesn't understand how strong you are, how indomitable—and he was so worried." Zazu reached out and hugged her. "He prayed all night, aloud; it was heartbreaking. I did the best I could, and he clung to me for a time, weeping."

Savina felt the tears begin, and for a moment could not choke them back. She sobbed on her friend's shoulder, but then heard voices and straightened, wiping her eyes with the back of her hand. "Thank you for looking after him," she murmured, kissing her friend's cheek. "To him, you're like another daughter, Zazu. Thank you!"

"We'll talk later," Zazu whispered.

The day went on, and Savina did her best to ignore the sensation that something was wrong, but she couldn't. She was unhappy, and her mind was tormented with doubts and fears. She and Zazu slipped away to the freshwater lake and bathed, washing their hair and clothes as best they could, rinsing away the grit and filth of the difficult night both had spent. After dinner—an abundance of steamed fish, since many had washed ashore in the storm the night before—and after tidying the dishes and pots, she walked down to the beach where the men were constructing their boat.

Her father, now that she was back, had returned to his task as Lord Gaston-Reade's second-in-command on the boat building crew. He waved to her, but she didn't want to interfere, so took a seat on a rock nearby.

Lady Venture was alone, out on her rocky promontory, and she scanned the horizon, looking for any sign of a ship. Savina supposed poor Annie must be off collecting wood for the fire, and Mr. William Barker, too, perhaps. The work of living never stopped, and all had been enjoined to gather wood, fruit and palm fronds whenever they had a spare moment.

The earl had bowed to necessity enough to remove his boots and stockings and take off his jacket, rolling his sleeves up over his forearms, and so Savina was treated to a shocking display of manly calf and ankle. He was, as the ladies of Jamaica had whispered, a well-set-up young man, and she supposed she should not be shocked, but titillated by the sight of so much of her fiancé's muscular flesh.

She sighed. All she felt was the same intense irritation he always seemed to inspire now. She couldn't imagine going through life in that state of constant vexation, though it seemed to her many women must.

The sun descended and Savina's father climbed the sloping beach, every line of his body expressing his weariness. He stopped at Savina's seat, laid one hand on her shoulder, and said, "Savina, my dear, I am not as young as I used to be. Your fiancé . . . now that is an untiring fellow. Bright future. Very bright future. You will be in good hands."

"You should go up and lie down, Papa," she said, gazing up at him with affection. His lined face was gray with exhaustion, and she promised herself to take better care of him. Even if that was all life held for her, she should be happy to love and be loved by such an affectionate, if occasionally misguided, parent.

"You're right, my dear. I shall lay myself down and pray to the good Lord to send us a rescue boat. I don't know how much more of this I can take." He wandered off, picking up his shoes and stockings from where he had left them, above the wet sand on a rock, and continued up to the encampment.

Lord Gaston-Reade stood staring at his raft. It was on the sandy beach, but up high enough that high tide would not reach it. Constructed of palm logs and lashed together with vines, torn strips of fabric and the chinks stuffed with whatever they could find, it wasn't pretty, but it would likely float. For a while. Until it became waterlogged.

Slipping from her rocky seat, Savina moved down the beach and joined him in staring at the craft. She dug her toes into the sand. "Do you really think you will be able to find help?" she asked.

"I do. We have talked it over, your father and I, and we think we are not too far from Turks Island; it should be south of us. We don't think we were blown so far north as the Bahamian islands."

"How sure are you?"

The earl cast her an exasperated look. "I do not like the tenor of your questions, Savina. You appear to be interrogating me. Do you doubt my powers of reasoning?"

Irritation chafed at Savina again, and she had to clamp down on her lip to keep from arguing. "Of course not." Unfortunately, biting her lip didn't work; she burst into speech again. "But are you willing to bet your life, and that of others, on it? Who will go with you? Not my father, I can tell you that with all certainty. And how do you know that after hours in the water this craft will not become waterlogged and sink? And what will happen if you face winds? Will it stand up to waves?"

He glared down at her, his hands on his hips, his feet apart. Dark with anger, his gray eyes were shadowed by his beetling brow. "Do you think I have not thought of all that? Really, Savina, you're going too far. You are questioning me most impertinently, and no wife of mine will take that tone with me."

Which made her next subject all the easier to introduce. Taking a deep breath, she faced him squarely. She had thought all day, and there was only one conclusion. "I don't think that you and I are really suited to each other at all. I cannot be less than I am just to satisfy your requirements. Albert, I don't want to marry you." She crossed her arms over her chest and stared up at him. His face was shadowed, since he had his back to the sunset, but she could see him turning scarlet at her defiant words.

"What nonsense! What absolute madness!" The earl looked down at her, then back at the boat, and then he turned to face Savina. "You're just hysterical," he said, his tone calmer. He reached out and touched her shoulder. "I can understand your fear. The night must have been awful . . . just terrible for you, and I do know how hard you work."

That he had no inkling of what had gone on between Tony and her, nor did he even seem to suspect or worry about it, irritated Savina, too.

He put both hands on her shoulders. "I know how hard this has been on everyone, but just trust me. I will find us a way off this island, I guarantee it."

Cold dread gripped her stomach. Her father believed so implicitly in the earl's judgment that he would willingly place his own life in Gaston-Reade's hands. But Savina would throw herself down in front of the boat rather than let her father go. She pulled herself from his grasp and stared up at him. "But the American captain . . ."

"Don't speak to me of that invidious coward!" the earl roared, throwing his arms up in the air in exasperation. "I have heard enough. He will *not* send word to our navy. Why should he? What has he to gain?"

"His own soul," Savina yelled back, clenching her fists against the inclination to beat at him, to try to make him see her point. "Albert, he was not some monster; I *will* not believe him so lost to all human feeling as to strand helpless people and abandon them to the elements with no hope of rescue."

Gaston-Reade's expression held pity and scorn.

"How little you understand of the world or the ways of men, Savina."

"I understand enough to know that you and I will never suit. Really Albert, even your own reason must tell you how little we think and feel alike on all subjects." She paced away and kicked at the sand. "We didn't have enough time to get to know each other, and the drawing room is such an artificial . . ."

"Enough, Savina!" he held up one hand as she turned back to him. "I will not listen to another word on this subject. When we get back to London you will feel differently, and I will not have you jeopardize our future by saying too much now." He gazed at his boat one last time, then said, "I'm going back up to the encampment. I suggest you do the same."

Savina watched him go, then glanced up at the rock promontory. On a whim, she strode across the sand, climbed the rocky outcropping, and made her way to Lady Venture's station.

Lady Venture, her hair windblown and her cheeks red from the sun and fire, turned as Savina approached. "Oh, I thought you might be Annie. Where is that girl?"

"I don't know." Savina gazed at the fire. As twilight approached, Lady Venture added dry wood to the heap, whereas in daylight, she used lots of green palm leaves, brush, anything that would give a lot of smoke. She had, to Savina's surprise, not shirked her duty.

"What happened during the night last night?" Savina asked. "That was a terrible storm."

"I stayed as long as I could, but the waves came crashing over the promontory and swept my fire out to sea. William and I rebuilt it today."

Savina stared at it for a moment, and when she looked up again it was to find Venture's prominent eyes fixed on her, her expression unreadable.

"You and Bertie were having a set-to, hmm?"

"How do you know?"

"My brother's voice carries when he is upset, which is fairly often, since he has a rather choleric disposition, just like our father did. When he is old he will be fat and angry and red-faced and die of apoplexy. Just like Father."

Savina almost laughed out loud at the satisfied tone in Lady Venture's grim pronouncement. On impulse, she asked, "Venture, do you love Mr. William Barker?"

"Love him?" The woman's gaze slewed around to Savina, but returned almost immediately to her fire. She threw another branch on it and stood back, dusting her hands off. "Good Lord, no. I would *never* marry a man I loved."

"Why?" Savina stepped back from the roaring blaze, keeping her balance on the rocky surface with difficulty.

Lady Venture stared again at Savina, her gaze holding longer this time. "You really cannot imagine?"

Savina shook her head.

The gleam of the fire lit the other lady's eyes with a cold, silvery glitter. "When you love them, they have you," Lady Venture said, holding out her hand, palm up. Then she fisted her hand. "And then they can make you do or feel anything, just by twisting you around into knots."

Taken aback by the vehemence of the other woman's tone, Savina said, "Not all men are like that, Venture. Really, aren't you being unfair?"

"No. You're too young."

"You aren't that much older than I."

"I'm twenty-nine, Savina." Her mouth was turned down in a grimace and she suddenly looked older than her years. "Or at least I tell people I'm twenty-nine," she admitted. "And I will until I'm married. Then I can get old."

The hurt was so firmly embedded in Lady Venture,

it was a part of her, Savina thought, sadly. That someone had hurt her in the past was clear, but it wasn't her place to pry. "So, do you think I should marry your brother?"

"Of course," Lady Venture said. "You're lucky to get him. Just make sure the marriage lines are drawn up so you have good pin money, jewels, and a carriage of your own, and hire good-looking footmen. Once you have borne the future Lord Gaston-Reade and another in case that babe dies, you can take into your bed whomever you please."

Shocked, Savina turned away and climbed back toward the beach. She couldn't face going back to the encampment just yet; she needed to sit alone and let the venom wash away from her. Lady Venture's outlook on life was repellent, but it was reflective of her own experience, it seemed. How justified was it, and how much would become her own experience in time?

She found a quiet spot on the beach in the shadow of the rock promontory and sat in the sand to watch the sun set while Lady Venture stood alone and stared out to the horizon.

Tony built a fire, teasing the banked embers into a blaze with dried beach grass and placing what wood he had gathered over it. Annie, Lady Venture's maid, had come back from the forest a few moments before, and was bustling around her and Lady Venture's pallet. Mr. Roxeter was already asleep, his resonant snores competing with the night noises of the tropical forest for precedence. A more different night than the one before could not be imagined, and the benign night sky, a blanket of stars overhead, seemed to beg forgiveness for its fit of temper. The earl, too, had returned from the beach and was just now lying down to sleep.

The flames leaped and danced, and Tony saw William Barker come out of the forest empty-handed. It had been Tony's impression that the fellow was gathering wood for his fiancée's fire, but it appeared that he was wrong. Barker came and sat down by the blaze.

"Barker," Tony murmured, sitting back on his haunches, "is it your impression that his lordship really does have a good idea of where an inhabited island is? You worked in the Jamaican government, you should have some idea. Does he know what he's talking about?"

"I don't have any better notion than you do, Heywood. I'm just going along with his lordship. He appears to know something about it all. You know him better than I do."

Tony nodded. That was what worried him. His employer was the kind who took a bit of knowledge, inflated it into certainty, and could bluster his way into making others believe him. In his business dealings that often worked to his advantage, and to some extent he was a natural born leader of men. Or, in this case, he could be telling the truth. He was not a stupid man by any means, but he did have that tendency to overconfidence. On a couple of memorable occasions since Tony had been his secretary that overconfidence had led to trouble. "So, will you get on the raft with him?"

"I have no choice," Barker said, with an edge of desperation in his voice.

"What do you mean, you have no choice?" Tony took a seat on the log nearby. "No one can make you if you don't want to. I tell you this, man to man; I will think no less of you if you refuse."

"No, I *have* to, Heywood. Venture will not let me be until I do, I just know it."

"She wouldn't want you to do anything you were uncomfortable with."

Barker looked at him with astonished incredulity. "You've known her longer than I. Do you really believe that?"

Tony considered the matter. "She will badger you," he admitted, at last. "But if you stand firm . . ."

But Barker was shaking his head. "No, you don't understand. She is a woman who will not be refused. I've tried saying no to her before. It doesn't work."

Tony fell silent, hearing an edge of desperation in the younger man's tone. He had been a witness to their courtship, and realized that Lady Venture made the decision, and then swept Barker along, like a crab on the tide. And yet, she had done much the same thing to him when first he began working for Lord Gaston-Reade and he had just refused to be impelled by the force of her personality; she had abruptly desisted and now treated him with frosty formality as if she had never implied that she would welcome him if he chose to court her.

"I'm tired. I'm going to sleep now," Barker said, rising and making his way back to their crude sleeping area.

Heywood sat and contemplated the flames for a while, then saw a dim shape approaching; it was Savina, he knew it by how his heart thumped just at her proximity.

"Come and sit by the fire," he whispered.

She did so, but on the far side, cross-legged on the ground, her tattered skirts spread around her. "I see you have put the tarpaulin back up."

"Yes. It was not damaged too badly, though some of the grommets were ripped off by the force of the wind. I think we were better sheltered last night than our friends." He fed the fire with more wood. "What do you think of the boat-building?" he asked.

She stared into the fire, the brilliant gold of the leaping flames lighting gold highlights in her dusky hair, which flowed over her shoulders in dark waves. The light burnished her cheekbones to glowing pink and lit a fire in her eyes, and he stared, unable to believe that just hours before he had held her and kissed her.

"I'm worried, Tony. Albert can't—or won't—answer any of my questions. He doesn't even know if the thing will float, or for how long, I don't think. Or what he will do if a storm comes up while he and whoever goes with him are out on the ocean."

"And how is he going to steer it? I must admit, I have some grave doubts myself." Tony paused and poked at the fire with the long stick kept nearby. "But what if he's right, Savina? What if Captain Verdun doesn't send help? We could be stranded here for years . . . or forever."

"I know. I've thought of *that*. I don't think my father could stand it, Tony, I really don't."

Her voice was clogged with tears, and he wanted to comfort her, but there was a wedge between them now, it seemed. She had avoided him all day, veering off when he approached and keeping her distance even at mealtimes. Their closeness of the night before had reversed into a sensitivity, on her part, that he didn't quite understand.

She cleared her throat. "So I think he may as well try, Tony. And he's going to anyway. He is implacable once his mind is made up to something."

"How well I know that," Tony answered. "But William Barker will likely be browbeaten into accompanying him."

"Mr. Barker is an adult male, quite capable of making up his own mind," she said, acidly. "Men have all the power, they may as well use it any way they please. But I will not," she went on, defying her own argument, "allow my father to take part in the expedition."

Tony stood, circled the fire and crouched by her.

"Don't worry, Savina, I will do anything I have to, to keep your father on dry land."

"Thank you, Tony," she said, leaning on his shoulder. "Thank you."

Fourteen

Morning light drifted through the canopy of palms and fruit trees. Zazu and Savina cut fruit and whispered together, while the others did their morning business. Savina's father had taken to tidying the sleeping area in the morning, his natural sense of order reasserting itself even in such primitive surroundings. Annie, with a shy smile, offered to take food to Lady Venture who, having volunteered to take a night as well as her usual day turn watching the fire, would be exhausted and looking for food and relief.

The other men wandered back into the encampment and the crude shelter of the oiled canvas tarpaulin. The various boxes and barrels of water, flour and utensils were pressed into service as benches and seats and placed around the perimeter of the refuge, with one barrel used as a table where Savina placed the platter holding breakfast. After their Spartan meal of fruit and water—tea was rationed ever more sparingly as the days passed, as were the food items Captain Verdun had allowed his captives—Lord Gaston-Reade stood and said, "I think that the raft is ready to set sail. I would like to do it at first light tomorrow, assuming the weather holds."

"You are still intent on this, my lord?" Tony said.

"Yes, Tony," he said, with exaggerated emphasis. "Your friend, the American captain, is not going to send help and unless we do something, we will be stranded forever."

Savina saw Tony's expression darken at the earl's taunting tone.

"Are you sure you know what direction you need to go to get to an inhabited island?" he asked, staring steadily at his employer. "And how are you going to steer the thing, anyway?"

"You have not been interested until now," the earl said, with an edge of resentment in his refined voice. "You have no right to question. It is sufficient that *we* think it's ready to go," he finished, indicating Savina's father and William Barker. "Now we need only decide who is to go along."

Savina held her breath, but her father did not volunteer.

"I should sink you like a stone," he said, ruefully, looking down at his paunch, which though deflating from a steady diet of fruit and fish, was still considerable. "And I don't think I would be a jot of help. I wouldn't be able to row very fast."

"You have already done your part, my dear sir. How about it, Savina," Gaston-Reade said, looking over at her, an unpleasant edge in his voice. "Shall we test our life partnership by setting sail alone?"

"Are you mad?" Tony said, leaping to his feet. "You can't mean to take Savina with you?"

"Why not? You spent the whole night with her in some deserted cave. Why shouldn't I have some time?"

"Don't be ridiculous, Albert," Savina said. "Tony and I had no choice."

"You and *Tony* seem to have become very close friends. I don't like it, Savina, and I won't tolerate it." The earl's enmity toward his secretary had finally been stated aloud.

"My lord," Savina's father said, staggering to his

feet, alarm on his gray, stubbly face. "Please, do not speak to my daughter in that fashion. Of course she cannot go with you. I know you wouldn't seriously suggest it."

"It was said in jest," the earl said, irritably. The shadows of the tarpaulin shrouded his face, but his petulant expression was clear in his tone. He crossed his arms over his chest. "I'm sorry some seem to have lost their sense of humor."

Savina watched Gaston-Reade, and realized that though he did not deign to show it, her night alone with Tony had rankled in some way. Though it was natural, if he cared for her, that he would be a little jealous of her and Tony's easy friendship—and more than friendship that she hoped he did not sense or suspect—still, she would have liked him better if he had shown his anger in a more forthright manner.

Mr. Barker, with a frightened look on his pinched face, stood. "Of course I will go with you, my lord."

"Good man," the earl said, clapping him on the shoulder. "I knew I could count on you. Going to be brothers, and now we will be companions in this grand adventure."

It was settled as easily as that, though Savina doubted that William Barker was enthusiastic about the adventure of it all, as Lord Gaston-Reade claimed to be.

The next day, though, dawned cloudy, and the earl deemed it too possible that a tropical storm would overtake their island refuge. They were in an uncertain time of year, when storms of vicious proportions could sweep through at a moment's notice. The next day, too, was thought to bring storms, though it was calm with only some gray clouds on the horizon. Savina wondered if Gaston-Reade was fearful, and perhaps not as certain as he pretended that he knew how to get to safety. She had hoped that his confidence was backed by a solid foundation of knowledge, but it seemed to her that he was delaying doing what he had so buoyantly planned.

The third morning she strolled down to the beach, thinking that she would help the indefatigable Lady Venture with the signal fire. The woman had not had much of a break, except to sleep at night, and she was becoming brown, drawn and tired looking, her bony face haggard, her sturdy frame gaunt, her prominent eyes bloodshot and wild. Savina, with an armful of green wood and bunches of leaves, was descending the sloped beach as the earl, Mr. Barker and her father again stood looking at the raft as if it would miraculously sprout wings and fly them to a safe place. Tony, now recovered completely from his strained ankle, was diving off the other rock promontory to spear fish for their dinner, and Zazu and Annie were still back at the encampment cleaning up.

Savina envied Tony his task that morning. She had learned to swim, much to her own surprise, and though she wasn't as proficient as Tony, she had managed to spear a fish on her tenth or eleventh try. Swimming under the water was the real joy, though, seeing a different world under the surface of the water, a world that teemed with life and vivid color, a world that swirled and moved and swayed to forces they didn't even notice above the surface. She and Zazu had shared the adventure privately, stripping off the heaviest of clothes so they could swim relatively unfettered in their chemises. She always paid for her underwater adventures with red, sore eyes the rest of the day, but it was worth it.

Though she longed for civilization for the creature comforts it had to offer—the deprivation was harsh and they were all losing weight and becoming drawn—she knew she would miss much of their life on the island for what she had discovered about herself, and would have to deny once she was constrained again by stays and societal expectations. The calm and prim demeanor she had assumed for her life in society was just a mask, and had so little to do with what was really inside of her; going back to that behavior would be arduous.

She looked up at Venture, who stood on the edge of the rock promontory, her eyes shaded, looking out to the horizon. Even she had lapsed some, her fastidious hairstyles a tangled mat brittle from the constant exposure to the sea breeze and sun. Venture stiffened that very instant and cried out, waving her arms, and for a horrible moment Savina thought she was going to fall from the edge to the dashing waves below, but then she turned, and called out to the rest of them, her words incoherent in the stiff breeze.

Turning back to the sea, the woman waved her arms and hopped up and down in a mad dance, and Savina, frozen, watched in confusion. She glanced down the beach at the men, and they appeared bewildered too, but then she looked up and Tony was standing, stiff and watchful, on the other rock promontory that framed the scythe of white sand. He shouted out and pointed to the horizon.

Finally Savina got the pantomime and raced the rest of the way along the beach, stumbling and losing precious leaves in the process. With one free hand she climbed the rocky outcropping and scaled the treacherous length to the signal fire.

Breathless, she approached Lady Venture. "Is . . . is it . . ."

"A ship! A ship, there, on the horizon!"

Savina strained her eyes, could see nothing, but then followed the line of Venture's outstretched arm and saw, glory of glories, distant white sails against the azure of the skyline. Feverishly, she fed the fire with the green banana leaves and palm fronds, trying to get the smoke going. In her haste she almost smothered the fire and fell to her knees, weeping and blowing at the tiny flame left, trying to get the greens to catch. She kept looking over her shoulder, but lost sight of the boat.

She stood. "Where is it?"

Lady Venture slumped in defeat. "It's gone. They didn't see us." She turned on Savina, fists clenched. "You were so slow! You just . . . just . . ." She fell to her knees and covered her face, wailing and knuckling her eyes with her grimy fists. "I can't do this anymore, I can't!"

Finally, the greenery caught and billowing puffs of smoke floated to the sky . . . too late. "Venture, I'm sorry," Savina said, patting her back, trying in vain to calm the hysterical woman. "I didn't know what was going on at first, and then the leaves wouldn't catch. I'm sorry."

Tony watched, incredulous, as the boat disappeared, slipping back over the horizon. No. It could not happen thus. He climbed down the rocky outcropping and pelted across the sandy beach. "My lord," he yelled, to the earl, "We can't let this happen. Why don't we use the raft . . . row out and try to get in sight of the damned thing."

Lord Gaston-Reade stared at him for a long minute, and Tony thought, given their recent strained relationship, the earl might refuse just to teach his underling a lesson. William Barker and Mr. Roxeter stared, their gaze shifting back and forth between the two men.

Finally, the earl said, "Let's do it." He leaped into action, grasping one of the rope handles he and the other men had looped around the palm logs. "Come on, Tony, help me drag the *Hopeful* to the sea."

As he and his employer did so, Tony caught Savina's eye as she held Lady Venture's shoulders. It looked like the older of the two women was having a breakdown of sorts. "Savina," he hollered. "Keep the fire going! Smoke. Lots of smoke! We're going to row out to try to catch their attention. Don't give up!"

She got his intent immediately and shook Lady Venture into awareness. The two women set to work fanning the flame into a roaring, smoky blaze.

It was possibly a forlorn hope, Tony thought, as he entered the water with the earl, dragging the *Hopeful*, as the raft had been christened. Both men jumped aboard and, using the crude paddles the earl's crew had fashioned, they paddled out, trying to catch a current.

The sun broiled down. Tony could see the puffs of smoke from the fire, but they dwindled in importance as distance was achieved, and he feared they could look just like puffs of dark cloud. He and the earl did what they had to do in grim silence, neither disposed to idle chatter and each bending all of his effort to the task at hand, despite the choppy waves and riffle of wind over the surface that threatened to capsize them every moment. It was in that moment that Tony remembered the things that he did respect about the earl: his industrious nature, his ability to grasp the importance of some things quickly, and his occasional capacity for rising above petty conflicts.

It didn't change his own feelings about the earl's inadequacies, but just at that second he was happy Lord Gaston-Reade was the other man on the raft with him and not William Barker. For the craft was becoming waterlogged and sinking below the surface, the effect hastened by their combined weight and vigorous movement. He was sure the earl had noticed it too, but he was not one to panic, nor would he need the obvious pointed out to him. Both of their knees were in water now, and soon their thighs would be, too, the salt water lapping at him, beckoning him to sink into the dark depths. If they didn't find the ship they would surely go under, and it was a long swim back to shore. He would make it, but would the earl? Would he be able to help him that long distance? He resolved then and there that he would do it or die in the attempt.

Where was that damned ship? He searched the horizon feverishly as he stroked and paddled. Had they imagined it? Was it even an English vessel or would it turn out to be an American ship, or worse, a French naval craft?

And then, like the Flying Dutchman, it was there, ahead, white sails billowing in the wind.

"Do you see a flag, sir? I can't tell what colors it is flying yet."

"I don't know," the earl said feverishly, digging his paddle into the riffled surface and pushing. "Right now I would even welcome your damned American."

"He is not *my* American," Tony said, through gritted teeth. "Hallo!" he shouted, though the ship was too far away for them to be able to hear. "Let's shout together," he suggested.

They paddled with all their might, the cold water rising to their thighs and every movement swamping the surface more. Both shouted, and they took turns waving their arms. Finally Tony saw a flash of glitter, the reflection of the sun off some glass, and he could make out someone up in the crow's nest.

He wanted to weep with relief when it became clear that someone had spotted them. He would not die in the black depth beneath them. Even if he perished in a French prison, it would be better than the slow horror of drowning, and it was humbling to realize how much he feared that.

Now, at least, they would be alive.

Savina, on shore with the others, saw the raft disappear and felt a pit of terror in her stomach. Her fiancé and the man she loved had gone out of sight. The others had rallied now, and Zazu, drawn to the beach by the shouting of the others, had orchestrated a relay of greenery to keep the smoky fire going.

Mr. William Barker, with the other two men absent, took command in a surprising show of leadership, and so Savina had time to think, not especially a good thing when her mind took a turn toward fatalism, something she had never allowed herself to succumb to before. Now, when hope should be highest, she was sure something would go wrong, and she could only pray it was not something lethal for the earl and Tony.

But as she stared off to the horizon she thought she saw a speck; she was afraid to raise a hope among the others if it was only to be dashed when it turned out to be her sun-dazzled vision. No, it was something. It was getting closer and larger.

"Hey. Hey!" She batted at Annie, who was closest. "I see something, it's . . ." She jumped up and down on the sand. "It's a rowboat! With men rowing! A dozen men!"

The others stopped and gazed out, and reacted in their various ways. Savina's father fell to his knees in the sand and wept, muttering prayers in a high-pitched wailing. Lady Venture stood staring, as if she was afraid to believe, silent tears streaming down her sunburnt face. Zazu came to stand beside Savina and they wrapped their arms around each other, and to Savina's amazement, so did Mr. Barker and Annie. He held the little maid close to him in jubilation at the rescue, and kissed her forehead. How oddly such an event affected them, she thought, glancing around at her castaway companions.

And she felt a pang of sorrow shoot through her breast. She would never again be here. Once she left, she thought, glancing back at the long sward of beach rising to the palm forest behind them, she would never again live like this, and all the hardships and discoveries and self-knowledge would fade into a distant memory.

They all stood silent as the sturdy rowboat beached and a uniformed man jumped from the prow and strode up the beach to them.

"Captain Henry Pollinger, his Majesty's navy, at your service, ladies and gentlemen. I've come to take you home to England."

Fifteen

The ship *Phoenix*, so named because it had suffered a fire in the shipyard when it was being built, but had arisen from the flames, was headed for England from Jamaica with some military families and others on board when it received word, through a long chain of circumstances, of the marooned party on the remote cay.

This Savina learned later, but as she was ferried out to the ship by rowboat, her thoughts were a wild tumble, and at first were mingled as much with regret for what she was losing as anticipation of what she was about to experience. The curious glances of the seamen who rowed she could understand; if she looked anything like Venture, whose wild hair, coal-smudged face and dirty, tattered clothing bespoke a sojourn of terrible suffering, then their stares held a mingled mixture of horror and pity. She resolved to ignore them as best she could. As they approached the ship, she and her fellow passengers silent and awestruck, she began to think of food and safety and comfort, and perhaps sleeping for a full day in a soft bed.

And yet her ordeal was not over.

Each one of them was raised in a rope chair, first Venture, who would allow no one else to go first, then Annie, and then herself. It was such a long way up; the journey seemed to take forever, and near the top she looked back and could see, etched against the blue of the ocean, the crescent beach of their island and the dark promontories. She said good-bye silently, and knew that her life would never be the same for having lived there.

Tears welled in her eyes and streamed down her cheeks, she didn't know why. She banged against the wood hull, the ropes creaking around her as she clung to them, quivering. Then, as strong hands reached down and caught her under her arms and drew her over the wide railing, she stared wildly, finding her every move watched by what seemed a throng of many fine ladies and gentlemen, all dressed in pale silks, expensive wool and gorgeous merino cloaks, who crowded the railing to watch the proceedings. They gaped at her as if she was an exhibit in a zoo.

Her limbs trembling from the long and fearful journey out to the ship by rowboat, and then the frightening ascent up the side of the ship by the perilous rope chair, Savina, set gently down on the deck by a compassionate seaman, stumbled and fell to her hands and knees on the deck. It was no good, her legs would not steady, and she had to sit for a moment, unable to rise.

One young lady in blue watered silk and with a parasol held over her by a maid whispered—though her high-pitched voice carried to Savina on the wind—to a beau at her side, "She looks quite wild, doesn't she, so brown and coarse and dirty, with her hair everywhere. And her dress is ripped! One has to wonder to what shocking practices they devolved in the time they were on that dreadful island."

"She looks quite untamed," the young man agreed. He held a handkerchief up to his nose. "Hasn't bathed in some time, probably."

The young lady laughed. Raised to her feet by a kindly seaman, Savina turned her gaze on the pair and stared at them, rage building in her heart at those who would taint the moment with their hateful malice.

"She appears savage, doesn't she? And she is baring her teeth at me," the young lady cried, falling back against the slender young man in a mockery of fear. "A lady savage. How amusing. I shall write that in my journal tonight."

"Write also," Savina said, before being led away, "that you have sunk to new depths of rudeness." Nervous tittering greeted her rejoinder as she allowed herself to be led to the hatch and taken below deck.

The next hours passed as if in a dream. She and Zazu ate with the others—toast with butter and marmalade tasted like manna to Savina—and drank hot tea with lemon and real sugar. Then they bathed; steaming, clean, lavender-scented water was supplied by two seamen directed by the captain's wife, a stout, motherly woman who took Savina and Zazu under her wing, scrubbing them as if they were her own helpless chicks. It was clear they could not put their ragged apparel back on, but Mrs. Pollinger bullied some of the passengers into giving up a few dresses for the castaway ladies.

Once they were presentable Henry Pollinger, the captain, welcomed them formally, in his teak-paneled rooms. "I thought," he said, "that we would hold a service of thanksgiving."

"That would be most appropriate," Savina's father said, at his diplomatic best once again now that he was wearing a handsome suit of borrowed clothes and his lined, sunburnt face was properly shaved.

"And a memorial service," the captain added.

"Memorial service?" Savina said, adjusting her stays, which felt most uncomfortable after weeks without them. She was much thinner than she had been, but the clothes were from one of the very slim young ladies aboard, and so were small and tight-fitting.

The bluff sea captain, his cheeks red in the candle-lit, low-ceilinged room, said, with a glance at his wife who stood at his side, "For the captain and crew of the *Prosperous,* surely, miss."

"What happened to the crew of the *Prosperous*?" Tony asked.

The captain cleared his throat and colored a deeper shade of crimson. "Forgot. You couldn't possibly know, could you? Hate to be the bearer of sad tidings, but . . . *Prosperous* went down in a hurricane, off Cuba. All hands—British, American, all of 'em—lost."

There was a profound silence. Weary and confused, Savina felt her vision blur, but it took a moment to realize it was tears. All those lives lost, and even the American captain who had been kinder than he had to be.

"If you had all been aboard," Captain Pollinger continued, his round face set in a grim expression, "you would be at the bottom of the sea now. Lucky that American captain marooned you all, or you would have gone down with them. We ought, I think, to give thanks that he was a man of his word and sent a message to the Jamaican office about you folks and about where you were stranded before meeting his untimely end. I'd like to pray for our British lads aboard, but I'd like to include a prayer even for the Americans, if you don't mind."

Savina felt all the eyes of her friends and family on her. She experienced a moment of dizziness and was afraid of fainting, but her vision cleared after a long moment and her tears dried. They were alive. Zazu's hand sought hers and gave her strength with its warm clasp.

"You saved all our lives with your decision," Zazu whispered in her ear.

"And you saved all of our lives with your knowledge,"

Savina said, refusing to take so much credit. "We all worked together, despite . . . despite our problems."

"I certainly think we ought to include the American captain in our prayers," Lord Gaston-Reade said, his face a mask of studied calm.

He glanced over at Savina, and she hoped he was thinking of all the disparaging things he had said about her decision to maroon them.

"And my valet," he went on, "Douglas O'Connell, who was among those poor men who went down."

"And poor Arthur, my own valet," Savina's father said, his voice trembling with sadness.

After the captain's private words with them, others trooped in and stood. The memorial service was attended by all available hands—the men were too aware of the danger of life aboard a ship to shirk their duties to the Lord on such an occasion—and by all the passengers, so the low-ceilinged room was crowded. Though the young lady and gentleman who had been so contemptuous of Savina were there, along one side of the room, their behavior was tempered by the presence of their families; they stood some distance apart from each other and only cast flirtatious glances to each other when the prayers allowed them to raise their eyes. Besides them there was one stout woman in mourning and her brood of six children returning to England after the death of their father from fever, a naval wife and her daughter, who was a pretty girl of about seventeen, and two other young men in their early twenties who were acquaintances of Savina's father.

Savina took it all in, her hand still clasped in Zazu's. She should be joyous, she thought, but her emotion was closer to melancholy. Perhaps that was appropriate, she thought, as the captain read the words of the service for those lost at sea. Joy would come later. At that moment she was overcome by an unutterable weariness of body and spirit.

For a few days Savina stayed in the tiny cabin assigned to her and Zazu, sick from the change in diet and water and the motion of the boat. She had never been so before and was distressed, finding it odd that the entire time on the island, with crude food, awful living conditions and fear as her daily companion, that she should only get truly sick, retching and feverish, when rescued.

But finally she and Zazu did venture above board and found the world a changed place. They had left behind the string of cays and the warm Caribbean sea and were speeding on their way to England, courtesy of the prevailing winds and the Gulf Stream, a handy flow of Atlantic water that carried ships faster home than out.

She clung to Zazu as they approached the railing, wending their way through ropes and barrels and bustling seamen, and felt her stomach flutter. Sails flapped above them, ropes creaked and the stiff breeze sang through them like fingers plucking harp strings; it was a cold song of the harsh life on board. Zazu was unnerved. Her whole body trembled and for the first time Savina understood her fears. Strangely, life felt within grasp on the island. Though natural disasters would occur, much could be avoided with careful planning and hard work. Clean water, shelter and food were the daily obsessions, and hard work could procure them.

"We're safe, Zazu," she muttered to her friend.

"As safe as the crew of the *Prosperous*?" Zazu said, scanning the horizon, her brown eyes wide.

Savina had no reply. Perhaps in life there was no assurance of safety. All of life was a gamble and a risk.

Tony Heywood climbed from the hatch and approached them as they stood near the railing gazing out over the sea. "Good morning, ladies; it's so good to see you above deck. Are you both well?"

"Well enough." Staring at him hungrily, Savina suddenly had a strong sense of the differences in her life heretofore, and her life as it had become on their tiny cay. Though her life in Jamaica had seemed free and easy to her at the time, she was still pampered, guarded, constricted and watched. On the cay she had been forced to fend for herself, to live and work alongside the others, and especially Tony, with no chaperoning. She could see now that her naiveté was what had led her to say yes to Lord Gaston-Reade's uninspiring proposal; others told her that was how it was done, and she had, as an obedient daughter and young lady, acquiesced. It had pleased her father and promised to provide a luxurious life for herself, free from worry. That her emotions were untouched had not occurred to her as a problem until she had been confronted by the fact that she had fallen in love with Tony Heywood.

She gazed at him and he stared back. He was brown and healthy looking, already gaining back some lost weight. The secret of her attachment to him was known only to Zazu, who squeezed her arm.

"How . . . how are you, Tony?" Savina asked.

"I'm well. It's so good to see you . . . both of you. But if I could have a word with Savina?" he said, glancing over at Zazu.

Zazu released her hold on Savina's arm and was about to stroll away, but just then Lord Gaston-Reade himself sauntered across the deck in the company of the young gentleman and lady who had ridiculed her appearance the day of their rescue.

"Ah, and there she is now," he cried out, on spying her. "My fiancée, Miss Savina Roxeter, daughter of Mr. Peter Roxeter, you know, very highly placed diplomat in Jamaica. And that very brown fellow standing with

Miss Roxeter and her maid is Anthony Heywood, my invaluable secretary," he continued to the young fellow. "I would advise you to find just such a one as him when you assume your majority, Mr. Collins. Tony is a very clever fellow, and not above even serving duty as my valet—my poor valet, you know, went down on the *Prosperous*—when necessary . . . isn't that true?"

Savina glanced over at Tony, who had stiffened at his employer's approach. Tony bowed, and said, "You must all excuse me."

"Wait, Tony, why don't you take Zazu with you. I'll take care of Savina, you know." He turned to the young lady. "Zazu is Savina's maidservant. Not unusual in Jamaica to have a . . . well, a servant like her, you know. But you were just there, Miss Gable! You would know this."

"I was not there long, just to visit my father," the young lady said in mincing tones, her gaze skipping over Zazu and alighting on Savina. "My mother and I would not stay in such a place long, you know. As she says, it is all very well to make your money from the plantations, but one doesn't actually need to live there in such tropical dissoluteness."

"Quite right, Miss Gable, and so I was telling my fiancée as we set sail for England."

"I don't think the air suits me above deck," Savina said, turning to retreat, noticing that Tony had slipped away and disappeared. "I shall return to my room." She took Zazu's arm.

"Wait, Savina," the earl said. He took her arm and led her aside, back to the railing. "You are giving the most peculiar impression, and I will not have it," he whispered, his tone fierce and harsh. "You looked very odd as you were brought on deck, Miss Gable says, almost wild. And if you do not stay, chat, and make friends, she will not have the opportunity to change her mind about you."

"I don't care," Savina said, pulling her arm from the earl's grasp and glaring up into his wintry eyes. "She is a rude girl, and so is the young gentleman rude. I can't imagine why you would be concerned in the least about their impression of me."

"I care because Miss Gable is a gossip, as is her mother." Lord Gaston-Reade looked past Savina with a tight smile on his face. "Once we are back in London I will not have your name bandied about. It is common, and will not do."

"I suggest, my lord, that you have never seemed comfortable with me as I am," Savina said, with as much dignity as she could muster. She clung to the railing, refusing to look down into the churning water below them. "If you wish to remake me in some pattern of simpering perfection, it would be simpler just to find a girl who already conforms. Perhaps one like Miss Gable."

"I have already announced you as my intended," Lord Gaston-Reade said, trying to take her arm again. "Word was sent back to the London papers, and we have spent a month together on a deserted island . . ."

"With six others," Savina retorted, pulling her arm away from his gloved hand.

"It matters not! No Gaston-Reade has ever had a hint of scandal attached to his name, and I will not be the first."

"Far better, then, to disavow me now, for I will not be a comfortable wife for you. You must know that by now." She was exasperated by his stubbornness, and thought that was the beginning and end of his insistence on marrying her; he had asked, she had accepted, and that was that. To change his mind would mean admitting he had been wrong.

He gazed steadily at her, the ocean wind ruffling his dark hair and lifting the carefully combed locks. They were interrupted by the arrival of Lady Venture, who was in the company of two of the matrons on board, both wide-eyed as she regaled them with stories of island life.

"... and I am so afraid my complexion is ruined forever!" she exclaimed, patting her face with one gloved hand. They joined Miss Gable and Mr. Collins. "I was intolerably sunburnt, but you know, if it had not been for my efforts, we would never have been rescued. I was the one who suggested that if we expected to be rescued, we needed to make a signal fire. I became the *mistress of the flame* as they all insisted on calling me!" She gazed off toward the horizon and smiled, the wistful, brave smile of martyrdom.

Savina sighed. She would not be the one to correct Lady Venture's story. At least a part of it was true; she had proven an admirable flame-keeper and if she had not been so dogged in her role they may not have been rescued in so timely a manner, for as they had learned, the lookout on the *Prosperous* had indeed seen the dark puffs of smoke and thought to investigate the source.

"I'm feeling ill again. I think I'll return to my quarters," Savina said aloud. She took Zazu's arm, and they returned to belowdecks.

"He simply refuses to believe I am calling off our engagement," Savina muttered to Zazu, as they descended and turned toward the passenger quarters.

"It's odd, isn't it? He is most adamant."

Negotiating the narrow hallways in the dimness was not easy, and they took a wrong turn. Like a bird flushed from a covert, Annie, Lady Venture's maid, erupted from an alcove, her pretty face pink and confused. She curtseyed, and bustled by them with a rustle of her borrowed skirts.

"I wonder what ..."

As they turned a corner, they came upon Mr.

William Barker examining the brass fittings of a lantern.

"Ah, ladies," he said, turning, his hands clasped behind his back. "How . . . how pleasant to stroll about knowing we are sailing ever closer to our home port, is it not?"

"I suppose," Savina said, thinking how odd it was that he was walking belowdecks when his fiancée was above. "Excuse us, sir. We are returning to our cabin." She paused and offered, "Lady Venture is on board, if you and Annie were looking for her."

"Ah, just so. Yes, just so," he said. "Thank you for that invaluable information," he said, and bowed, then passed them. "I shall find her directly."

Savina watched him go; he disappeared down the dim corridor, and she turned to Zazu. "I think I know enough of men and women now to know that he was not looking for Lady Venture."

"Very true," Zazu said, gazing down the passage after him. "The lady is in for a nasty surprise one day, if she keeps Annie as her maidservant."

"You don't suppose he's forcing the poor girl into an intrigue, do you?"

"No," Zazu said, with a dry tone. "I rather imagine *she* was the one who began the flirtation."

"Oh." Savina considered it, but it still mystified her, since it seemed an affair with no honorable or reasonable end. "To what end?"

Zazu shrugged. "Many a woman has used her charm on a man for the gifts he can bestow. Or, perhaps she genuinely likes him."

"Mr. Barker?"

Dryly, Zazu replied, "Better him than a third footman in Lord Gaston-Reade's household, I suppose."

"I see what you mean," Savina said, looking down the corridor thoughtfully. "I do see what you mean."

Savina spent most of her time with her father and

Zazu, after that. Tony seemed to be avoiding her anyway, and she was confused and uncertain about everything concerning him and her feelings toward him. The trip seemed long, but it was actually very speedy, and one gray, breezy, chilly morning early in November, with the mist like a shroud over the city, they made port in Bristol and from there hired a few carriages to take the two-day drive to London.

It had been almost ten years, Savina thought, gazing out the window and shivering as they entered London and her father eagerly chattered on about the house he had leased—knowing he was retiring and returning to England he had made elaborate plans many months ago by mail—and all the old friends he hoped to see. But for her, all her friends and plans and dreams had been left behind in sunny Jamaica. London wasn't home, to her; Spanish Town was more her home. And for Zazu it must be even worse, she thought, glancing over at her maid, who solemnly gazed out the window taking in her first sight of the city. She hadn't complained, but did appear to grimly accept her fate as one taking a tumbrel ride to the guillotine.

It had been a dreadful mistake to come back to England, Savina feared. But what choice did a young woman have, hemmed in by social obligations and strictures, condemned to lead the life her father, and then her husband, said she should? Life was simpler on their deserted cay.

She gazed out as they pulled up to their gloomy, gray limestone house in what her father was saying was a good section of London, very near Mayfair, and with a park just opposite.

"There are bars on the windows," Savina exclaimed.

"Well, all kinds of rogues around, you know," her father said. "Just a precaution, I'm sure."

"But is it to keep the rogues out, or us in?" she asked.

Zazu chuckled, but it was a grim sound in the gray day's dim light.

Sixteen

Savina despised their London house. It was gloomy, labyrinthine and cold; the chill settled into her bones and made her miserable most days. Although she did her best to conceal her feelings, not wanting to dampen the joy of her father's homecoming, he sensed her distress and offered to find a house to lease in the country. But she knew she needed to stay in London, and so she stared out at the gray city beyond her window and mourned the loss of her life in Jamaica. It was as if, she thought, gazing out on the gloomy sky clouded by smoke from thousands of coal fires, her spirit was being faded by the dreariness of each successive day.

She was beginning to understand how fundamentally different she and her father were from each other. He was enjoying their return to London, and the dismal weather only seemed to revivify him. Where tropical heat and constant sunshine had made him irritable, rain, sleet and frost made him rub his hands with glee and claim there was nothing like a proper coal fire and good old-fashioned English cooking to make a man feel young again. The notoriety of having survived a marooning on an exotic tropical island at the hands of the American navy had transformed him into a dinner guest much sought-after in his circle of old acquaintances, and even introduced him to a more lofty class of society. Far from melting into obscurity, as he had thought he would do after retiring from public service, he was now a personage of great importance.

Savina observed his enjoyment of his fame and though she did not understand it, she appreciated it for his sake. For herself, she despised the whispers, the pointing and the invitations that came only because she was "Lady Savage." That silly title was Miss Gable's doing. The earl had correctly identified her as a gossip, and so the name had been whispered from her lips to every person of her vast acquaintance; a gossip-starved London had taken up the appellation. Her fame had grown to the point that she could not go anywhere without being accosted and told all about her own story. Among the more serious-minded the turn of the war was the topic of interest, but among those with lighter tastes, Lady Savage was the rage.

Many were kind and congratulated her on her remarkable recovery from the feral state, for she had, they assured her with serious expressions, been unable to walk upright the day of her rescue and had crouched on the deck of the *Phoenix* grunting and pawing at the boards. Her dress had been ripped to reveal much of her bosom and all of her legs, they said, and her eyes had been bloodshot and wild. She had been as brown as her Jamaican maidservant.

She would have enjoyed obscurity, for there was much she needed to sort out. There were things she should have done immediately, first among them demanding a private meeting with the earl to ask that he release her from their engagement. But Gaston-Reade was her only conduit to Tony. It hadn't taken her long to realize how constricted her life was to be in London; it would be impossible to see Tony Heywood once her ties were broken with the earl. A young lady risked every shred of her reputation if it got about that she had corresponded with a young man, or had arranged a meeting with him. If she didn't care about that fragile reputation for her own sake, then she had to care for her father's dignity.

So she was still, in the eyes of society, engaged to Lord Gaston-Reade, and he insisted that as his fiancée she must be seen at all the proper events; though London society was very thin there were still balls and dinner parties, and he escorted her everywhere. She tried to pull back. She knew she was doing wrong by continuing the sham of an engagement, but she couldn't think how to right things and didn't dare to reject the earl until she had spoken to Tony. She should have taken advantage of their time on board ship to talk to him, but there was always someone about in such close quarters; she had mistakenly thought things would be simpler once they got to London. It showed how ill-prepared she was for life in the metropolis that she could have thought so.

What she wanted from the secretary she did not know. Did he love her as she loved him, fervently and completely, or had it been tropical madness, induced by the sun and heat and the relentless fear they had suffered? What was there for them anyway, in a world where wealth—or at least a competence—was needed before marriage could even be considered?

She didn't have any answers, but still, there were things between them left unsaid. Ten minutes alone with him would have sufficed, if she could have counted on her own courage to pour her heart out and expose all the raw emotions she was suffering. Her fear was that she would look an idiot, feeling everything while he felt nothing. She had no encouragement from him. Although she had been to the earl's London home three times with her father and had seen Tony twice, so far, that was only in passing. Surely if he cared for her he would have tried to see her? She had thought he might even love her, after the many instances of tenderness between them, but if he cared he didn't deign to show it; he merely bowed to her remotely and wished her a good day when they had chanced to meet, though she stared at him and tried to show him with her expression that she needed to talk to him privately. That coolness left her more confused and sad than even the grim weather and almost as much as Zazu's unhappiness.

On that front she had made up her own mind. Zazu must return to Jamaica; the poor girl was fading, her vivacity dampened, her inner light extinguished. Savina vowed to canvass every friend and acquaintance she had back in Jamaica to see if there was a position among them that would allow Zazu and Nelson to wed. She didn't know if Zazu would agree to go back, and it would be like tearing her own limb off to see her go, but she loved her friend and couldn't bear to see the sadness in her warm, brown eyes. The grand plans she and Zazu had, of seeing Florence and Rome, of traveling and exploring the world, had died with Savina's decision not to wed Lord Gaston-Reade—though given the earl's disposition, they likely had little chance of seeing fruition anyway—and she grew certain that the chill austerity of a servant's life in England would destroy Zazu's spirit. It would not do. Perhaps love was a stronger force than she had judged it to be and was worth making some sacrifices for.

Late November brought Lord Gaston-Reade's thirtieth birthday, and it was to be celebrated with a dinner party at his London home. Zazu, who had accompanied her—her father was suffering a cold and wished to stay home by his fire with a close friend to comfort him—helped her out of her cloak, necessary as London's chilly fogs closed in. Savina glanced about at the room of the earl's London home set aside for the ladies' comfort during the evening, and shivered.

"I hate this house," she said, gazing around at the dark-paneled walls and ornate fireplace. "It's so gloomy. I don't think I could ever bear to live here."

With a throaty, humorless chuckle Zazu replied, "You will be mistress of it soon enough, and then you can tear it down."

"Even if I still planned to marry Albert I couldn't destroy this old pile. It is, as his lordship calls it, a 'gem' in the string of jewels of Mayfair." She turned, allowing Zazu to right her twisted sleeve, and said, "You *know* I'm not going to marry him; I can't, not feeling as I do. It's just . . . how do I get him to believe me? And how do I do it—jilt him—now that he has announced to everyone I am his fiancée? I don't wish to hurt his feelings, nor do I want to cause a scandal of any kind." She sighed, heavily. "And you know I have another reason. I must speak to Tony once more before I end my engagement."

A couple of ladies entered the withdrawing room with their maidservants, and they collected in a tight knot on the far side, near the windows, whispering and pointing at Zazu and Savina.

"Pardon me," one of the young ladies said, approaching but still keeping a safe distance. She nervously smoothed the pale lavender fabric of her dress skirt down. "But you are the earl's fiancée, the one they call Lady Savage, are you not?"

Savina sighed. "I am that unfortunate creature," she admitted to the young lady before her, derision heavy in her voice for anyone perspicacious enough to take note of it. There was no danger of that in the present company.

"I told you she was," she said, over her shoulder to the other girl, her friend. The girl threw another look over her shoulder, then leaned forward and whispered, eyes wide and gleaming with fascination, "We have heard that you all lived together on the island and behaved like natives. Is that true?"

Savina exchanged an exasperated look with Zazu.

Zazu took the hint and said, "Miss, if by behaving like natives you mean we survived awful weather, gathered fruit, fished for our meals and slept on the ground, then that is true enough."

"You can speak English," the girl cried, staring at Zazu and clasping her gloved hands to her thin bosom.

They were called, at that moment, to dinner and Savina reluctantly left Zazu behind. She learned, as they strolled through the corridors to the dining room, that the two young ladies were distant cousins of the earl's. Their rapid conversation was full of names Savina didn't recognize and topics of no interest to her, so she was not sorry when they were parted by the seating arrangement at dinner.

There were thirty people seated in the grand dining room of the earl's London home, but conspicuously absent was Mr. William Barker. Lady Venture, flanked on one side by an elderly uncle and on the other by a foppish cousin, looked bored and angry, eating a lot, drinking more, but not seeming to notice what. Savina endured sitting at the earl's right hand. After innumerable courses, many toasts, and far too many clever speeches—including one long one by the earl in which he thanked everyone but Savina for their rescue from the remote cay—the dinner was finally over.

In the drawing room the ladies sipped coffee and gossiped; Savina sat down next to Lady Venture on a hard Jacobean seat with a high back. She was going to make an effort, she promised herself. The earl's sister was difficult, managing, and hard to like, but she already knew the woman had some admirable characteristics. Even though Savina did not intend to marry her brother, it surely was worthwhile to cultivate the friendship.

And there was not another single person in the drawing room she felt she knew well enough to sit down with. That was the true charm of Lady Venture's company this night, she admitted to herself, ever willing to be ruthlessly honest.

"Lady Venture, where is Mr. William Barker this evening?"

The woman turned a basilisk glare on Savina. "I hope he rots in hell," she slurred, "and his guts are plucked out piece by piece by ravening wolves."

One of the earl's cousins, seated quite near to them, gasped and tittered, then whispered to her friend. As shocked as she was by Lady Venture's wild manner, Savina still managed not to let her social face change. "Venture, what is it? What's wrong?" she murmured, leaning forward.

The other woman, her plain face set in a grimace that seemed an attempt to keep the tears from rolling down her cheeks, merely shook her head. She smelled strongly of wine, and perhaps more powerful spirits than even that. Her prominent eyes were bloodshot and red-rimmed. That, though, Savina surmised, was from tears and not spirits.

"Come to the lady's withdrawing room," Savina said, pulling the other lady's arm and forcing her out of her seat. She hustled Lady Venture away from the ill-mannered giggles of the other young ladies, and they moved to a sofa in the dim room where the ladies' maids stayed to tend to their mistresses. "Now, Venture, tell me, what is it?" she asked, as Zazu approached.

Lady Venture collapsed on the seat and moaned, "He's gone. William is gone!"

"Gone? Gone where?" Savina asked, sitting beside Venture and taking her cold hand and rubbing it.

"He is gone to hell, I hope," the woman growled.

Zazu offered a handkerchief, which the lady snatched and dabbed at her coursing tears. She took a deep breath and stiffened her frame.

"William Barker is a depraved animal. He has jilted me and absconded with my poor, sweet, innocent Annie. They have gone to Italy, his letter said, and have m-m-married!"

A torrent of tears followed this pronouncement, and Savina, with Zazu's help, did all she could to staunch them. Would it be better for Venture or worse, Savina wondered, if she knew that Annie was no innocent victim, but likely the instigator, and that the affair probably had its start in the informality of their island stay?

Not knowing the answer Savina stayed silent, preferring to tend to the lady and let her cry the inevitable tears of humiliation with a sympathetic audience. At least she would be of use to someone that evening. Instead of returning to the assembled company, Savina and Zazu helped Venture to her luxurious room in the family quarters of the house and found a maid to attend her in her misery. It was the least she could do, her conscience shrieked at her, considering that she had in mind to do much the same to Albert as William Barker had to Venture, if in a more straightforward manner.

Her goal that night of seeing Tony and talking to him for even a moment in private was doomed from the start, she had learned from Venture. He had apparently gone down to the earl's estate in the country for a couple of days to see to some estate business. He wouldn't be back until the next morning, or perhaps even a few days later. With no chance of achieving her main objective, seeing Tony in private, Savina left a message for Gaston-Reade that she was not feeling up to company that night and was returning to nurse her father, and she and Zazu departed.

Gossip about Lady Venture's misfortune spread rapidly through the thin winter society, and Lord Gaston-Reade, tense and angry at his sister—as unjust as it was, he perceived her as the initiator of the scandalous chatter—raged ineffectually at the unfairness of his ancestral name and title being dragged through the muck and filth. Listening to one of his lengthy tirades in the parlor of her and her father's leased home, Savina knew that the time had come. She was being unfair to him by keeping up the charade of an engagement when she had no plans to marry him, and her own motives—her need to sort out her feelings and see Tony one more time—were insufficient to carry on. She was being selfish. So, though there would never be a *good* time to break the engagement; she just had to do it.

Perhaps jilting Lord Gaston-Reade now would have one good consequence in easing Lady Venture's lot as a pariah among women by shifting attention to her brother. One would have thought Mr. Barker's scandalous elopement was something catching, the way affianced young ladies avoided the contamination of the lady's company. Though the earl would suffer in the short run by being the object of malicious gossip, Savina knew that being a man and an earl, his freedom from his colonial engagement would make him a much-sought-after personage, especially among those who had a daughter, granddaughter or niece unwed.

Her decision made, she had only to do the deed. But she did have one more thing to do before she was free to follow her conscience. She rose from her seat by the window and formally said good day to the earl, who stamped out of their rented house to go to his club; before she broke her engagement, she needed to tell the one person who would be most hurt by it.

"Papa?" she said, slipping into the parlor, where she thought her father was reading the morning paper.

"Savina!" Her father leaped up from the settee, his pouchy face red.

"Oh, Mrs. Beacom," Savina said, crossing the floor and extending her hand to her father's old friend, a frequent visitor at their town house.

That lady, a widow of hennaed and wobbly charm, burst into tears and snuffled into a handkerchief. She took Savina's hand and squeezed it so hard it began to go numb.

"What's wrong?" Savina cried, glancing from the seated lady over to her father, who paced by the fireplace. "Is there bad news?" She knew Mrs. Beacom's two sons were in the navy and feared the worst. Everyone was on edge and worried, it seemed to her. Negotiations to end the war were underway, but the outcome was uncertain.

"My dear," Savina's father said, approaching and putting his arm around her shoulders, "nothing is wrong; everything is quite wonderful in fact. Mrs. Beacom . . . uh, Maude, has agreed to be my wife! Isn't that the most marvelous thing?"

Taken aback and forced into a hug by the weeping widow, Savina was breathless, but soon concluded that this was the perfect time to break her own news. Any sadness or concern over it would be lost in the tumult, she hoped. "I'm so happy for you both, particularly you, Papa," she said with all sincerity.

Her father had long been lonely, and she had always feared he stayed single for her sake; he was a favorite among the widows of Jamaica for his courtly manners and sincere enjoyment of feminine company. He had always championed marriage as the ideal state, and indeed, Savina's mother was his second wife, his first having died after a happy, if childless, ten years of marriage. There were a couple of ladies in Jamaica that he had come close to marrying, but Savina had disliked both. Mrs. Beacom seemed a harmless, sentimental lady, and was a very old friend of her father's, so his third wife would be the joy and comfort of his declining years. This was her rapid conclusion. "But . . . Papa, I have some news of my own I must tell you. I hope it will not taint your own joy."

Mrs. Beacom's tears dried and she gazed at her soon-to-be stepdaughter with something like suspicion.

Savina took in a deep breath. "I cannot marry Lord Gaston-Reade," she said. "I am going to break our engagement."

Mrs. Beacom gasped and fainted dead away.

As she and her father tended to the insensible lady, she hardened her resolve. She had been intolerably vacillating until now and it was unfair to everyone, herself included. It was as if the London fogs had infiltrated her brain, clouding her normally sensible nature with self-doubt and fear. No more. She would make decisions about her future.

Mrs. Beacom recovered and sat with her feet up, sipping a restorative cup of tea as a handsome footman fanned her.

"Papa, you do understand, don't you?" Savina asked, pulling him away from his intended bride.

"No, I don't," he said, staring at her, his gray brows pulled down in puzzlement. His expression cleared. "But I don't have to, do I? You have always been your own girl, Savina. When your mother chose your name I warned her such an unusual choice would make you headstrong, but she didn't listen to me. You're very much like her, and will do what you want, I suppose. I was frankly surprised when you agreed to marry the earl and come back to England. I very much feared you would demand to stay in Jamaica."

She didn't answer that it was what she had really longed to do. "I wanted to make you happy."

"My dear, you can only do that by making yourself happy. That's all I've ever wanted," her father said, patting her shoulder. "His lordship seemed, to me, to be a very capable, kind-hearted fellow, and I knew you would find no better in London."

Savina sighed as her father went back to sit with Mrs. Beacom. The very next morning she was going to do the deed and break her engagement to Gaston-Reade. And try to see Tony. He was back in London now, she knew, from something Gaston-Reade had said, and would be at the earl's residence the next morning, with any luck at all.

Even with her mind made up on one point, she was still in the same quandary; did Tony think of her often? Was he as miserable as she? Did he even care, or had he forgotten their night together and the kisses that had revealed so much to her about her own feelings? If she found that his feelings were similar to her own, even though she knew they could do nothing about it—with no money on either side wedding would be folly—at least there would be something to hope for. Her resolve firm on one point, she went up to her room to write promised letters to friends in Jamaica.

Seventeen

Tony sat at a desk in the earl's library, sorting through a stack of letters that had piled up in the few days he had been down in the country for estate business. Some contained information, some inquiries about the plantation, and others held assorted business-related queries. The very mundane nature of the task allowed his mind a portion free to ponder his situation.

Life as he was living it was close to intolerable, and he couldn't take much more. He had made impulsive and sudden changes in position before when bored, but he was older now, and more cautious. That was the only explanation he could think of for why he had not already told the earl to stuff his sheaf of quill pens up his nose and departed.

Unless it was that he feared if he left the earl's employ he would never see Savina Roxeter again.

But Lord Gaston-Reade had used Tony's every waking minute, filling it with endless work; Tony had expected much of it. They had been away for seven months, after all, and there was a lot of estate business to catch up on. But he hadn't even had a moment free to see any of his friends yet.

Worse was the fact that he had barely seen Savina since arriving in England three weeks before, and when he did see her it was only for a moment in passing; he was so afraid of showing too much of his emotions that he had been forced to keep his greeting to a bow and a "good day." He hungered for a moment alone with her, but feared it would only lead to disappointment. It seemed to him that she had changed. She was now completely quiescent and agreeable to the mockery of an engagement the earl insisted was still valid. Perhaps in England she had seen how powerful and well-thought-of the earl was, and had become acquainted with the vastness of his holdings and the lofty elevation of his old Norman title. He had not thought her burdened by cupidity but the simple fact was, women needed to look out for themselves in a world where their worth was generally not calculated by any true measure, but relied on their own fragile beauty and the consequence of the man they could attract with it.

And even if she cared for him, as he had thought she did, she would not be the first woman to go into a marriage in love with another man. He hadn't thought her capable of it, but then, he only knew one side of her. Regardless of any of that, his own situation was becoming unendurable. Lord Gaston-Reade, still offended by Tony's behavior on the island, made him pay in small ways and constantly reminded him of his own possession of Savina Roxeter, as if he knew more than he ever admitted about their mutual attraction.

As Tony sat, trying to come to grips with the torturous nature of his life as it was, he heard voices in the parlor and crossed the room, entering by the sliding door between the two rooms.

"Savina," he said, staring at her, drinking in the delicious sight of her attired in a deep gold velvet cloak and petite hat. Her dark curls dusted her shoulders, brown ribbons from the hat cascading down the back and reminding him of her unbound hair on their island paradise.

She looked up, and Lady Venture, seated with her,

raised her eyebrows. "So, you call her by her Christian name? How . . . enlightening."

"We fell into the habit on the island," Savina said, her chin rising at the glittering challenge in the other lady's hard stare. "You must have noticed, Venture."

"I didn't. But then I was so very busy, you know, tending the fire that aided our rescuers. It seems," she said, archly, "that perhaps I should have paid more attention to what went on around me on the island." She rose, walked to the door, and passed by Tony, giving him a sly smile that looked more like a grimace. "Why don't I go and see if I have any mail yet?"

Tony kept his temper. Her recent disappointment had made the woman even more severe and captious. Though Lady Venture was being sarcastic, he had wished for this opportunity and would not waste it. She exited, he waited a second, then crossed the room and stood before Savina.

Though he had been acquainted with her as his employer's fiancée before they were marooned, it was on their little cay that he had really come to know her, and so this polished, poised, elegant young lady before him did not seem like Savina . . . *his* Savina.

"How have you been?" he asked, hearing the coolness in his own voice and hating it, but unsure of how to conduct himself given her own behavior of late.

"I've been very well, thank you. And you?"

He watched her face, but in her averted eyes and still demeanor there was no hint of the lively young woman he had come to know and adore during their month or so marooned. "I'm well." He sat down in a chair opposite her. "How kind of you to visit Lady Venture."

"I came to see Albert, really," she said, her eyes downcast. She fiddled with the string handle of her reticule and looked away to the window.

It couldn't be clearer to him that she regretted their previous association and wished to distance herself from it. Not only that, but judging from her current behavior, she was wishing him anywhere but with her. "I'm so sorry," he said, moved by his own needs to stay, even if she wished him gone, "that some in society are being unkind and calling you Lady Savage."

"It's despicable," she exclaimed, her tone low and trembling. "Simply awful. I am the center of attention wherever we go; you cannot imagine how awful that is. I wish . . . I wish so many things were different. I wish *I* had done many things differently."

He nodded. There could not be a clearer message to him that she wished to forget about their liaison and the passionate kisses they shared. Perhaps she was even afraid he would tell Lord Gaston-Reade about it. That thought became certainty, for it would explain her uneasiness in his presence. She probably longed to warn him to say nothing, but didn't know how. "I think you can safely trust that nothing that happened on that island will ever be spoken of again. It is all sealed and forgotten."

She looked up at him finally, but he could not make out her expression, which appeared to mingle consternation with doubt. "Truly? Is it all forgotten?" she exclaimed, her tone breathless.

He took in a deep, quivering breath. "Yes," he reassured her. "More than forgotten; it never existed."

"Oh." She looked down at the fur that lined her cloak and stroked it. "Oh. All right."

The door slid open and Lord Gaston-Reade strode in. Tony leaped up from his seat. The earl frowned.

"I understood you were with Vennie, Savina. What are you doing in here, Tony? Do you not have enough to occupy your time in the library? You should have told me; I can think of many more tasks for you. Until you find me another valet you should be at the very least ironing my cravats."

"Albert!" Savina said, coloring faintly.

It was enough. Being humiliated in front of the woman he loved after finding out she no longer cared for him was enough. Tony whirled on his heel and moved back into the library, but not to stay. No, not to stay. He sped into the hallway past Lady Venture and took the stairs two at a time up to his room.

Savina turned back from the door to the earl. "How could you be so unkind?" she asked. Even if she was feeling the full extent of a broken heart, it did not make her want to see Tony hurt. It had been her mistake, after all, not his, to think what they did the night they spent together in the cave, all of the kissing and sweet closeness, meant he might care for her. It was she who had allowed herself to fall into so precarious an emotion as love with no inkling of it being returned. "You seemed to deliberately wish to humiliate him."

The earl shrugged. "It is quite evident to me, Savina, that you think you care for Tony in some way, after the two of you made fools of yourselves on the island. That island did strange things," he said, his cheeks red and his voice harsh with anger. "Even William, whom I thought a sensible chap, has gone and done the unthinkable by marrying that little . . ." He broke off. "I will not offend you with the word I would have chosen."

"No, don't." Savina stood. His rude behavior had made what she now had to do easier, and there was no further reason to wait. She needn't ever come back to this house again, now that she knew Tony didn't care for her. "It has become clear to me, Albert, that the engagement we entered in Jamaica was based on a fallacious understanding of each other's character. We would make each other miserable and you would regret marrying me. I have been trying to tell you this for some time, but apparently subtlety will not do. I release you from our engagement, Lord Gaston-Reade."

She took a deep breath, feeling the freedom of her words and rejoicing in them. "I will inform the papers, just so people know you have not 'done the unthinkable' and jilted me."

"You cannot end our engagement!" the earl bellowed. "Everyone knows we are to be married. What will they say?"

"That you have had a fortunate escape." She moved to the door, but stopped and turned back to face the fuming and sputtering earl. "Give my best to Lady Venture. And tell her by jilting you, I hope that it takes some of the attention away from her own failed engagement."

"Savina! Savina Roxeter!" the earl hollered as she left the room, but she ignored him.

She met Zazu, who awaited her in the hall, and left.

Tony closed his traveling desk and folded the letter he had written. Glancing about the narrow room that had been his home for the three years he had worked for Lord Gaston-Reade, barring the time they had spent at the earl's plantation in Jamaica and the estate in Oxfordshire, he felt ready for the task at hand. There was nothing left for him there. It was time for his life to take a new direction. He picked up his greatcoat and opened the door. "Jem," he called out to the young stable lad sitting on a hard chair in the hallway, waiting there at his behest. He waved at his valise and said, "Take this bag down to the front hall for me, will you? And see if that stiff-rumped old butler will find a carriage for me."

The fair-haired lad darted into the room, hefting the bag easily for such a slender sprig. He hauled it out and headed for the back stairs, the servants' stairs.

Tony, his traveling desk under one arm, greatcoat over the other and hat in hand, descended the front staircase for the last time, pausing to gaze up at the portraits on the wall, each more grim and long-nosed than the last. They all bore an unfortunate resemblance to Lady Venture even more than Lord Gaston-Reade in their long hooked noses and prominent eyes. As he turned to descend the rest of the way, that lady was standing at the bottom of the stairs waiting for him.

"I have an idea that you are about to leave us, Mr. Heywood. Is that so?"

Her eyes glittered strangely in the dim hallway, and Tony wondered if she was drinking again, a habit she had taken to since William Barker's defection. He descended the last few steps and said, "Why do you ask, my lady?"

"I just was wondering." She caressed the balustrade and smiled hugely, her teeth bared.

He circled her warily, laid the desk on a table, placed his greatcoat and hat on top, and headed toward the library. "Is Lord Gaston-Reade still entertaining Miss Roxeter?"

"Oh, 'Miss Roxeter' is it now, and not 'Savina'?" She leaned against the balustrade and stared at him. "No. No, Savina has gone home, I do believe."

He watched the lady a moment, trying to decipher her odd behavior, but shook his head finally, at a loss. "Good. I will have a private conversation with his lordship, then."

"Do so," Lady Venture said with a giggle. "You do so, Mr. Tony Heywood." She danced away, humming a tune under her breath.

The woman was utterly unfathomable, far too much like the black depths of the sea to comprehend. In the first months of his employment as the earl's secretary, she had often cornered him and let him know, in terms far from uncertain, that if he chose to pay her court and dared to think he might climb to so elevated a position as her husband, he would be most welcome. He had soon disabused her of any notion that he would be so bold, and she had retreated with some resentment. Since then they had found an uneasy truce, but this behavior . . . he shook his head. Unfathomable. Tony took in a deep breath and entered the library, not sure if the earl would be there or in the parlor, but he found him at his large desk.

The earl looked up, his expression cross, his brows beetling over his humorless gray eyes. "Are you over your filthy temper yet, Tony?"

"*My* filthy temper? I think, sir, you have mistaken my behavior for your own."

His erstwhile employer glared at him. "You are treading the line, Tony . . . beware."

Tony strolled across the room and laid the letter in front of the earl. "That is my notice, and the direction where you may send my last quarter pay, minus, of course, the two weeks for lack of notice. I am leaving your employ, my lord, and I feel free now to tell you that though your good qualities are there, they are so buried under your haughty, arrogant, unpleasant manner and your conceit, that they pale in comparison." A weight lifted from him and Tony felt free. He took a deep breath and let it out in a long sigh.

The earl stood, his face red and his cheeks puffing in and out. "Now see here . . . you can't . . . I won't . . ." He babbled incoherently for a moment, then abruptly sat down. "Get out," he said, spittle flying from his mouth. "Get out of my home! And you can forget your pay. I won't give it to you."

"Then I will see your solicitor," Tony said, calm in the face of such vented spleen. Though Lord Gaston-Reade had nothing of which to complain, his irritable reaction was to be expected, given his disposition. "Mr. Hemmings is a most gracious and fair gentleman and will not see me without payment for work brilliantly done."

"Brilliantly done?" the earl leaned over his desk and glared at Tony. "What have you ever . . . just get out!"

With that Tony walked to the hallway, shrugged on his greatcoat, placed his hat on top of his head as he picked up his desk and exited, with the earl hurling imprecations after him and blustering that there would be no doors open when Tony looked for another position, for he would make sure every last man jack left in London would hear about such despicable, traitorous—

The rest was lost as Tony strode out the front door to find his bag on the step and a carriage waiting. The blustery wind cut into him and he pulled his greatcoat closer, but as he looked back up at the earl's gloomy town house, he felt deeply that he had done the right thing. He couldn't stay there any longer being humiliated by the earl in front of the only woman he could ever love, dwindling every day in her eyes into some buffoon of a man.

Savina paced and fussed for two days, not knowing what to do. Was she willing to live without Tony, or was there any possibility, even despite his cold behavior toward her, that his feelings could be reanimated and he could be made to feel again what she had thought he felt on the island? She didn't know. How could she? She'd never had any experience of mind-reading, and his reception of her certainly gave the impression of one who regretted his foolishness in the heat of the moment. And yet she loved him; what if he was her only love? What if this feeling, this wholehearted devotion to one man, was her only chance at happiness of that kind?

Even if she had the chance to make Tony feel again what he felt on the island, what different ending did she expect? She had only a modest dowry, not enough to keep them both, and he depended on his job for a living, a job he could not keep and marry her. There seemed no solution to her dilemma, and perhaps, if he had decided he didn't care for her, it was what he needed to feel to be able to go on with his job and his life.

Since she was now not going to be marrying the earl, Savina would be living with her father and his new wife in the rented house he had leased for an additional year, and if that lady had not seemed overjoyed at the prospect, Savina supposed she couldn't blame her soon-to-be stepmother for not wanting a grown daughter living with them.

On the third day, the day after her announcement of the broken engagement had been delivered to the paper, she was called in to the library by her father, who was sitting with his solicitor, papers spread all around them.

"Savina, dear, the most extraordinary thing," her father said, looking up over his magnifying glasses from a long paper he held in his hand. "Come in, sit down. You know Mr. Chandler, I suppose."

"No. How do you do, Mr. Chandler?" she said, crossing and taking his hand. She examined him with interest, noticing his bald head and red-veined cheeks. They had been in Jamaica so long that she had no memory of meeting Mr. Chandler, though she had heard his name often enough. He was solicitor for many in the family, and had some connection, she thought, to the maternal side. He had handled her father's affairs in England during his long absence in Jamaica.

The elderly man nodded. "How d'ye do, Miss Roxeter," he said, his tone business-like.

"What's going on, Papa?"

"Well, for one thing, it seems I am a wealthier man than I expected! Our Mr. Chandler, here, has invested my savings wisely, and we've a tidy sum to begin with, Maude and I."

"That's wonderful, Papa," Savina said.

"Ah, but there is more, young lady, and it concerns you," Mr. Chandler said. "This little item in your father's hands . . . have you ever heard tell of a lady by the name of Miss Lydia Ponceforth Harpington?"

Savina sat in the other chair across the desk from her father and next to Mr. Chandler. "No, I can't say that I . . . wait . . . mama's maiden name was Harpington."

"Yes," her father said. "Good girl. See, told you Chandler, quite sharp, she is."

"And I seem to remember . . . Papa," Savina continued, looking over to her father. "Is she not my aunt who gave you the money for my little coral cross?" She fingered the cross; it was her good luck charm, she had always felt, and had kept her safe even during their island adventure. Though she didn't *really* believe in such things, the cross had always given her comfort, and still did. "I seem to remember before we left for Jamaica . . . did she not come to see us?"

"She did," her father said, an encouraging smile on his face.

"She was very old, and our housekeeper said she was very rich." Savina looked back into the solicitor's eyes. "And she patted me on the head and said I was a fine girl. She said that she was my old aunty, and she hoped I would remember her when I was all grown up."

"Yes," the man said. "That would have been the lady herself; actually, Miss Lydia Ponceforth Harpington was your mother's aunt, your great-aunt. I was her solicitor, too, as I was for a great many of the older generation. All that grand old generation dying off now, sad to say." He shook his head and made a clicking sound between his yellowing teeth. "She left an extraordinary will when she expired earlier this year. All her possessions are bequeathed to one young lady in the family, and that young lady must have achieved her twenty-first birthday."

"Oh," Savina said. "I just turned twenty-one several weeks ago while we were stranded on the island. With all of the excitement I quite forgot about it myself until a week ago when I attended the earl's birthday celebration. It was a bit of a shock, but we were all occupied with other worries on the island, you know."

"Quite right. Well, she did not make the bequest known—for reasons that will be clear in one more moment—but it was for the first young woman in her family of your generation to achieve her twenty-first birthday unmarried. You have cousins," he said, looking at another paper and glancing down it, "but of them several are already married, or reached the age of twenty-one before Miss Harpington's passing, or have some years yet to go. Miss Harpington did not make her bequest known, for she did not want it to influence the young ladies' behavior, you see. It has become clear after exhaustive examination of the extant family, that you are the one." He looked up and into her eyes. "I do not approve of such conditional bequests, but then Miss Harpington was a very hard lady to cross, you know."

"What does it mean?" Savina asked.

The solicitor took off his glasses and polished them on a white linen cloth as Savina's father shifted in his chair.

"Come, Chandler, out with it," her father finally said. "What is it all about? What is the bequest?"

"In good time, Mr. Roxeter. As I was saying, she had something against early marriages for girls; she spouted some rubbishy nonsense about females not knowing their own mind 'til they turned that age. As if young ladies ever know their own mind until it is decided for them." He sniffed. "But that is neither here, nor there. The bequest is yours, Miss Roxeter."

"Oh," Savina said, not sure how to feel or what to think at such an unexpected turn of luck. It was quite like something out of a romance; the forlorn young maiden is bequeathed an old manor house and must go to see it, thereby placing herself into a perilous situation and meeting a brooding, dangerous man. If that was the case, she didn't think she would take the bequest. She had no taste for brooding, dangerous men and wouldn't want an old English manor house . . . far too expensive to keep up, she had always thought, if they were falling into ruins as they so often were in that kind of tale. But perhaps she could sell the house, the one possibility that never seemed open to the young ladies in the novels. "Is the legacy a house?" she asked, her curiosity piqued. She leaned over and tried to see the paper, but the solicitor snatched it from her father's hands.

"Oh, no, Miss Roxeter," Mr. Chandler said, pushing his glasses back up his nose. "It is money. Rather a lot."

He named a sum, and Savina, feeling faint, sat back in her chair. "And it is all mine?"

"Until you marry. Then it becomes your husband's of course." He shuffled the paper together with some other documents. "I will be your trustee until such a time as you decide what to do."

"Oh, but I already know what I'm going to do with the money," she said, in a most unromantic way. She should have fainted, or at least needed smelling salts, but the brief dizzy spell had passed quickly and she felt stronger than she had in weeks. With a happy sigh, she said, "I'm going back to Jamaica."

Eighteen

Tony, now resident of a dingy coffeehouse, bought a newspaper from the lad outside, then sat and ordered coffee from the landlord. He needed to find another position. He had already jotted down a list of names, his valuable contacts. He had gone many places with many people over the years since his sixteenth birthday. A personal secretary, he had decided when he was very young, was a much better position for a man of his desires than an estate agent or land steward. He liked to see places, not be mired in England, and he had been farther than most young men of his acquaintance. He had been to Canada, and had seen Persia and Greece and Italy, parts of the Orient and, finally, the West Indies.

Even if employment with the earl had not become intolerable due to the fatheaded idiot's treatment and his continuing engagement with Savina, Tony would have left. He wouldn't stay in cold, damp, dreary England, not after he had seen Jamaica. His goal now was to find work that would take him back there and allow him the opportunity to build his life in the one place he had found that offered everything he could want.

Almost everything he could want, he corrected himself. One chapter of his life was closed forever. Love was something he had thought was unnecessary for a man, but he had found that strange, feverish emotion came over one and once beset, a man was sometimes permanently changed. It was so with him, anyhow. If he had had money, or power, or prestige he would have fought for Savina Roxeter, but he could offer her nothing but penury. His pride would not allow him to beg for her love when he had nothing of any value to lay at her feet but his own heart.

If, one day after he made his fortune, she was still unmarried—unlikely given her engagement to Lord Gaston-Reade—then he would approach her, but she would probably refuse him anyway. He had no reason to think her as enamored of him as he was of her.

The landlord set a thick earthenware mug down in front of him and Tony took a deep gulp of scorching coffee to warm the freezing temperature of his own body after spending another night in his damp attic room, the cheapest in the house. He shook open the paper. He wanted the page where positions were listed, but the society page was first and a familiar name caught his eye. He read the piece once, twice, thrice. And then once more.

The meaning did not change. Miss Savina Roxeter had ended her engagement to Lord Gaston-Reade . . . of her own volition, it seemed, for it was simply a statement of the dissolving of the attachment. His heart thumped and hope blossomed, only to be squashed by common sense. Well, good for her. But it didn't change anything, did it? It just meant that she had come to her senses, and it left her free to find a man who could make her love him. And a man who could afford to marry.

A harsh but familiar voice pulled him from his reverie and he looked up to see Lady Venture at the doorway to the coffeehouse arguing with the landlord and waving a paper in front of his nose. Tony bolted from his chair and approached the embattled two as people tried to push past her.

"May I be of some assistance, Lady Venture?" Tony said.

"There you are," she said, with a harumph. She glared down her beaky nose at the landlord and said, her voice loud and her hand waving, "This idiot claimed you were not resident here, even though I saw your direction that you gave Bertie."

"Pardon, milady," the landlord said with a deep bow, "but you was askin' after a Mr. Hayward, an' this here gent is Mr. Heywood, y'see."

Tony smelled the spirits on the lady's breath, just as the unhappy landlord clearly had. He took Lady Venture's arm and guided her back to his table by the window, meeting the curious stares with a stony one of his own. Each coffeehouse resident turned his gaze back down to his paper. He sat her down and took the chair opposite her. "What is it, my lady? Is something wrong? Can I help you?" Though he and Lady Venture had never been more than casual acquaintances, he knew how badly William Barker's defection had hurt if not her heart, then her pride, and he felt for her.

"No, but p'raps I can help you," she said, with a look intended, he thought, to be full of mystery and intrigue.

"Oh?" He waited, not sure how to proceed.

With a triumphant flourish she handed him the paper she had been waving at the landlord, and he glanced down at it. The writing was a lady's, and he took in the address and signature. It was to him from Savina.

"Bertie read it and discarded it, you know . . . wasn't even going to forward it. He is an overstuffed ninny," she said her voice rising in volume. "Been intolerable to me lately, blaming me for William's defection. Deserves whatever he gets."

With that cryptic statement she stood and wobbled away, the plumes on her hat bobbing as she wove unsteadily between chairs and tables, only striking a few in her perambulation.

"Lady Venture," he called after her and started out of his chair. "Let me . . ."

But as the landlord followed her outside, Tony saw that her private carriage was waiting, and the coachman, a steady old man by the name of James who was devoted to the family, was there to help. He sat back down in his chair, relieved that she had someone with her who would take care of her. James waved at Tony through the frosted glass and winked as he aided Lady Venture's precarious reentry from the icy cobbles up into the carriage. The coachman climbed the box and with a flourish of his whip they were gone back down the narrow street.

Tony sat down, finished his cooled coffee and stared at the folded note. Did he dare read it? As long as he didn't, he could imagine it contained high-flown professions of love and adoration from Savina. She would say she was desolate without him, and that she had broken her engagement with Lord Gaston-Reade because she loved Tony so much and could no longer bear living a lie.

Taking in a deep breath, he admitted how foolish was a man who would still dare to dream after all hope was extinguished, and unfolded the letter. He read it, nodded once, and refolded it. As with all fools, he had been doomed to disappointment. The note was a simple request to see him at her father's house. It said nothing further, and he could only guess, since she had thought he was still employed with the earl, that she was going to use him as an intermediary, perhaps, to return gifts the earl had given her during their engagement. What else could she want?

He ruthlessly suppressed his yearning hope that she would confess a deep and abiding love and her intention to wait for him forever. That was idiotic. He had no evidence since their passionate kisses on the island that she felt anything at all for him. But he could at least tell her he was looking for a position that would take him away from England. What had felt unfinished between them would finally have an end.

The note in reply to hers had made her heart thump and her stomach clench. He was coming to see her. He had left Lord Gaston-Reade's employ, the note said, but Lady Venture had been kind enough to bring him her request, and he was coming to see her if she was free this afternoon between twelve and one.

She looked up at the clock on the mantle of the gloomy little parlor as she paced, wringing her hands together in front of her. It was twelve-thirty. She caught herself, made herself stop, and started all over again when she heard the footman answer the door and usher her guest into the entrance hall. She glanced over at Zazu, who sat in the corner, her dark eyes bright with mischief.

"Don't stare at me so, Zazu, or I shall never get through this." She touched her hair to make sure it was tidy and smoothed her dress down, trying to calm the quivering of her hands. "I'm afraid I shall stammer and make an utter fool of myself."

Zazu grinned, her sweet, full lips turned up in a smile that had not been there before knowing they were both going back to Jamaica. She stood and crossed to Savina and took her restless hands in her warm, calm ones. "I'm going to leave you alone," she said, searching Savina's eyes. "I don't care what the servants think, nor should you, about you being alone with Tony. We shall be far away from them all soon, and far away from this damp and dreary island to our sunny, warm island. And we will walk on the sand arm in arm and see the misty Blue Mountains, and . . ."

"And you'll marry Nelson." Savina joyfully clasped her in a hug. "And you'll be my friend and partner, and we'll work together to prove that a plantation without slaves is possible. It all may be a dream, but we'll succeed or fail together." They were silent for a moment, clasped to each other. "I love you, Zaz," she whispered, inhaling deeply her friend's cinnamon scent.

Her former maid, now just friend, pushed away from her and walked to the door into the dining room. The murmur from the footman was louder as he and Savina's visitor approached the parlor. Zazu paused and said, gently, "I love you too, my sister. Now, do what you can for your own happiness."

Savina composed herself as her friend exited and the door to the hall opened.

The footman bowed and said, "Mr. Anthony Heywood for Miss Savina Roxeter."

"Thank you. Please shut the door on your way out, Jenkins."

The footman ushered Tony in, bowed again and closed the door. Savina heard a whispering in the hall beyond the door and could imagine the scandalized staff, but she didn't care anymore. This island, this *city* was not her home and never had been. Jamaica was home. She gazed steadily at Tony. He was so very different from the man she had come to know on their little cay in the Caribbean. Immaculately dressed, his boots shining, his face shaved clean, his brown hair close-cropped, he was the stiff and formal secretary Mr. Anthony Heywood still, not her own exciting, enticing, barefoot Tony.

"I received your note," she said, trying to begin a conversation. "You have left Albert's employ."

"I have." He took a few more steps toward her. "And I understand from the paper that you have renounced your engagement."

"I have."

They stood and stared at each other for a long moment. Savina could hear her own heart pound. Could he hear it, too? Would he wonder at the cause?

"Lord Gaston-Reade has had a rather disagreeable week," Tony finally said.

Savina grinned. "I say he is a fortunate man, for I wouldn't have made a suitable wife, and certainly a scandalous countess." Tony did not respond to her smile, and she turned away. This was going to be much more difficult than she had even anticipated. She turned back. "Will you sit down, Mr. Heywood . . . Tony?" What had once been easy between them was now awkward, since they had come back to England, and she wasn't sure how to correct it.

He bowed, indicated with a gesture that she should sit first, and then followed suit at the other end of the settee she chose. Cold, hard sunshine shone into the dim parlor, illuminating their corner and dancing off gold threads in his hair. She stared down at her clasped hands, then fiddled with her dress, pleating the blue and white striped fabric in her fingers. Her hands were cold and numb, a perpetual state even with the fire blazing in the hearth at the end of the room. Jamaica would solve that, and she would never be cold again. "I have been the fortunate recipient of a bequest," she began, then didn't quite know how to proceed.

"I congratulate you," he said, his furrowed brow showing plainly how confused he was by her beginning.

This was awful, worse than she had imagined. What

she wanted was before her, tangible, within grasp, and yet so very far away. She could feel him, and remembered the strength of his arms, the sweetness of his mouth on hers, and yet there was a barrier between them. She had asked him once, on their deserted island, what there was between them, but if he had answered, she didn't remember, and now she was afraid all of the emotion and longing was on her own side. If she could just know how he felt . . . but that was impossible.

"Zazu and I are going home," she said, meeting his gaze, but then faltering as she lost herself in the warmth of his brown eyes. "We're going home," she repeated, looking back up at him, her voice stronger, "to Jamaica."

The corner of his mouth lifted in a crooked smile. "How wonderful for you both! Zazu must be happy."

"She is. And so am I. England isn't my home. Father is happy here, and now that he is to be married, I can feel sure he will be comfortable. He and his new wife can come and visit, perhaps. Or . . . perhaps not." That had been part of her struggle, the knowledge that going back to Jamaica could possibly mean seeing her father for the last time. But if she had had her way they would have stayed in Jamaica. Coming back to England had been her father's desire. It was time now to do what she wanted.

Tony steadily watched her and she longed to be closer to him, to feel his warmth, to feel any kind of comfort in his arms again. But she was so uncertain; their time on the island had been time out of mind, a step away from real life. What he felt now she had no way to tell by his reticent behavior. How he greeted her proposition would, she hoped, teach her much.

"I think your father only wants your happiness," he said, slowly, watching her.

She nodded. "He does; I think he understands why

I want to go back to Jamaica, though he would rather I stay in England." She stopped, and silence descended between them again. This was ridiculous, she thought, shifting impatiently and turning to face him on the settee. She needed to say what had to be said. "What about you, Tony? You don't have any family here, do you?" She knew the answer, remembered it from their conversation that memorable night in the cave, with the wind whipping the trees and rain slanting into their shelter.

"No, my parents died many years ago." He met her eyes and gazed deep into them, but when he lost the thread of his conversation, he looked away and fastened his gaze on the window. "I have a brother, but he's attached to the war office and is in Belgium now. He has married a Flemish girl, and even when the war ends I think he'll stay there, where her people have land. We correspond occasionally."

"Oh." This was getting more stilted and awkward by the moment. "But . . . but you have a friend, I remember."

"Yes. An old friend."

"I'm . . . I'm buying a plantation," she blurted out. "In Jamaica. One I know of . . . close to our old home." The information came out in pieces, her voice quavering. She had a question . . . an offer to make.

His gaze jerked back to her. "Oh?"

"Yes. There is a derelict plantation close to my old home, and I always did love it." She felt the excitement build as she spoke of it, and could picture the vine-choked grounds, the long drive overrun with weeds, and the crumbling stone walls of the manor house. She supposed it was her own version of the haunted old mansion house she had imagined would be her bequest, but this she knew what to do with. "I would wander there for hours and plan grand renovations. There is a house, a groundskeeper's cottage, quite a few outbuildings, and many acres that used to be devoted to sugar. I'm buying it, and Zazu, Nelson and I shall run it with only free labor, freed slaves, Maroons, anyone we can get. We won't plant sugar; we'll grow coffee, for the plantation land runs right up into the mountains, and the terrain is suitable for coffee bushes. The worker families will be able to earn a plot of land to raise a family by working with us on Liberty. That will be the name of the new plantation." Her chin went up, but then she took a deep breath. She had already had to defend her plan to people she required to help her, including the solicitor and her father. She had defeated every argument and stubbornly insisted on her way; her father had seen that further argument was futile, and had finally given in, reluctantly. But she relaxed, then. She knew enough about Tony to know she didn't have to defend her vision to him.

His eyes shining, he said, his voice gentle, "How wonderful." He slid closer, reached out and took up her hand, squeezing it. "I'm so very proud of you, Savina."

"Will you help me?" she asked, getting it out quickly before she had time to become frightened of the risk, and encouraged by the warmth of his handclasp. She slid even closer to him on the settee until their knees touched, still holding his hand. "Will you help me, Tony?"

He stared into her eyes, silent for a long minute. The clock on the mantle ticked. Somewhere in the house someone dropped something and it crashed on the floor. But his gaze never wavered.

"Of course I'll help, any way I can. How?"

"I-I-I know very little about . . . about financial affairs and such. I understand reasonably well the day-to-day running of a plantation, but I know nothing about money, nor does Zazu. I'm afraid of losing everything without someone there I trust to guide me. I need a partner."

"A partner?"

Her heart pounded and she felt sick, but she had come too far now to back away. She clung to his hand when he would have withdrawn it and stared into his eyes, the brown so warm, with crinkles at the corners as he squinted at her in puzzlement. "Yes, someone to run the financial aspect while Zazu, Nelson and I run everything else. It will be a risk, you see, and . . ." She trailed off, seeing the mystification in his expression. She had to say it, had to make it clear. "It would only work, of course," she said, raising her chin, and trying to catch her breath, "if we were married. We could marry and be partners, you see. The money would go to you as my husband and then you would be able to manage it for me; you could travel to Jamaica and live with me at Liberty. As . . . as partners."

In such bold words it sounded cold and selfish, and she scrabbled around in her mind trying to find a way to soften such a plain statement, but she could think of nothing short of throwing herself at his feet and confessing her undying love. But that would end everything if he said he didn't love her and so wouldn't marry her, knowing he couldn't return her feelings. No, she had had to approach the offer this way. He liked her, didn't he? And cared for her in some way? Would the idea appeal to him?

From the shocked and frozen expression on his face, she couldn't tell.

Tony felt worse than frozen, he felt as if he was encased in mortar, unable to move even to pull his hand away from Savina's tight grasp. But finally, as anger flooded him, he felt his joints loosen and he pulled away his hand, stood and said, "How could you think I would agree to such a mockery of the marriage state? For money? What kind of avaricious fortune-hunter do you take me for?"

"You misunderstand," she said. "I merely meant . . ."

"Meant to insult me, clearly," he ranted, "with an offer so immoral . . ."

"Immoral?" she cried, standing and facing him. "How is it immoral? Are you saying that every arranged marriage between men and women is immoral? Is my offer not what women are offered every day, when they are asked for their hand in expectation that their dowry will aid in the establishment of a family's wealth?"

"This is different. This is . . ."

"I fail to see how it's any different," she interrupted. "I need your help. It will only work if we're married and able to live together on the plantation. We're friends, aren't we, and like each other well enough? How is that any different from other marriages?"

"It's just different," he said, whirling on his heel and striding toward the door. He grabbed hold of the porcelain doorknob but didn't turn it. If he was honest, he would admit to her that he hoped she would want something more from him than his help in establishing a plantation, but if that was all he could offer her, financial advice and guidance, he would rather starve. He supposed she had really asked him as a sop to her father's fears for her, some misguided worry on his part that she would be prey to money-grubbing colonialists. She trusted him and knew what he was, and if he was calmer he might be flattered, but the insult lay at the core of the offer, that marriage to Savina Roxeter would be a wise business move for him, much like taking a position as advisor to some wealthy nabob.

And it stung because he loved her so very much and wished she loved him, too, wished she felt for him one tiny iota of the emotion he held within his breast for her. But she couldn't love him and offer him her hand as a business partner in such a cold manner. It wasn't possible.

He looked back at her. Her cheeks were pink and her breathing quick, and she appeared to be furious, her hands clenching and unclenching at her sides. There were tears in her eyes . . . tears of frustration and anger that he was being so obstinate? But then so was he furious, and devastated. He stood by the door, uncertain of what to do, but then decided there was nothing else but to leave. And so he did, yanking the door open and charging out, hearing her call his name, wanting to go back, but needing to leave more.

He walked out forgetting his hat and stick, forgetting anything but the need to get away. He strode out the front door, down the damp walk and across the street to a tiny enclosed park opposite; he paced the length of it, remembering the island, *their* island, and their night together, the bond that they had forged and that he still felt. The little park was brown and dead. Jamaica was lush and green, filled with life and promise . . . and love that could be his some day.

Was he a fool? He paced anxiously, his boots thumping along the stone walk, the dead chill of the air freezing the tips of his fingers and his ears. Carriages rattled by, the clop of horses' hooves loud on the cobbles. He sat down on a stone bench and buried his face in his hands. What was he doing? The girl he loved more than even his own life had offered him marriage, and all he could do was climb on his prideful conceit and refuse, choosing to feel insult when he should be grateful she felt anything for him at all, even if it was just trust and reliance. There were worse beginnings to marriage than friendship, mutual reliance, trust and caring. Pride would be a cold and lonely meal when she was far away in Jamaica and he still in England, perhaps.

He gazed back at the house from the park entrance. The cold stone facade repelled him, but within it was a warm, vivacious woman, the lady he loved. Without thinking he walked across the street, leaped up the steps and threw open the door. The footman stalked into the hall, but he pushed past the man and entered the parlor. She was still there, and her expression was even more frozen.

"I . . . I have thought it over," he stuttered, "and have decided I would be an absolute fool to put aside your kind offer. It is far too good an opportunity for . . ." How to say it without confessing everything he felt and longed for and making an even greater idiot of himself? "Far too good an opportunity for a . . . a man in my position to refuse. If I have not mortally offended you—and I could not blame you if I have, for I was unforgivably rude—I would like to take you up on your offer."

She stood stock-still in the middle of the room, her lips pressed together and her hands clenched at her sides. Tears streamed down her face, and it pained him to have caused her any such emotion, even if it was rage that had inspired the teardrops. He saw, then, in the shadows, Zazu gazing at him like he was some kind of imbecile.

Savina stood staring at him. His expression was unfathomable, but had the look of desperation in the wrinkled brow and haunted eyes. He was out of work and had no income. He was living at a coffeehouse, and though he didn't want to take it, clearly, her offer of marriage must have seemed like the best of possible futures for a man with no money and no immediate prospects.

But she knew that he liked her, at least. And in time they could perhaps rekindle the attraction they had shared during their night together. Her life and future hung in the balance, the choice now hers.

Should she calmly agree, or should she tell him that given his outburst, she had changed her mind and the offer was no longer open?

The clock on the mantle tock-tocked the minutes away while she tried to be calm, tried to consider her answer rationally. Instead her thoughts tumbled around her brainbox like mutinous kittens. She searched his eyes. He was hoping she would accept, now; she could see it in his eyes.

"All right," she said, forced to a conclusion and hoping for the best. "I suppose it will do." She put out her hand, not quite knowing what else to do. "There is nothing to wait for then; let us get married soon and sail at the first opportunity."

He took her hand and they shook, a business deal sealed and done.

Nineteen

He and Savina spoke for a few minutes to work out the details. He was willing to wait to marry once they reached Jamaica, but she said she wanted her father to be able to attend the ceremony. It left them little time, since she wanted to leave England and sail before the weather made it impossible. It meant there were only a few opportunities left on ships already scheduled. She had a ship in mind, and it was sailing in one week.

Everything was rushed. She told her father of her plans, and then sent Tony into the library speak to him. The meeting was stiff and awkward, with Mr. Roxeter understandably perplexed at the turn of events. He called his daughter back in, and she made plain to her father that marrying was her best option to be taken seriously by the other plantation owners in Jamaica, especially since they would be doing something radically different in their use of paid labor. Every time she made her sensible plans plain, it was like another knife in his heart, for he was certain no woman who was in love could have used such cool language in referring to her marriage. It truly would be a marriage of convenience for her.

Tony left soon after that to begin the task of severing his ties in England and saying farewell to those of his friends he had still an acquaintance with. He was considered, among them, as they gathered that evening at a tavern, singularly fortunate to have snagged a woman of wealth, even if she did only wish to marry him for propriety. How could he explain to those friends slapping him on the back and buying him ale that what he really wanted from Miss Savina Roxeter even more than her hand in marriage was a confession of undying and eternal love? He would sound a complete sap.

But he had plans. With his saved funds he exited his coffeehouse abode the morning after his engagement to a little known shop in an unsavory section of town few of the fashionable knew of and even fewer deigned to enter. He entered the Stygian gloom, the floor creaking under his feet better than any bell to announce his presence. The old man behind the counter looked up from his task, his eyes huge behind thick glasses.

"Mr. Gold," Tony said, striding forward.

"That is still my name, though some would dispute it."

Leaning on the counter, Tony gazed down at the project the old man, wizened and bent with age, his hands hobbled with arthritis, was laboring on. "It's beautiful," he said, of the intricate broach in which the jeweler was setting precious gems that sparkled in the light of his peculiar lamp.

"It's not so bad," the man grudgingly admitted. "And what would you be wanting, young Mr. Heywood?"

Even after so many years, even with all the affection between them, it was still Mr. Gold and Mr. Heywood. This hobbled old man on the other side of the worktable had stood in as the father he had lost, had paid his schooling, had supported him in what he wanted to do, even though Tony was supposed to be working for him as an apprentice and learning the jewelry trade. When Tony had expressed his determination to travel, it was Mr. Benjamin Gold who had used every contact he had to find him a good job, his first position as secretary. It was unspoken between them, but there was a bond of reliance and love that would never break, even if they never saw each other again. "I wanted to see you. I've been away a long time."

"You are famous, my young friend. Famous and with adventures. Tell me about them."

Tony sighed and sat on a stool across the workbench as the old man worked. He told him everything—or almost everything—and they filled in the year since they had last seen each other. Though their attachment was an old one, and strong, Tony had not felt the need to come see the goldsmith immediately; he knew that all he had to say to him would wait, and now he had even more to tell him. He eased back into their friendship like an old worn coat, and finally made them both tea on the little stove at the back of the shop.

They sat companionably and shared a midday meal, and the tea, and their conversation wandered far afield. Savina's name came up often, of course, and once or twice the old man had looked at him sharply, but had not commented.

At long last Tony took a deep breath and said, "I am to be married." His tone, he realized as he said it, was one of hesitation, for he was still muddled about his feelings. It hurt, in a most peculiar way, to be marrying Savina, knowing she didn't care for him the way he cared for her. What if she never did? Could he bear that?

"Should I congratulate, then, or express my condolences?"

"What do you mean?"

Mr. Gold's face, deeply lined and etched with pain, twisted in what may have been a grin. "So much courage it took to even say it that you had to take in a deep breath, like you were announcing you had been arrested for murder."

Tony smiled and leaned his elbow on the worktable as Mr. Gold went back to his patient and methodical task. "I'm not exactly in a normal situation for an engaged fellow."

"How is that?"

"Well, she is the loveliest young lady in the world."

"I have heard the same sentiment expressed by many a young gentleman, and many an older one, too."

"How many of them can say that the lady is the one who proposed?"

Mr. Gold looked up and squinted. "She did? Do you mean through her solicitor, or her father?"

"No," Tony said, enjoying the relation of his story for the first time. "No, she herself did the asking . . . it is Miss Savina Roxeter. What she proposed was a partnership. You see, she has received a bequest and is buying a plantation back in Jamaica."

"Ah, yes, she is the young lady who was with you during your marooning on the deserted island, and your dramatic rescue. Now I have heard some gossip . . . she wouldn't happen to be the most famous Lady Savage, would she?"

"So you had heard all about my adventures before I even told you?"

"I hear much. But always it is better to hear it from the source, you know. I find much was exaggerated, as I had suspected. Some had it that you all reverted to nature, palm skirts and strange lingo, unsavory practices. Such nonsense people believe. So, is it the young lady who is this Lady Savage?"

"Yes," Tony admitted, "she's the one." He shouldn't have been surprised, he supposed. Mr. Gold's connections went deep and wide and everyone talked to him, perched on this same stool as he worked away creating his masterpieces.

"And is she as wild as her sobriquet would imply, young sir?"

Tony thought about that. "No, she's not wild. That was a bit of silliness on the part of some very flighty young ladies among the passengers of the ship that rescued us."

Gold shrugged. "I thought as much."

"But she is very intelligent, and beautiful, and . . ."

"And she has asked you to marry her."

Tony sighed. "Yes. For all the wrong reasons, I fear. I am to be her business partner, the financial genius, you see, in her bold experiment, her new endeavor, a plantation in Jamaica that will not use slave labor."

Mr. Gold looked up and stared into Tony's eyes for a long minute. "I think such a young lady is a rare gem indeed, Mr. Heywood. You know how I feel about slavery; to find a young lady who is so lovely, intelligent, but also with such a good heart . . . and how fortunate that she has chosen you, since you are already so in love with her that you cannot bear the pain of her asking you for strictly financial reasons or to satisfy society's notions of propriety."

"Is it so apparent, Mr. Gold?"

"Only because I have known you these many years," he said, setting aside his tools and straightening his back with a wince and a grimace. "So you come to me for something more than to tell me your good news, yes?"

Tony sighed. "She doesn't love me yet."

"This you are certain of?"

Nodding slowly he said, "Yes. She likes me, she respects me, but love . . . don't you think I would know if she felt that way?"

"Women, who can understand the way their minds work? And they would say the same of us."

"But I love her." The words echoed in a whisper up to the high, dim reaches of the crowded shop. "And so I'm going to marry her and . . ."

"And make her fall in love with you?"

Tony grinned. "That's my intention."

"If anyone can do it, you can. Will you take something from me? I would like to be a part of it."

"I would be honored if you would make something for Savina. And . . . will you come and see me married? It will be in Bristol, before we sail."

Mr. Gold nodded. "I surprise even myself now, but yes."

"I intend to woo her once we are safely wed and on our way back to Jamaica. I'll do everything in my power to show her how I care, and make her care for me, too." He paused and stared at his old friend. The light, directed down at the worktable, left his bony features in relief, the deep-set eyes dark, the cheeks high and jutting. "I won't ever be coming back here to England, Mr. Gold, not that I know of, anyway."

The older man gazed at him steadily and nodded, a world of sad understanding in his pouched and bloodshot eyes. "England will be the poorer place for your defection. What we create must be most wonderful, something befitting such a fascinating young woman who could capture the heart of such a fellow as you. And though I know you will insist on paying for it, I would ask that you let it be my gift to you both."

Tony stuck out his hand. "Thank you."

"It's been days, Zazu, and I've hardly seen Tony."

"He must have much to do, more than yourself, for England has been his home his whole life."

"I know, I know. And at least he's coming this morning. We have some details to work out." Savina turned away from the window and the dreary scene of frost and blight. She rubbed her arms. "I can't get warm. I can't even feel my fingers, I'm so cold."

Zazu, quietly mending a dress hem, looked up at Savina. "You're worried. Sit and talk to me."

Savina flung herself down next to Zazu and thought over the last few hectic days. Her father and Mr. Chandler had quite frankly not believed her when she announced her plans. But she had, with the solicitor's reluctant help, arranged for the purchase of the vacant plantation. The English owner was quite willing to get rid of it, but it was still at great cost and took much of her inheritance. Her father had hoped she would change her mind; it had come as a great blow to him, she thought, when she announced her engagement to Tony minutes after proposing to him. She should not have taken her fiancé in to her father right then, after making such a momentous announcement, but she knew time was going to be tight, and she needed her father to get used to the idea of her upcoming nuptials. He had reacted badly and had made his disapproval known to both of them.

She had tried to soothe things by telling him that she would at least be settled and safe; wouldn't he want her to have protection and companionship, since she was set on going back to Jamaica with or without it? Tony had acted oddly for the rest of his brief visit and had left the house with no more than a handshake from her, the most intimate contact they had had since agreeing to marry.

Each day since, her father had tried, at every opportunity, to talk her out of the "whim," as he insisted on calling it. With his continual badgering added to her own worries, she felt as if she had made a few decisions in haste, and now could not be sure that everything she did had been for the best. She expressed all of these worries to Zazu as the younger woman sewed; Zazu calmly told her to take each action step by step, then, and decide if it had been all right.

"That sounds logical," Savina said, sitting up straight and folding her hands on her lap. She ordered her thoughts. "I came back to England only because I felt I had no other choice. Father was coming back, and I became affianced to Lord Gaston-Reade, and so had to return also."

"First," her friend said, cutting her thread and tying it off. "Do you feel you made the right choice in breaking your engagement to Lord Gaston-Reade?"

"Yes," Savina replied, sure of her ground. "I could never have cared for him, and it was wrong of me to agree to marriage with him in the first place."

"Then you did what was necessary and right."

"Correct," Savina said with a nod. "That was the right thing to do. Then I learned of my bequest." She bit her lip. "It's so much money! I never expected to have so much. I want to go back to Jamaica with you, and I want to live there."

"So, buying the plantation was a good idea and you don't regret that."

"No, I'm happy to do that. It was a dream, that place, and now it's mine." She reached over and touched Zazu's arm. "Ours."

"And then there is Mr. Heywood . . . Tony," Zazu said, setting her sewing aside.

"And then there's Tony," Savina agreed. She examined her hands, now recovering from all the hard work on their little cay in the Atlantic. Soon it would be as if all of that never happened. What if the love she felt for Tony was the same, merely a passing thing that needed the desolation of their deserted cay to keep it burning hot as it had then? In that moment, sitting in the cold dreary parlor of a London house, she could not feel everything she had once felt for Tony, the powerful physical attraction, the respect, the admiration, the utterly helpless feeling of falling in love. Had it gone for good? Or had fear driven it deep in her heart? How would she ever know? And how did *he* feel?

"That's what it is, of course. I'm afraid."

"Afraid of . . . ?" Zazu encouraged her.

"Afraid I will regret marrying Tony . . . or worse, that he'll regret marrying me. It was like an interview for a position, not an offer of marriage." She twisted her hands together. "Zaz, what am I going to do? I don't think he loves me. And I'm no longer sure I love him."

Zazu examined her friend's face, searching her expression. "Are you not just afraid right now?"

"Of course I'm afraid," Savina cried, leaping up and pacing to the window. "I'm terrified! Terrified he won't ever love me. Terrified I've made a dreadful mistake. Terrified I don't really love him, that it was just the experience . . . being on the island, being together so much, his kindness, that made me feel as I did." She turned away from the window toward her friend. "He hasn't kissed me a single time since we were rescued. What if . . . what if he never does again? I made it sound like a business arrangement, and I don't know how to . . . what if he comes to resent me for the marriage and feels he was unfairly pressured into it?"

Crossing the room, Zazu took Savina's hands in her own and squeezed them. "You should talk to him, tell him your fears, let him know how you are feeling."

Jenkins entered and bowed. "Mr. Anthony Heywood for Miss Savina Roxeter."

Tony followed him in, hat in hand. Zazu squeezed her hands and released them, said hello to Tony, and then followed Jenkins out to the hall, winking at Savina and closing the door behind her.

She was left alone, staring at Tony who gazed steadily back at her, his brows drawn together and his mouth twisted in a puzzled frown.

"I'm . . . happy you came," she forced herself to say. "I have something I want to ask . . . or say to you. Please, have a seat."

He set his hat on a table and sat on the settee near the window. She paced in front of him for a moment, then turned and faced him. What to say? In that moment she had come to the absolute certainty that he did not care for her the way she cared for him. If he did, he would have shown it somehow. He hadn't had any trouble on their island, after all, and she didn't think him a shy or reticent man, and he had rejected her marriage offer first, after all. That had to have been his first instinct. He didn't love her. Whatever attraction he had felt was fleeting, and instigated only by their odd surroundings.

"I hope you're well, Tony?" she said, stiffly, sitting down on a stool in front of the settee.

"I am, thank you. What is it you wished to say?"

Panicked, she blurted out, "I don't think this is going to work out at all well." Taking a deep breath to steady herself, she clasped her hands together tightly between her knees so he couldn't see them shake. "I'll be still going to Jamaica, but I'm breaking off our engagement. You're f-free."

"What?" he cried, leaping to his feet. "No! You can't do this. You can't dismiss me as if I'm some employee who didn't suit."

Stung by his language, she jumped up, too, and faced him. "Whyever not? I'm sure you'll find another position, Tony, one that will suit you better, perhaps." She didn't think it in her to be so spiteful, but all of her fear and pain of the past week came pouring out.

"A talented young man such as yourself . . . many will find themselves in need of your services." Tears welled up in her eyes and she was horrified at her own words. Did she want to hurt him?

Yes, it seemed she *did* want to hurt him, if she was honest and searched her own heart. She wanted some emotion from him perhaps, even if it was anger. His coolness of late had been more hurtful than any amount of anger could ever be.

He turned, grabbed up his hat from the table and headed toward the door without another word. But when he got there, he stopped, and then he turned back on his heel.

And strode across the floor, flinging his hat aside as he did so. He pulled her roughly into his arms and before she could catch her breath he had her bent backward and covered her lips in a smothering kiss. One became another and then many. He held her tightly, and she surrendered once more to the enchantment of his ardent kisses. It was as if her clothes tattered and the sound of waves on the shore filled her ears. The scent of sea and jasmine blossoms drifted around her and the tropical heat filled her frigid form. She threw her arms around him, a burbling joy welling up into her heart at the waves of passion she felt flowing between them. She closed her eyes as they sank to the carpet; he pulled her so close she could feel every muscle of his body flex and he took her lips again in expert passion, his breath ragged and her own mingling with his until they blended.

"You're not going to do this to me," he said, shaking her until she opened her eyes and gazed up into his. She was disoriented by the sight of the ceiling and the wood paneling, having expected blue sky and sunshine. He framed her face with his strong hands and kissed her more gently. "You're not going to do this. I won't let you," he croaked, his voice hoarse and quavering. "I'll steal you away. I swear it, Savina; I'll kidnap you and take you to Scotland and bribe some hedge parson into performing a ceremony, but I won't let you destroy me."

"Destroy . . . what do you mean?" Her voice sounded odd and breathless, as if the air had been squeezed out of her lungs. The oddly prosaic surroundings of the cold, dreary little parlor shimmered and wavered in her gaze.

"Destroy me! I have never loved a woman before, never . . . not until my own Lady Savage. I thought I'd lost you forever, but now I'll die before I let you get away. Say you care for me." He kissed her again, hard, pinning her to the carpet and covering her mouth. "Say it. Say it!" He kissed her again. "You *must* care for me! Say it!"

Laughing, breathless, pushing him away, she gasped, "Let me catch my breath! How can I speak when you keep kissing me like that? Oh, Tony! I do! I do love you." She tightened her grip and buried her face in his neck. Her voice muffled, she cried, "I do! I love you so. I *love* you! I do."

Twenty

"I do," Savina said, softly, and then louder, her voice carrying on the cold breeze that swept through the harbor. "I do!" She laughed out loud, the joyful sound carrying above the creak of the deck and whine of wind in the ropes.

The vicar spoke again, shivering so badly his voice quavered, and then was silent.

"I do," Tony said, clear and loud, in answer to the parson's question, and then, as the vicar pronounced that they were joined in holy matrimony, he took Savina in his arms. The ship, loaded and ready to sail out of Bristol harbor on the next tide, shuddered and moaned underneath them, and the friends gathered on deck and the crowd assembled down on the dock clapped, hooted, stamped and whistled as they kissed.

It was not a moment to repeat the passion of their usual caresses, though, and Tony quickly released Savina; she gazed around at the gathering for the first time as a married woman.

Lady Venture stood alone and watched. Savina had been hesitant about the lady, especially given their past altercations, but they met at a dress shop and Lady Venture was, after all, responsible for making sure Tony knew of her letter to him. In gratitude, Savina asked her to attend their shipboard wedding just before they were to sail to Jamaica, and the lady had said she would come, even though it was all the way in Bristol. She seemed recovered from the perfidy of Mr. William Barker, but Savina would not probe what could still be an open wound, and the lady didn't offer any information.

Savina's father, his arm linked through that of the new Mrs. Roxeter, was smiling at her, and she was grateful for that. Once she and Tony had come to a true understanding of all their various worries and fears and had discussed their future, Tony had gone to Savina's father and spent two hours closeted with him in his library. At the end of it, her papa had had nothing to say but that she was a fortunate young woman to inspire such great love in so worthy a young man. And it had reconciled him, he said later, to losing his daughter to Jamaica, for he would always know she had someone who loved her to look after her.

Savina did not reply with what she truly thought, that she knew she didn't need anyone to look after her, that what she wanted and had found in Tony was an equal, a partner, a love to last through all hardship and toil that could be in their future. Her father wouldn't understand that, and she was intent on leaving him happy.

Zazu, standing next to her through the ceremony, was grinning widely even though she, too, was shivering from the frigid air. They were going home, and Zazu and Nelson would be the next couple marrying. When Savina had asked, gently, if she was sure the young man would have waited for her, after all that had happened, Zazu was unshakably confident.

On the other side of Tony was a bent old man, a "Mr. Gold," Tony had introduced him as. He had looked grim through the ceremony, but when she glanced at him now, she saw a tear glisten in his rheumy eye. Someone, at least, would miss Tony as badly as her father was going to miss Savina.

"I have only one thing left," Tony said, facing Savina and commanding her attention, even as the stiff breeze whipped his words up into the sky, "and that is to give you this." He took her left hand and slipped on a gold ring to go with her wedding band.

She gazed down at it. Two gold hearts, linked and embossed, were flanked by sapphire-studded wings.

He glanced over at Mr. Gold and smiled, then captured Savina's gaze again. "That is for how my heart took flight when I met you, and how every wish and prayer I have ever had has been answered by your heart to mine." He leaned over and kissed her again, and she knew that from that moment on she would have the confidence that Zazu had in her own love for Nelson, that it would withstand any challenge of time or travail.

Their farewell was emotional and the voyage long, but every day she discovered something new to love and admire about Tony, not the least of which being that he was indefatigable in his love for her. They had long hours to talk, and longer hours to make love, as they planned their lives together and the family they would create.

On Christmas day, just days after making harbor in Spanish Town, they stood on a palm-dotted hilltop near the ocean as the sun set, and listened to vows being read as Zazu and Nelson stood hand-in-hand. The golden sunset cast rosy glows on the cheery faces of the wedding guests and the palms swayed in the tropical breeze that swept up the hill.

"Zazu doesn't show it, but she's nervous about tonight," Savina whispered to Tony, twining and tangling her fingers with his. The warmth of the sun at her back filled her and she sighed and leaned against her husband.

"I didn't think she was afraid of anything other than the ocean," he whispered back.

They stood close to the ceremony, but both Zazu and Nelson had large families that were crowding closer and closer, her grandmother and mother proudly seated in places of honor. His parents, their physical freedom purchased in a deal wrung from Lord Gaston-Reade's plantation manager by Tony, smiled broadly from their own seats by Zazu's grandmother and mother.

"She'll be all right. I was able to assure her that there is nothing at all to be afraid of," Savina said, primly.

Tony chuckled in her ear and whispered, "How good of you to share your hard-won knowledge." He pulled her against him and held her tight as he kissed her ear.

At long last the ceremony was over and the newlywed couple retired, after a raucous party, to the groundskeeper's cottage on the grounds of Liberty plantation. Savina had offered a place in the main house, since they were all partners in the plantation, but the newlyweds wanted to build their own home and were going to use the comfortable cottage for the time being as their private nest.

It was late. Savina retired to her bedroom and shivered when she heard the latch click open. Tony slipped through the door dressed only in a shirt and breeches, his shirt loose and his feet bare. He padded silently over to her and stood behind her, gazing at her reflection in the dressing table mirror.

She turned and put her arms around his waist and laid her head on his bare stomach, kissing the warm skin under her lips. He threaded his fingers through her hair and kissed the top of her head.

"I love you so much, Tony."

"No regrets, my Lady Savage?" he murmured, cradling her head against his stomach.

She smiled against his skin, feeling the inevitable burgeoning of his unfailing passion for her. Her fingers fumbled with the buttons of the fall of his breeches and he quivered under her feather-light touch.

"You love to torment me with that awful name. No . . . no regrets," she whispered, slipping one button from its buttonhole. She kissed his stomach and undid another button.

With a groan he stopped her fingers, swept her up in his arms and carried her to the enormous bed they had inherited when they bought the plantation, laying her down gently and pulling the flimsy nightrail from her lithe body. Warm tropical breezes swept the gauzy curtains aside; they fluttered in the windows, and the brilliant moon shone bright. But wound together in the sheets, Savina and Tony failed to notice anything but the love in each other's eyes and the sweet melding of their bodies.